ANGHARAD HAMPSHIR
1972. She has worked as a radio]
honorary lecturer in journalism
and regular contributor to the *S<*
Kong. Angharad has a Doctor
the University of Sydney and is now a research fellow at York St
John University. She lives in York with her family.

THE
A NOVEL
MARE

ANGHARAD
HAMPSHIRE

Northodox Press Ltd
Maiden Greve, Malton,
North Yorkshire, YO17 7BE

This edition 2024

1
First published in Great Britain by
Northodox Press Ltd 2024

ISBN: 9781915179821

This book is set in Caslon Pro Std

To those who stand up.

The most frightening news brought about by the Holocaust
and by what we learned of its perpetrators was not the
likelihood that 'this' could be done to us,
but the idea that we could do it.

Zygmunt Bauman, *Modernity and the Holocaust.*

Explaining is not excusing; understanding is not forgiving.

Christopher Browning, *Ordinary Men: Reserve Police
Battalion 101 and the Final Solution in Poland.*

Lift up your faces, you have a piercing need
For this bright morning dawning for you.
History, despite its wrenching pain
Cannot be unlived, but if faced
With courage, need not be lived again.

Maya Angelou, *On the Pulse of Morning.*

The knock on the door changed everything. Until then, we were happy; we knew who we were.

You've got the wrong person, I told him. My wife is gentle and kind. She wouldn't hurt a fly.

After he left, we sat side by side on the sofa and I held you tightly as you sobbed into my neck. Your shoulders heaved up and down and your tears soaked my collar.

This will be the end of me, you whimpered. I only did what everyone else did back then. I was no different. You have to believe me; I've done nothing wrong.

I shushed you and calmed you and told you I loved you. I had no reason to doubt you. But after that knock, everything around me started to wobble and bend. All that was solid became molten. It was as if we were standing in front of the funhouse mirrors on Coney Island, looking at our reflections, distorted, distended versions of ourselves.

My whole sense of who I am, who you are, all of it shook.

Russell.

July 1957. Velden am Wörthersee.

We meet over seeds. I'm sorting through packets of black yarrow, winter heath, saxifrage and alpine snowbell, asking a shop assistant for advice in broken German, when I hear a voice behind me.

If you are looking for an Austrian flower, then you must take this.

I turn around. You are standing right next to me. Your dress is cornflower blue; it matches your eyes. You hand me a small rectangular pocket of paper with a picture on it that looks like a white star of snow.

This is no good! the shop assistant says and plucks the packet straight out of my hand. Edelweiss likes altitude. This plant will not grow in New York!

I look at you and you shrug.

You could try it anyway, you say in accented English, taking the packet out of the shop assistant's hand and holding it towards me. Edelweiss is the most Austrian flower. If that's what you're after, only this will do.

With that, you turn and walk out the door.

The second time we meet, I'm sitting reading a newspaper on the terrace of Schloss Velden, in the shade of its mustard-coloured walls. I recognise your accent and the pitch of your voice.

So, did you buy the Edelweiss?

You busy yourself round my table, clearing up crumbs. This time, you're in uniform, a white shirt, black skirt and apron, and when you pass near me, I smell your perfume.

I didn't know you worked here, I say.

Well, yes, I do.

I look up at you. Your eyes are strikingly blue.

Can I get you a coffee?

Yes, please. A coffee with milk. And to answer your question, I bought the Edelweiss, though I don't know if it will grow in my back yard. It's about as far from a mountainside as you can get. What seeds were you looking for?

Oh, just some vegetables. I have a small garden at the back of the hotel. I'll bring you your coffee.

As you head back to the hotel kitchens, I feel a recklessness that comes from being so far from home. I call out to you.

Could you show me your garden? I'd really like to see it.

You turn back towards me and flash a huge smile.

I can show you on Sunday, you say. That's my day off.

When you return, you are carrying my coffee. You place it in front of me and then stand there and wait, looking straight at me. It feels like you're willing me to say something bold.

How about we do something else on Sunday? I ask. Could I take you for a row on the lake?

You tip your head towards me and pause for a second. My heart dances between us like dust in the breeze.

Alright, you say. If you do the rowing. I'll meet you at nine by the pontoon.

Hermine.
October 1934. Nußdorf.

I'm fifteen years old, the youngest of seven. I live on the outskirts of Vienna, in the last rows of houses before the city gives way to the hills. My parents, my elder sister and I share a three roomed apartment at the top of a tall, narrow house that is painted bright yellow. Our apartment is above Herr Fischer, the shoemaker. He is above Herr Köhler, who works in the beer factory. Swallows nest here in the summer, and when it rains, it sounds as if someone is playing piano on the tiles of the roof.

Each day, I walk along the brook to Frau Lackner's house, where I work as a maid. I watch for the birds: treecreepers and finches, wagtails and pipits, tits and sparrows, martins and swifts. My sister Luise works as a maid too, for Frau Brünner. She walks to work with me but comes home much later now that the baby's been born. Frau Brünner beams with pride, a boy after four girls, an oak among acorns. Mutti washes and delivers laundry all around Döbling. Her knuckles look like walnuts, wrinkled and chafed. When I get home, I help her. We take much longer now without Luise, but I don't mind; I like the time alone with my mother.

Vati drives a truck for Herrn Gruber, who owns the beer factory. He delivers crates of beer into the city, bottles clinking behind him on their way to the shops and the pubs. He likes it. It is a good job.

On Sunday, Mutti busies herself cleaning and cooking while Luise and I walk to church, laughing and chatting. I see Luise sometimes during the week at the butcher, but we don't stop to talk. She buys better cuts of meat, flank and rump to my blade and knuckle; the Brünners are much better off than the Lackners.

Today, as I walk home, I'm thinking about All Saints Day. Each year, we tend the graves of the Braunsteiners, Knodns and Sachslehners in the cemetery at Nußdorf, laying wreaths and lighting candles until the whole graveyard flickers with splinters of light. So it is that I'm deep in thought about decorated gravestones when I find Vati home from work early, complaining of a pain in his chest.

The next day, he takes to his bed. His skin is sallow and his breathing uneven; it sounds as if he's sucking in air through a sack. Mutti tends to him, but he refuses her broth. She calls for the doctor, a sign that it's serious because we don't have that kind of money. The doctor announces pleurisy and pneumonia, and Mutti falls to the floor. Vati reaches out towards her from the bed. Outside the window, starlings rise like a wave across the darkening sky. Their chattering mutes Mutti's sobs.

When I get home from work, I go straight to Vati's bed. Hair clings to his forehead and sweat sheens his brow. I tell him about the kingfisher that I saw perched by the brook, russet and azure, eyes watching the water down a well-defined beak. Vati likes to watch the birds too. He looks at me weakly and closes his eyes.

Three days later, the priest comes to read Vati's last rites. Luise puts her arm round Mutti and holds her like a baby while she rocks on her heels. Outside it drizzles. The leaves sag with dampness.

A place is prepared for Vati in Nußdorf cemetery. The apartment fills up as Inge, Erika, Franz, Dieter and Josef return. My brothers bow their heads, too tall for this room now. Inge and Erika fuss around Mutti. Though she is happy to see them, soon she is overcome with sadness, and tears fill her eyes. How will she manage without Vati by her side?

I take hold of her hand and tell her that I'll look after her. I will find a better job and help pay my way. But inside I'm frightened. My heart is a boulder. I'm a girl of fifteen whose father has just died. Everything around me is going to change.

Russell.

July 1957. Velden am Wörthersee.

I wake before 6am, full of nerves and excitement. It is already sunny; thin wisps of cloud fade into the blue. Out of the window, the lake sparkles blue green in the morning light. The weather bodes well for our outing.

When I reach the pontoon, you are not there. I wait for you anxiously, telling myself that you're not coming. Suddenly, I see you walking towards me, wearing the same blue dress that you wore in the seed shop. Your blonde hair falls to your shoulders and the straps of a bright red swimsuit loop up from beneath your dress round your neck.

I brought us some cider, bread and cheese, you say, pulling a dark brown bottle from your bag and passing it to me. Also, some apples and Kipferls. I made them myself. I hope you like them; they're an Austrian treat.

I'm sure I will, but hang on a minute, I didn't bring my swimming trunks. I'll run and get them.

I sprint to my room and fumble with the key. Inside it's messy. Clothes are strewn all over the floor. My trunks, damp from my last swim, are rolled up and stuffed under a towel. I wrestle them on under my shorts, grab the towel and run back down the stairs. By the time I reach the pontoon, I am panting. You look relaxed and serene, leaning down to the water, holding onto the edge of the boat.

Sorry! I say as I catch my breath. Please, you go in first.

The boat wobbles and then steadies as you climb in and sit down at the back. I put my foot in too far to one side and the boat lurches. You look at me, alarmed.

Hey careful! you say.

I feel my face redden, embarrassed by my clumsiness.

Don't worry, I say. I've done this before.

I centre myself and drop the oars into the rowlocks, then push off and pull out into the lake, propelling us away from the shoreline. The water below deepens, changing from turquoise to topaz, malachite to emerald. I feel more in control and start to relax. The sun rises and I begin to sweat, but you don't seem to notice; you're far too absorbed with looking out over the lake. A fish jumps into the air not far from the boat, catching both of us by surprise. You look at me and smile.

The water's so clean here, you say. You know, you can drink straight from the lake.

You scoop up a handful of water and put it to your lips, then put your hand back into the lake and trail it next to the boat. You look so European and elegant sitting there in your sundress, such a far cry from the girls I know back home.

We don't get many Americans in the hotel, you say. I think you're the first we've had this year. What brings you here?

I want to impress you, to puff myself up.

I worked as an electrical engineer for the U.S. Air Force during the war, servicing airplanes, I say. When the war ended, I worked in the American zone in Vienna for a few years. I've always wanted to come back for a holiday. I saved up and decided to do it this year. I spent a couple of weeks in Vienna and then came out here to Velden for a two-week vacation before going home.

You lean forward towards me and look at me, interested. I can see the curve of your breasts through your dress.

Do you work with airplanes still in America?

No, not anymore. I still work in electronics, but nowadays I work for a television company in New York. I test the electronics in TV sets. It's detailed work.

That's a good job, you say. You must be very clever.

Your compliment warms me. I pull on the oars.

I would love to go to New York, you say. I bet it's amazing.

New York's great, but Vienna's more beautiful, I say. Europe's so different from the States, the architecture, the music everywhere. I play the trombone and I enjoyed all the music in Vienna. When I lived there, I went to lots of concerts and I learnt to speak German. I like speaking another language, though it's a bit rusty now.

I come from Vienna too, from a suburb at the edge of the city.

So, what made you move here?

After the war, it was hard to find work in Vienna. I have some relatives here who said they would help me find a job. I've been working here for seven years.

Do you miss Vienna?

Not really. My mother died not long after the war and staying there without her was too sad. I like it here. It's a nice place to work. I like being by the lake and I love the mountains.

You point towards the peaks in the distance, dark triangles, forested with green.

My mother died too, I say. Same as yours. Not long after the war. I know how that feels.

You smile at me softly. The lake starts to narrow, bringing us closer to the shore. As we round the next corner, a small wooden jetty comes into view. Trees grow behind it in a small copse.

That's a good place to stop, you say. We can tie up the boat and go for a swim.

As we near the jetty, you pull off your dress. The red of your swimsuit contrasts with the cream of your thigh. I look away, not wanting to be caught staring. The boat rocks suddenly, making me look up. You've jumped over the side, into the water.

Come on! you shout and then you dive underneath the boat, flicking your legs up into the air.

When you surface on the other side, your hair is slicked onto your face. You tread water and look up at me with a smile, broad and white.

Hand me the rope, you say. I'll pull us in.

I grab hold of the rope and throw it to you. You scoop through the water, pulling the boat with ease, your legs kicking strongly. When we reach the jetty, you wrap the rope round one of its struts.

Jump in! you shout. The water is perfect!

I pull off my clothes, sling them into the hull and leap over the side. My skin shrinks with the cold and the wet. By the time I resurface, you've already swum out into the lake. I follow, but I'm not a strong swimmer; I cannot keep up. When I finally reach you, I watch in admiration as you dive down to the bottom, your body carving through water and light.

The afternoon passes as we swim and sun ourselves, stopping only to picnic, and then lie side by side lazily on top of the jetty. I fall asleep in the sunshine. When I wake up, you're lying on your stomach next to me, looking at me intently. My arm has draped over yours in my sleep. I move it off you, embarrassed by my touch.

So, what do you think of it here? you ask.

It's beautiful, I say. I really love Austria and this place is the best.

And what about me?

The question throws me completely; it is so unexpected. I want to tell you that you are perfect, so beautiful, so fit and so strong, but I fumble for words. All I can summon is, You're a very good swimmer.

You snort with laughter.

My swimming. Is that all?

I get up and walk to the end of the jetty, unable to look at you, and lean into the boat. In the pocket of my shorts, I've stored two tiny packets of seedlings: cucumber and pepper.

These are for your garden, I say as I hand them to you.

You turn them over carefully in your hand and your expression changes, as if your face has been covered by cloud.

Did I do something wrong? Are you OK?

No, no. Please don't think that. It's just that nobody has given me a present in a very long time.

You lean in towards me and kiss me gently on the cheek.

Hermine.

December 1937. London.

The journey from Vienna to London takes three full days. Traute Graf is my travel companion. She's short with a freckled face and brown eyes. Traute is Luise's friend. She's three years older than me and full of self-confidence; she's already worked in London for two years. I'm to be a scullery maid, the lowest of domestic servants, which irks me because I've worked as a maid in Vienna for four years. I don't see why I should start again at the bottom.

Keep your chin up, Traute says. Just think of the money. There's a shortage of good maids in England. They promoted me to housemaid in less than a year.

It's true that the money for housework is much better than in Vienna. I hope I'm promoted as quickly as Traute so I can send more back home. My employer is called Mr Miller. He's an American engineer who lives in London with his wife, their fourteen-year-old daughter and a Swiss governess. As Traute shares tales of life in London, I unwrap the wax paper packages that Mutti prepared for the train: potato dumplings, Schlosserbuben and Vanillekipferl, and worry out loud whether my English will be good enough and whether the job will be too hard.

Don't worry about English, she says. You'll pick it up quickly and you won't have much direct contact with the family, anyway. The most important person to please is the cook. She runs the house and if she likes you, she'll promote you. Best to tell her the food is delicious even if it's slop.

As we cross Austria, frost drapes green pine forests with its bright wintry shawl. Fields covered in fawn-tinted stubble break into settlements dusted with snow. Strings of icicles hang from the timber of farmyards and spires mark out villages, reaching upwards like fingers into the sky. I marvel at this landscape of fairy tales, but Traute is indifferent. She reels off advice.

The water in the scullery must be scorching. If it's not, fat from the pans congeals in the drainpipes making everything smell. Always tread on the wooden slats to protect your shoes from the wet and the cold.

We pass through Salzburg into Germany. Clouds billow above furrows of rufous earth. A goshawk wheels high above a solitary fir, scanning for prey. Munich passes into Stuttgart and the land flattens into vast open plains. The earth is heavier here, clumped in dark sods.

Traute has moved on to how to wash clothes. I know this already, so I start to doze off. When I awake, we're in France, on the outskirts of Paris. Factories puff ash-coloured smoke into the sky.

The time off is wonderful, Traute continues. We'll picnic in Hyde Park and go to some dances!

The train slows right down. As we pull into Dunkirk, a woman leans out of a window in a line of brick houses, beating a rug until it coughs out black dust.

By the dock, there's a strong smell of seaweed. Waves slap angrily against the harbour wall. Out at sea, white horses toss great sprays of spume skywards. Traute hands me a brown paper bag.

The boat starts to pitch as soon are we're out of the harbour. The first time I vomit, it's into my hands. Stinking liquid drips through my fingers onto the floor, which is swaying beneath me. The second time, I manage to get it into the bag.

You need some fresh air, Traute says and leads me up to the deck.

Freezing air pulls at my face as I lean over the railing, hands tingling with cold. The sea roils far below, dark as oil. I long for the warmth of my mother and home. Slowly, the nausea lifts.

Rain pelts the side of the train as England passes in a patchwork of fields. At last, we reach London. Row upon row of terraced houses line the track, grey with red roofs and tiny backyards. From Victoria Station, we make our way to Notting Hill Gate and walk the final stretch, dragging our suitcases along the wet streets. Vienna feels a lifetime away.

Traute stops and points at an enormous four-storey building.

That's the Millers' house, she says. In you go!

I look at the building nervously. Black and white tiles pave the way to the door.

I'll meet you here on Sunday, she says and gives me a shove.

When I ring the bell, an elderly woman wearing an apron comes to the door.

You must be the Austrian girl, she says. I'm Mrs Cooper, the cook. What are you waiting for? Come on in!

Russell.

July 1957. Velden am Wörthersee.

You catch me at the back of the hotel, bent over the soil. The garden smells muddy, of sunshine and earth.

Hello, you say. What are you doing here?

I jump backwards, startled, feeling immediately guilty, and look down at my feet. But then I hear you giggle. It turns into a laugh and before long both of us are laughing harder and harder until I'm too weak to stand. I sit down in the mud. You lean forward and offer me your hand. I take hold of it gently and you heave me back up.

Come on then, you say. I will show you my vegetables. I think that must be what you're looking for.

We walk past rows of onions and carrots, shoots pointing skywards, leaves feathered with delicate fronds. Beans twist tightly round canes like green ribbons, leaves parted round plump crimson flowers. We reach the back of the garden, where there's a small area containing potatoes and cabbages and a few herbs.

This is my patch, you say as you pick up a watering can, take it to a rain barrel in the corner of the garden and fill it up.

Aren't you working today? I ask.

Yes, but it's my break before dinner. I have a few hours off.

You tend to your vegetables. Water spills out of the can and sinks into the earth in dark patches. You see me watching you and smile.

Would you like to go for a walk? you ask.

I feel myself flush.

I'd love to, I say.

Alright then. I need to water the rest of the vegetables. I'll meet you at the front of the hotel in ten minutes.

I walk back through the garden, buoyed with possibility, and wait on the terrace for you to arrive. When you join me, we walk down to the lake. The water is clear in the shallows, then graduates out in deepening shades of green and blue.

Your English is so much better than my German, I say. Did you learn it in school?

No. I learnt English in London. I worked there for a short time before the war. I think your German is just fine, but if you want to improve, you just need to practise.

It was fluent when I lived in Vienna, but I've lost a lot of it since then. Maybe I could practise with you.

Why not? you say. That would be nice.

I smile at you as we walk together along the waterfront. The path takes us past gardens that roll down to the lake. Sculpted box hedges and flower beds punctuate neatly mown lawns. We come to a park that is grassy and tree lined. A bench looks out over the lake in the shade of some trees.

I don't think we can go any further, you say. Otherwise, I'll miss my next shift. Do you want to sit here for a minute?

We sit on the bench and look out across the lake.

Oh look! you say in excitement, pointing to the tree nearest to us. I love that bird.

A small brown bird is moving up the trunk in a series of small hops.

It's a *Baumläufer*, you say. It's looking for insects in the bark with its beak.

The bird disappears round the back of the tree then reappears further up, hopping and prising away at the trunk.

I don't think I've seen one of those before, I say.

Don't you get this bird in America?

I don't know.

I love birds, you say. They are my favourite thing.

I don't know very much about birds at all.

I could teach you about the birds we get here if you like.

Yes please, I say far too enthusiastically.

You laugh and glance at your watch.

I need to go back to work, you say. But if you are really interested, I have a very good book about birds that I can show you later.

You stand up and lead the way back to the hotel. When we arrive in its gardens, you stop to look at me. I can tell that you are weighing me up.

Will you show me your bird book after your shift? I ask hopefully. I'm in room number twenty-five.

Alright, you reply, and then you are gone.

When you knock on my door later, you are in your work uniform and your hair is tied back. You're carrying the bird book. As you enter the room, I notice your cheekbones and the curve of your mouth. You sit on the bed, indicate for me to sit next to you, and open the book. The mattress bows and sags, pulling us in towards each other. Our legs and shoulders touch; our faces are less than a foot apart. I struggle to concentrate. All my attention is drawn to your body touching mine.

Are you looking? you say, tapping the book earnestly.

There's something about the timbre of your voice. I look down at the page. Thankfully, it's a bird that I know.

A kingfisher! I say triumphantly.

In German, we say *Eisvogel*.

Eisvogel, I reply, mimicking your accent.

You smile and my heart jumps a beat. To keep the conversation going, I ask you where the best place near here is to see birds.

For water birds, the lake, you say. But my favourite place to birdwatch is the mountains.

You continue to leaf through the book. Each time you turn the page, your arm brushes against mine. I put my hand on the book to stop you from turning the pages. Your eyes meet mine and your face flushes.

Could you show me? I ask.

The birds?

No, the mountains. I mean the birds and the mountains.

That would be nice, you say softly, closing the book.

I lean in towards you. You don't lean away, so I lean in further until we are kissing. Your mouth is soft and warm, gentle against mine. After a minute, you pull away.

I'd better go, you say. I will get into trouble if my boss finds out that I'm in your room.

I hold on to your arm gently. I don't want you to go.

Please would you take me to the mountains? I've only got one weekend left here. Can you get next weekend off work?

I'm immediately embarrassed by the desperation I can hear in my voice, but you look at me kindly.

There's a mountain not too far from here called Hochobir, you say. It's a beautiful walk to the peak, but you need a car to get there. Do you have a car?

No, I say. But I'll find one. If I get hold of one, will you take me there?

Alright, you say. If you find a car, I will ask for the weekend off work.

Hermine.

December 1937. London.

The house in London runs by routine. I wake at 6am, wash, put on my clothes and my apron, and then go downstairs to report to Cook. I clean the fireplaces, polish the grates, fill buckets with coal, lay the kindling and light all the fires. The rest of the day is spent in the scullery and kitchen, washing clothes and dishes, and helping Cook with the food.

In the scullery, I set the pot boiling, fill one tub to soak clothes, another tub to scrub them and a third one to rinse. At first, I forget to stand on the wooden slats and my shoes become drenched. They rub against my feet all day long, giving me blisters. I soon learn better and make sure they're dry. After washing the clothes, I put them through a mangle, a clever machine that wrings out the water. Each time I use it, I think of Mutti and how much she would love this device - it saves so much time.

In between washing, I take in deliveries from the grocer and butcher and peel and chop vegetables. By the end of the day, my hands are chafed red from the cold and the wet. I rub in goose fat, but still they throb. By the time I have finished, it's late in the evening. My legs feel like stone as I head up to my room. I'm sharing with Betty, a housemaid from Lancaster, a city in the north of England. She finishes before me, so she's already here. She told me that she's not one for chatting when we first met, and she was not lying; she doesn't even look up when I enter the room. Instead, she faces the wall and turns out the light. I long for my mother and my sister. During the daytime, I'm so busy with work that I don't have time to think, but at night my mind turns to home. I think about Christmas in Nußdorf: the Krampus parade, the candles on the wreath, the carols, Sachertorte and Spitzbuben, and Vati, dear Vati, and how much I miss him. I look forward to Sunday when I can see Traute.

Russell.
July 1964. Maspeth.

It's Saturday morning. The radio's on in the kitchen; the Beach Boys are singing *I Get Around*. I hear you downstairs making a hash of the lyrics; it makes me smile into the mirror as I shave.

Hey, honey, I shout out. Those aren't the right words!

Don't ruin my fun, Russ! you shout up to me. It's good for my English to sing along.

You're busy downstairs re-painting the hallway, changing the colour from white to pale yellow. Suddenly, I hear a sharp knock on the door.

I'll get it! You call out.

I wipe off the shaving soap with a washcloth, rinse it, wring it and hang it to dry. When I finish, I can hear you talking to whoever it is at the front door. As I walk down the stairs, I see you through the banisters; your hair's up in curlers and you're wearing a top that matches your shorts, striped pink and white like candy. A man stands in the doorway. He looks like a door-to-door salesman: young, professional, wearing a suit. It's then that I see it: the paintbrush dropped onto the floor next to you; it's spattered yellow paint all over the floor like broken eggs. I look at you more closely. Your shoulders are raised and you're clasping your hands. With primeval instinct, I rush down the stairs and pull you away from the man, putting my arm around you protectively. You cling on to me tightly. Your whole body is shaking. The man's foot is wedged firmly against the door, preventing it from closing. My hands snap closed into fists.

Who are you? I say fiercely. What are you saying to my wife?

Hermine.
March 1938. London.

This morning after breakfast, Mr Miller calls me into his study. It's the first time he's spoken to me directly and I fear for the worst. Is my cleaning not good enough? Am I using too much coal? At least my English has improved enough now to understand what he's saying. I knock on the door and he calls out to me to come in.

Mr Miller is sitting at his desk reading a newspaper. He doesn't look up as I stand in the doorway and look around the room. I've never been in here before. The walls are painted a deep bloody red and rows of bookshelves line the walls, filled with hundreds of books. A huge globe sits to the left of his desk.

Hello Hermine, he says and sets down his newspaper. Please come in.

I had no idea that he knew my name, nor that he could pronounce it correctly. It is comforting, like eating warm cake. I smooth down my apron and enter the room.

Sir, I reply, waiting to be scolded.

Do you know what's going on in your country? he says.

Fear quickly replaces my initial relief.

No, sir. Is my mother alright?

He picks up a silver letter opener and spins it in his hand. It catches the light.

No, no, it's not that. I'm talking about the political situation. A wave of relief.

I don't know anything about politics, sir. What's happened?

Three days ago, German troops entered Austria. Your country's been annexed and your chancellor's resigned. Austria belongs to Germany now.

The news comes as a shock. I feel completely overwhelmed and don't know what to say. What does this mean for my family? Mr Miller looks at me, then taps at his newspaper.

The Times of London says many Viennese are happy about it. What do you think?

I stand there in silence, unable to talk. I'm debilitated by worry about Mutti, Luise and the rest of my family. Mr Miller looks at me intently and continues to speak.

This means that you are a German citizen now. I don't want to alarm you, but there is some talk of war. Right now, it seems unlikely that Mr Chamberlain will do much about it, but if tensions do rise and Britain and Germany end up at war, you will have to leave. If war breaks out, it is possible that you could become a prisoner of war.

My heart starts to pound. I hold on to the edge of the desk to steady myself and look out of the window. Outside, an apple tree holds up branches covered in dark furry buds. Some buds have begun to open into pastel pink flowers. Soon the whole tree will be covered in rose-tinted snow. I look back at Mr Miller. Though he is talking, I can't make out words. His mouth is opening and closing as if he's a fish.

Hermine, he says, louder this time. Do you understand?

I look down at his desk, avoiding his eyes.

Yes, sir, I say. I'm just worried about my family.

Your family will be fine for the time being, he says. I will keep you informed. That is all. You may go.

Over the next two weeks, I listen through doorways and hear Mr Miller talking to his wife about the *impact of rearmament* and the *shadow of war*. I try to talk to Betty, but she has less than no interest.

Don't be so ridiculous! she says. There will be no war.

On Sunday, I meet Traute in the communal gardens. Daffodils

line the borders with soft yellow bonnets. We sit on a bench. A wren perches nearby on top of a bush, feathers puffed out and wings slightly lifted, its high-pitched warble surprisingly loud.

It's good news, Traute says. Schuschnigg was weak. He should never have made concessions to the Italians. Hitler's much stronger. The first thing he will do is help us to take our country back.

Take it back from what?

Traute looks at me with disdain.

The Jews, of course, Hermine! Don't you know anything? Vienna's in their hands. It's because of them that Austria's a mess.

She leans in towards me with evident delight.

Haven't you heard? The Jews are being made to clean the streets of Vienna with toothbrushes. I wish I could see it.

That seems quite pointless to me, but I say nothing. There's no point saying anything to Traute.

That night, I go to bed worried. The day's events tumble together in a horrible dream in which I'm scrubbing the fireplace while Mr Miller shouts at me over and over that it's not clean. I wake with a start and realise I'm sobbing. I look over to see whether Betty's awake. She's fast asleep; her bedcovers rise and fall gently. I close my eyes and pray to go home.

Russell.

August 1957. Eisenkappel-Vellach.

The hotel manager finds me a car. He's allowed you to take the weekend off. If he realises our requests are linked, he says nothing.

We meet just before dawn. As darkness lifts, pale tinges of colour paint the hotel gardens in pastels and greens. You're wearing shorts, a sweater and sturdy boots, looking athletic and healthy. Your hair is tied up in a scarf and you're carrying a rucksack. We're heading to Hochobir, in the direction of the Yugoslavian border. If we leave first thing, we will have enough time to walk to the summit and back in a day, staying overnight in Eisenkappel-Vellach, near the start of the walk. I take out the map and hand it to you.

This is the start of the hike, you say, pointing at the map. If we leave now, I think we will get there by eight. That should give us plenty of time to get to the top and back in time for dinner. What do you think?

Sounds good, I say. You be the navigator.

We set off. I'm driving and you're in the passenger seat. The route takes us along the north edge of Wörthersee. Swans sun themselves by the lake, wings splayed out in the first warmth of day. Soon, we pass into farmland. Field upon field of wheat and sunflowers sway in the breeze. I want to find out about you, so I start to ask questions, but my line of questioning immediately falls flat.

So, how old are you?

You look at me horrified.

That's a rude question! I'm not going to tell you. You'll think it's too old.

I'm sorry, I say. I shouldn't have asked, but you're definitely not old! I'm gonna guess you're thirty or thirty-two.

You let out a sigh.

I'm thirty-eight, you say. So, you're wrong. I am very old.

You don't look thirty-eight, I say. Anyway, that's not old.

It's far too old to be alone, you say, looking out of the window.

I'm not sure how to take this. Does this mean that you're alone and you don't want to be? Perhaps you've been married before and your husband has died. Are you looking for someone to love? I wonder if I'd be too young for you and then why I'm even thinking about this.

So, what about you? you ask in return.

I'm thirty-three, turning thirty-four in a few weeks.

You take in this information but do not reply. I steal a glance at you, but your face gives away nothing. Perhaps you're not looking for anything at all.

We reach Völkermarkt. Orange roofed buildings surround the central square. We turn to the south, cross a small lake and head towards the mountains. I push for a bit more information.

Have you ever been married?

Well, that's an even worse question! First my age and now if I've been married!

I feel suddenly hot. My skin crawls as if it's covered in ants. I stop talking and look straight ahead out of the windshield, minding the road. You look forward too, but after a few minutes you decide to reply.

I had some boyfriends during the war, but afterwards I never met anybody, so I haven't been married. The war made a lot of things difficult for me. What about you?

I'm not been married either, I say. I've never been all that good with the girls.

You laugh merrily.

I don't believe that, you say. That cannot be true.

Just look at me, I say. I'm hardly a Romeo. I'm kind of weedy-looking and I'm not very tall.

I don't know what weedy-looking means, you say, patting me on the knee. I think those American girls are crazy. They must all have rocks in their heads.

I can't believe you just said that. I feel suddenly lighter, like my body is made of air. I start to whistle. You pick up the tune and hum along. I've never felt this good in female company. Usually, I feel awkward around women, but you're making me feel so at ease. As we drive through Eberndorf, white rectangular houses prop up red-tiled roofs. The road continues, banking up on each side until we find ourselves in a valley with views of the mountains off to the right. When we reach Eisenkappel-Vellach, it is just before 8am. We find the start of the track, check that we have enough food and water, and then we set off.

The path climbs through a shaded pine forest. The air is thick with the smell of damp earth. Past the forest, the track continues to rise through Alpine meadows dotted with purple and white flowers. As we hike, you ask me about my life in New York. I tell you how my father died when I was young, leaving my mother to raise four children, how hard she worked to raise us and how sad I was when she died shortly after the war. I tell you how my brother and sisters moved away, leaving me with no family in New York. I tell you all about my childhood, what I did during the war and about my work. You listen to me with genuine interest as I describe my house and my garden, my neighbours and friends. It makes me feel special. We reach a mountain hut and you suggest that we stop for a break. I take an apple out of my pack and hand it to you. You polish it on your shorts, take a bite, and then stretch out your long slender legs and lean your face towards the sun.

I've told you pretty much everything there is to know about me, I say. What about you?

Your eyes are still closed, your face lifted upwards.

I don't have so much to tell, you say. Like I told you, I was a maid, first in Vienna and then in England. I had to come back because of the Anschluss. I wanted to be a nurse, but there were no jobs. The only work I could find was in a beer factory, but I didn't like it much, and the pay was very low, so I took a better paid job in a factory in Germany. I ended up living near to a prison, so I took a job there because it was much better paid. I worked there during the war. Afterwards, I came here.

You open your eyes and look at me directly.

My life is not very exciting.

Don't be silly, I say. Working in a prison must have been interesting. What was it like?

Interesting is not the right word. It was hard, but then it was wartime, so everything was hard.

What kind of prison was it? I ask, intrigued.

A prison for women.

What did you do there?

I lean in towards you. You lean away from me and cross your arms round your body before you respond.

After a while, you say quite simply, I was a guard.

Wow! What was that like?

You look at me carefully, scanning my face.

At first, it wasn't too bad, but the conditions got worse as the war went on. It was very overcrowded and there was a lot of sickness, a lot of typhoid. I kept getting sick. They were very difficult years.

You stand up abruptly.

I don't like to think about it. Could we talk about something else?

Of course, I say. I'm sorry. I don't mean to pry.

Hermine.
May 1938. Nußdorf.

Luise is waiting for me at the station. I run at her, shoes clacking against the platform's edge.

Hermi! she rasps as I hug her, struggling to break free. I can't breathe!

She pushes me back, holds me at arm's length, and looks me up and down. I look at her too. She is noticeably thinner.

My goodness, I say. Have you stopped eating?

Nobody is eating well anymore, she says. Food is so expensive now. Even the Brünners only buy meat once a week.

We head out into the street. Vienna looks so beautiful. I hadn't realised how much I'd missed her archways and pillars and domes. A man cycles past with a whirring of wheels. We wait for the tram and Luise tells me about Horst, the youngest of the Brünners, how she adores him, how well he can talk.

The tram arrives and two men get off, looking dishevelled. Their eyes are cast down.

Jews, pronounces Luise loudly. If it wasn't for them, Austria would not be so poor.

The woman standing next to us nods in agreement. She leans in towards me and whispers dramatically, The Jews kill Christian children and use their blood in their rituals.

I lean away from her in disgust. As the Jews shuffle off, Luise spits at them. I have never before seen her spit.

Don't do that, Luise, I say. It's disgusting.

They are the ones who are disgusting, Hermine. They've been taking all our money, getting rich while we remain poor. Don't ever go near them; they're as dirty as rats.

As the tram glides through Vienna's wide avenues, slowly my discomfort fades. We pass into Döbling, and once we reach Nußdorf, the tram clunks to a halt. We descend into the square and walk home along Kahlenberger Straße. Summer has filled the gardens with cloudy white heads of yarrow, thick yellow bushes of St John's wort, purple campanula and blue bugle herb. The drone of bees stirs the air. I'm so desperate to get home that we run the last few metres. As soon as I open the front door of our building, the scent of Mutti's cooking hits me square in the face. After months of English food, it smells so good. I run up the stairs and fold into Mutti, breathing her in. She wipes her hands on her apron and then strokes my hair.

Come and eat, mein Liebling, she says. I cooked especially for you.

I missed your food, Mutti, I say as I fork great mounds of potato into my mouth. It's so good to be home!

When we've finished eating, Luise holds out some papers to me.

It's not such a bad time for you to come back, she says. The Germans have a programme for mass employment, so there will be more jobs. This is an application form for nursing. I've applied, as have a lot of girls in this area. I kept it for you, so you can apply too.

I take the papers and go into the bedroom, remove my clothes from the suitcase and fold them neatly onto familiar shelves. Outside the window, a swallow delivers mud to its nest under the roofing; its wings whir blue-black like the smudging of ink. By the time I get into bed next to Luise, I'm exhausted but full of hope.

Tomorrow, I think. I will fill out the form.

Russell.

August 1957. Eisenkappel-Vellach.

The summit of Hochobir looks down over Carinthia. Sunlight and cloud shade the mountains with greys and greens. As we descend, you point out the flowers: bright blue gentians, yellow alpine anemones, purple pasque flowers, delicate white Alpine buttercups. You stop and bend down to pick a tiny blue flower.

This one's my favourite, you say. It means don't forget me. In German it's *Vergissmeinnicht*.

It's the same in English! I reply in delight. We say forget-me-not. It's such a cute name. I suppose nothing wants to be forgotten, not even a flower.

You speed up a little and start to walk on ahead, deliberately going faster when I try to catch up. When I reach you, I take hold of your arm and turn you towards me. There are tears in your eyes.

What's wrong? I ask.

You'll forget me as soon as you go back to America, you say. I'll be left here cleaning hotels.

I feel deeply protective of you. I don't want you to be upset. I place my hands on your shoulders.

I could never forget you, I say. Listen, this is going to sound crazy, but why don't you come with me when I go back to New York?

Your expression shifts, like the wind on the water. You turn away from me and look up into the sky. Two huge birds wheel and soar above us, spiralling upwards into the clouds.

Buzzards, you say quietly. People are afraid of them, but they do not harm humans. They only eat animals that are already dead. Let's stay here and watch them. We can eat our lunch.

We sit in silence, watching the buzzards. They glide and lift overhead in a magnificent display of choreographed companionship. I shouldn't have asked you that question. What was I thinking? Of course, you'll say no. I break the silence.

I'm sorry, I say. That was a completely crazy idea. This is your home; you have family here. You don't know me. We only just met. Just forget I said that.

You shake your head.

It's not that, you say. I would love to come with you. I like you a lot. Both of my parents are dead. Two of my brothers died in the war. My surviving brother and my sisters are all married and busy with their work and their children. I hardly see them anymore. No, it's not that. I can't come because I don't have any money and I wouldn't know how to get a visa.

I pull you towards me and kiss your forehead gently, then lean you back and look into your eyes.

You don't need money, I say. I have enough money for both of us. I'm sure we can sort out a visa. New York is full of immigrants from Europe. I'll work out a way to get you in, and then I'll look after you. You will never clean a hotel room ever again.

Your eyes fill with hope. I feel myself spinning. Above us, the buzzards twist and turn around each other as clouds build and billow, casting huge shadows onto the land.

Come on, I say. Let's head back down the mountain. We can have dinner somewhere nice while I persuade you to come to New York.

In Eisenkappel-Vellach, we find a wooden chalet with vacancies at the edge of the town. The building rises upwards to a high pointed roof. Bright flowers spill out from tubs below all the windows. I squeeze your hand as I check us in as Mr and Mrs Ryan. This is what it would feel like if you were my wife.

After dinner, we head back to the chalet, tired but content, full of plans for New York. I turn away while you undress and get into bed. When I turn back, you are under the covers. I climb into the bed and lay myself next to you; your body is warm and soft against mine. I reach out and touch you, gently at first, but soon my touch becomes urgent. I push myself into you and both of us groan.

Afterwards, I hold on to you tightly and whisper into your ear, Marry me. Come with me to New York.

Hermine.

September 1938. Nußdorf.

The post box remains empty for more than six weeks. Nothing arrives for Luise or me. She continues to work for the Brünners, but I cannot find a job. Despite all the talk of falling unemployment, people are not taking on housemaids. I'm desperate for money; we need it for food.

In the end, the only place that will take me is Nußdorf Brewery, where memories of Vati press like a bruise. The work is hard and monotonous; ten hours filling bottles, then stacking them into crates. The beer splashes onto my clothing and dries on my hands, sticking like syrup and smelling stale like bad breath. But something good happens; I make friends with the girl who stands next to me. Maria Müller is eighteen, one year younger than me. She lives nearby in Döbling with her three younger brothers. The money she earns keeps them all in school. Maria is friendly and kind. We take to meeting outside the factory each morning and at lunchtime we share our food. Her friendship makes the work much more bearable. She tells me that she also applied for a nursing position and heard nothing back. One day Maria announces that she's applied for factory work in Germany.

Come with me, she says. It's much better paid.

Russell.

July 1964. Maspeth.

The man shuffles backwards, but his foot remains stuck in the doorway. The blood is pumping hard in my neck.

Who are you? I ask him. What have you been saying to my wife?

My name is Joseph Lelyveld, the man replies. I'm a reporter for the *New York Times.*

I look from Lelyveld to you and back again. He looks uncomfortable and you start to cry. You lean in so close to me that your hair curlers tug at the skin of my neck.

You can start by taking your foot out of my doorway, I say to the reporter.

Lelyveld moves his foot and takes a step back but continues to stare at you while you sob.

Could someone please tell me what the hell's going on here?

Finally, you break the silence.

This man wants to talk about my work in the prison during the war. I told him that I only did what everyone else did back then. I just did my job.

I tighten my arm around you. One of your curlers falls out of your hair and bounces off your leg onto the floor. It lands next to the paintbrush in a pool of yellow paint.

With respect, sir, Lelyveld says. I'm writing a newspaper article for the *New York Times.* It would be better for both of you if you let me come in.

Hermine.

October 1938. Fürstenberg.

The train is unheated. Maria and I travel together, huddled close in warm winter coats. It's the first time that Maria has left Vienna. She's extremely excited.

This is an adventure! she says. I hope we like our new jobs.

Two weeks ago, the Magdeburg Polte-Werke offered us work at its munitions factory in Grüneberg, an hour to the north of Berlin. The pay is almost double the beer factory and the company has found us accommodation nearby.

This news was especially hard to break to Mutti. Like Luise, she's become far too thin. However, she agreed reluctantly that I should go when I told her how much money I'd be able to send home. I promised her that I would only stay away for a year or two, just enough time to save up some money. Luise told me firmly to take it and go.

Times are hard now, Hermi, she said. The money you send can be spread through the whole family. Think about how much it would help.

Austria rolls past through the window. The greys of the Danube give way to the greens of the plains. Maria asks me if I think Germany will be different.

Not so much, I say. At least we speak the same language. England was difficult for that. And anything is better than the beer factory.

Outside, it darkens. Forests of pine swallow the light. In Berlin, we stay overnight in a hostel right next to the train station, sharing a dormitory with twelve other women. The night is stuffy and restless and we're both tired when we board the train the next day for Fürstenberg, a small holiday resort two hours north of Berlin.

As the city dissolves into flat, open farmland, deer lift their heads as our train rattles by. Both of us doze and by the time we awake, we're slowing down to pull into Fürstenberg. Out of the window, a lake catches the blue of the sky. Our landlord, Herr Schmidt, is easy to spot on the platform; he's the local police chief and is wearing his uniform. Herr Schmidt is much shorter than I expected but surprisingly strong. He insists on carrying both of our suitcases, sweeping them up, one in each hand, and then leads us through streets lined with pastel-coloured houses.

It's so pretty! I say. I can see why people come here on holiday.

Fürstenberg is the gateway to the Mecklenburg Lake District, replies Herr Schmidt. It's a beautiful place.

He leads us to a house at the end of a terrace. A woman opens the door with a welcoming smile.

This is Frau Schmidt, he says.

Please call me Anna, she says, and she shows us around.

Downstairs, there's a dining room, sitting room and kitchen. Outside, the outhouse and washroom. Upstairs there are two bedrooms: the Schmidts' on the right, ours on the left. Our room is just wide enough for two single beds either side of a small table. At the end of the beds is a wardrobe and chair.

I'll leave you to unpack, says Anna. When you're ready, come downstairs for some tea and cake.

Maria smiles at me. Both the Schmidts seem very nice.

Russell.

October 1957. Elmhurst.

The sound of the telephone ringing jolts me awake. I turn on the light. The hands on my clock show it's 4:30am. I hurry downstairs to the living room and reach for the phone.

Honey? I say. Is that you?

There's a series of crackles and then I hear your voice.

I'm sorry, Russ. Did I wake you?

That's no problem. Is something wrong?

Another crackle and pause, the delay on the line. At first, I think it's static then I realise you're crying. My chest tightens instantly, as if I've been punched.

Where are you? What's wrong?

I stretch and coil the loops of the telephone wire round my forefinger tightly. It turns my fingertip red.

There's a big problem, Russell. My visa has been rejected.

I pause, digesting this news. I expected your visa application to go through easily. I've no idea what the problem can be and I feel so far away from you, unable to help. I need to come up with something quickly to make this OK.

Don't cry, honey, I say. I promise I'll find a way to work this out. Just give me a few days to come up with a plan. I'll call you back when I've worked out what to do.

OK, you say. I've got to go, Russ. This call is going to be very expensive.

You put the phone down. I return to the bedroom. I'm far too awake to get back into bed, so I pull on some clothes and make my way down to the kitchen. The bare skin of my feet sticks to the cold linoleum floor. I pull up the blind on the window; it's still dark outside. A dog barks in a neighbouring garden. People are starting to get ready for work. I fill the kettle at the faucet, put it onto the stovetop and sit down at the table to think. It must be possible to get you into America. I'll go to the Immigration Service as soon as it opens to get some advice.

Hermine.

October 1938. Fürstenberg.

The train from Fürstenberg to Grüneberg takes an hour each way. Maria and I have requested to work the same shifts so we can travel together. Each shift lasts ten hours. We start off loading machines that make fuses, but soon volunteer to work putting phosphorous into the metal tips of munitions because that gets us a special ration of milk. We're given tongs and protective gloves so that we don't get burnt. The work is much more rewarding than filling beer bottles, and working the same hours means that we have company and don't wake each other up when we come in.

When we have a day off, we help Anna to prepare some meat or a pie. She's a very good cook. She chats away in the kitchen as we assist her, telling us that she met Herr Schmidt as a child. Their families are friends and they were married last year. Herr Schmidt was promoted to town police chief two years ago. He is very well liked in the community and Anna is hugely proud of him and his work.

You're so lucky to have a good marriage, I say. I hope one day I will have your good luck.

Anna smiles at me.

I'm sure you will, Hermine, she says. Both you and Maria. You're such nice girls.

A few Sundays later, we all attend church. Afterwards, the Schmidts go to visit their families, so Maria and I make a picnic and head to the bandstand, which is in the park right next to the lake. Each Sunday, a band plays and people come from all over to dance. Swans glide along the lake's surface, occasionally dipping their heads into the weeds. As we near the bandstand, we hear the band playing. The music is fast and uplifting, causing a communal tapping of feet. After a while, Maria indicates a tall, dark-haired man wearing a uniform sitting opposite us on a bench.

He's been watching you, she whispers.

I check him through glances until our eyes meet. The man gets up from the bench and approaches. He's remarkably handsome. My face feels suddenly hot.

Good afternoon, ladies, the man says. My name is Dieter.

He turns to me and I giggle.

Would you like to dance?

And so, I meet Dieter. He tells me that he's from Berlin and has been sent here from Sachsenhausen to help build a women's prison on the edge of the lake. He's a good head taller than me, with raven black hair, light green eyes, sharp cheekbones and a very white smile.

I'm in charge of a group of male prisoners, he tells me. The prison we're constructing will re-educate female criminals and enemies of the state.

As we dance, I tell him about my work in the factory and my life in Vienna. The afternoon passes so quickly that I don't even notice that it's getting dark. When I finally look up, Maria has slipped off without me. Like a gentleman, Dieter escorts me home. Just before we get to the door, he stops me.

Can I see you again?

That would be nice, I reply with a blush.

Next Sunday then. The same time at the bandstand.

I open the door and creep up the stairs. Maria's already in bed. She begs me to tell her all about Dieter. I lie down on my bed, swathed in happiness, and recount the afternoon. Even though the days at the factory are long, I'm happy here.

Russell.

October 1958. Halifax.

A layer of fog rests over Halifax Harbour, undulating gently in a grey wave. The morning air is salty and cool as I pace the dock and peer through the mist, wondering when your ship will arrive. It turns out the easiest way for you to gain entry to America is to come into Canada as a visitor and for us to get married here. Once we are married, you can apply for an entry visa to the United States as my wife. The voyage from Europe takes just over two weeks.

Over the past months, I've made all the arrangements, from the ship you are sailing on to booking a registry office wedding in a week's time. I would have preferred a proper church wedding, but this is the quickest way for us to get married. The whole of my body aches to see you, but at the same time, I feel nervous. I haven't seen you in more than a year. I hope this is going to work. The last time I felt this mixture of trepidation and elation was the end of the war.

The bow of the SS Maasdam comes into sight, puffing smoke out of its stack. The port comes alive as the ship edges her way into the dock. People line the ship's deck, wrapped in warm winter coats. I scan the disembarking passengers looking for you and almost don't recognise you under your hat and your coat. You walk down the gangway carefully, watching your step. When you catch sight of me, you wave at me furiously and my whole being sings.

You made it! I shout, running towards you.

I pull you close into me and breathe the scent of you in. You cling onto me hard until eventually I prise you off me. We kiss, warm and promising. All the doubts I've had about whether you still love me evaporate into the morning sun.

Hermine.

November 1938. Fürstenberg.

Dieter and I walk by the lakeside. Autumn has stripped the trees bare and spume tumbles across the lake in great gusts. Dieter takes my hand and rubs it a little to keep it warm. We're discussing the birds.

The greatest of all the birds is the kite, he says, but I disagree.

It's the pied woodpecker, so colourful and quirky, or maybe the kingfisher, so fast and full of grace.

We keep walking and talking until eventually we turn back towards the town. In the backstreets of Fürstenberg, we come across a cemetery that's clearly been vandalised. Gravestones lie toppled and smashed to pieces all over on the ground. Rough-edged chunks of stone have flattened the flowers. The rest of Fürstenberg is so orderly. It's so out of place.

What's happened here? I exclaim. What a terrible mess! What a horrible thing to happen to a graveyard!

Dieter looks surprised.

You must sleep very deeply! Didn't you hear the commotion the other night? This is the Jewish cemetery. It was destroyed a few nights ago, as was the hotel in town that's owned by the Jew.

Why did this happen?

A Jew shot a German in Paris. It's in retaliation for that.

But why Fürstenberg? Did the Jew come from here?

No, he didn't, but that's of no consequence, Hermine. The action's being taken across all of Germany. The Jewish problem's been growing. The shooting in Paris is the tip of the iceberg. The Jews must be stopped. They are *Untermenschen*, far worse than vermin. If we're not careful, they will wipe us all out. It's about time we addressed this problem all over the Reich.

I didn't even know the hotel owner was Jewish, I say.

They're hiding in plain sight, Dieter replies. That's what's so dangerous about them. We need to weed them all out. Come on, let's leave this disgusting place.

We walk away from the wreckage and start to head home, cutting through the alleyway that leads to my road. The passage is lined with high brick walls; the mortar between them is furred with deep green. The air is cool and mossy and damp. Dieter stops, leans his back against the wall and pulls me towards him. His kiss tastes yeasty, like almost-cooked bread.

Russell.

October 1958. Halifax.

In the week before our wedding, you busy yourself finding work in Nova Scotia while we wait for your visa, seeking advice from the hotel staff. One maid is particularly helpful. Her brother-in-law runs a farm about eighty kilometres northeast of Halifax in Middle Musquodoboit. He's looking for a farmhand to help with the Brussels sprout harvest and is happy to employ a hardworking woman.

I'm not afraid of physical labour, you say, standing squarely before her, clearly capable of the job.

I don't like the idea of you doing manual labour, but we agree you should take it so that you have an income while we wait for your visa to arrive.

I hope your visa doesn't take too long to process, I say. I hate to think of you working out in the fields while I'm living comfortably in New York.

Don't worry about me, Russ, you say. I'm perfectly capable of working outside. All this will be worth it when I get to America as your wife.

The wedding ceremony takes place in Halifax City Hall, a cream and red building not far from the waterfront. You wear a green dress and brown shawl, and I wear a suit. As we walk in through the hall's huge wooden doors, I hold your hand tightly. The registry office is up on the third floor. We sit outside the office on a row of wooden seats and listen to the murmur of voices coming from inside the room from the previous ceremony.

I wish we could get married properly in a church in front of

God, I whisper. I could choose the music and you could wear a white dress.

I don't mind where we get married, you reply. All that matters is that I'm getting married to you.

I hold your hand and pray silently for our marriage to be blessed, and that God understands why we're here.

This may not be a church, I say. But I will take my vows just as seriously as I would if I said them in front of God.

Me too, Russ, you reply. Who's to say that God is not here?

Our conversation's interrupted by the registry office door opening. A young couple comes out followed by a cheerful looking man.

Hermine Braunsteiner and Russell Ryan? he says and we nod. Your turn! Come on in!

The ceremony takes less than ten minutes. We read through our vows and sign the certificate in front of two council witnesses.

Afterwards, you say, Well, that was quick and easy. Come on, let's celebrate!

Though it's only mid-morning, we go to our hotel room, order room service and spend the rest of the day in a haze of husband and wife.

Hermine.
June 1939. Fürstenberg.

Herr Schmidt makes a suggestion while we're returning from church.

The commute to Grüneberg is tiring you both out, he says. Why don't you apply for work here in Fürstenberg? The new women's prison is open now and the *Kommandant* is looking for guards.

Dieter has told me all about Ravensbrück. It's filling up fast. Over the past month, truckloads of women and children have been transported there. The numbers have increased so much that they come in by train too. Guards with dogs meet the trains at the platform and march the prisoners through the streets north from the station and east around the lake. The prisoners look ragged. The children with them hold their hands out, begging for food. Maria wants to give to them, but I tell her not to because they are criminals.

How can a child be a criminal? she asks me in horror. They're only children. What do they know?

Dieter says it's their mothers' responsibility to look after them, I say. They're not our problem, Maria. Their mothers should have thought about their children before they committed their crimes. If they go unpunished, what sort of example does it show their children? They'll end up becoming criminals themselves. That's what Dieter says and I think he is right.

Maria looks at me, unconvinced. I know there is no persuading her; she's as stubborn as she is kind.

Herr Schmidt tells us that he's met the prison commander,

Max Koegel.

He seems like a decent man, he says. The salary is 185 Reichsmarks a month after the training period, plus you get accommodation for free. You pay a small amount for clothing and food, but you would still take home more than working in the factory. You girls should apply.

Our current salary is seventy-six Reichsmarks a month, out of which we pay board and lodging and for the train. By the end of the month, there is not much left. Working at Ravensbrück would more than double our salary; we could send so much more home. It would also cut out two hours of commuting each day.

The timing would be good for us too, Herr Schmidt says. We're going to need your room back in a few months' time.

He looks at Anna, who is blushing and holding her hand to her belly.

Oh! Congratulations, Anna! we say and she smiles.

We discuss the idea later in our room.

I'm not sure about working in a prison, says Maria. I don't think I'd like that kind of work.

It would just be for a year or two, I say. I'm sure the work isn't too bad. Think how much money we would save.

In some ways, Maria is much stronger than me; she never seems to miss home, but in other ways she is quite soft. I agree immediately, but she takes a week to mull it over. In the end, she cannot turn down the pay. I'm so glad. We've shared so much in the past year and become such good friends. This feels like something we should do together. We put in our applications and wait.

Russell.

July 1964. Maspeth.

The man fumbles in his pocket, pulls out his wallet and takes out his card. He hands it to me and I look at it closely. His name, Joseph Lelyveld, is printed underneath the newspaper's logo. I feel a sudden panic. The *New York Times* has a wide circulation. I don't want us mentioned in the paper at all.

Hermine, I say. I think we better let this guy in. Then we can clear this all up.

I show Lelyveld into the living room. He sits in the armchair, pulls a pen from his jacket pocket and opens his notepad to a fresh page. I sit on the sofa and you sit right next to me. You hunch your shoulders forward and turn to me, eyes haunted with fear.

This will be the end of me, Russ, you say.

Hermine.
June 1939. Ravensbrück.

A message arrived yesterday from the *Oberaufseherin* of Ravensbrück, asking us to come in for an interview. Maria and I are filled with nerves and excitement as we walk to the prison. It's a warm summer's day and the path is layered with hundreds of footprints baked in the dry mud, all leading towards the camp. The sound of a cuckoo cuts through the forest, echoing round the trees.

When we arrive, we're taken into a room for a medical examination, after which we sit a written test containing questions about mathematics, history and geography. It takes a full hour. Though it's not too hard, there's a question about Napoleon that I can't answer and one about the discovery of the printing press that I'm certain to have failed. I hope this doesn't prevent me from getting in. Next comes an interview with *Oberaufseherin* Langefeld. We're led to her office and I go in first. She stands when I enter. Though she looks intimidating in her uniform, her face has a softness. Her hair curls to her shoulders in perfect blonde waves. Langefeld sits back down behind her desk. I remain standing. The interview is short, less than ten minutes; she asks me about my work in Vienna, London and Grüneberg, plus some additional questions about my political beliefs. I tell her that I'm happy Austria's united with Germany and that I will serve the Reich in the best way I can. She looks pleased with this answer.

Ravensbrück rehabilitates prisoners through hard work, Langefeld says. The prisoners come from all over Germany: criminals, anti-socials, homosexuals, communists and the work-shy. Your job as an *Aufseherin* is to make sure that they're working. You'll accompany them on their daily assignments and keep them under control. The day is long. It starts before dawn and it ends after dusk. It's hard work, but it's also a very good job with the future possibility of promotion. Do you think you can do it?

Yes, I say. I'm used to long hours and hard work.

Good, Langefeld says.

She taps at her desk and asks if I have any questions. I cannot think of any.

Well then, that is all, Braunsteiner, she says as she shuffles some papers. After I finish with Müller, I will get one of the *Aufseherinnen* to show you around.

Once Maria's interview is over, a guard called Schultz leads us to a square which is being dug by prisoners wearing blue and white striped dresses spattered all over with mud. Four large white villas line the square on either side. Schultz waves the prisoners out of the way so we can enter one of the villas.

These are the guard houses, she explains. You will live here.

Schultz shows us around.

Each house has rooms for eight *Aufseherinnen*, she says. You get your own room.

The food in the canteen here is good, Schultz says as she shows us into a small kitchen. But this is a nice place to meet colleagues for tea and a snack.

She leads us up the stairs to look at one of the bedrooms. It's spacious and light, split into two sections. In one half, there's a bed, sofa, desk and chair; in the other, a line of wardrobes and a sink. Maria smiles at me. It looks very comfortable.

You can write your letters home from here, Schultz says, pointing to the desk. And you can put your uniform and other clothes in there. The prisoners do all our washing and ironing. Ravensbrück's a very good place to work.

Maria and I can hardly contain our excitement. Any reservations Maria had about working here disappear as soon as she sees the accommodation. Both of us will have our own room!

Russell.

April 1959. Elmhurst.

You peer out of the windshield as we drive through New York. Excitement radiates from you like summer heat.

Oh my goodness! you say. These buildings are so high! How is it even possible?

Welcome to the United States of America, Mrs Ryan! I say. The land of the free!

You arrived this morning on the SS Stavangerfjord. The journey from Halifax took less than three days. The route I've chosen takes us around Columbus Circle and along the south end of Central Park. I'm desperate to show off my city. We drive past New York taxis, the colour of egg yolk. Horse-drawn carriages line the edge of the park.

Do we live near here, Russ?

No, honey, this is Manhattan, the most expensive part of town. Queens is a bit further out and much more suburban than this.

We cross the Queensboro Bridge. The water beneath it shines indigo blue. You look out over Roosevelt Island, so far from your old home, so near to your new.

We're coming into Queens now, I say, as we come off the bridge.

The edge of the road banks up to Calvary Cemetery. I continue on Queens Boulevard until we reach Elmhurst, then take a right down Grand Avenue and a left onto 82nd.

My neighbourhood's a mixture of red brick and homes clad with wood. Some houses are built right up to the sidewalk and some are set back from the street behind yards. You take it all in and sigh with delight. We cross 54th and I slow down to pull up outside my house. It's small but homely, painted cream under a triangular shingled roof. I turn off the engine and search your face for signs of disappointment, but I need not have worried.

Oh Russ, you say, flinging your arms around my neck. I love it!

Hermine.

August 1939. Ravensbrück.

My room's on the top floor under the eaves. I love it here. The pitch of the roof reminds me of home. Maria's room's on the floor below me. We step out together on our first day of work. Prisoners are digging flower beds and planting trees in the *Aufseherinnen* square. They do not look up as we walk past them into the prison.

I'm guard number thirty-eight and Maria's number thirty-nine. For our training, we are each allocated to an experienced guard. Maria's assigned to Dorothea Binz and I'm put under Maria Mandl. Mandl's dark hair is pulled back off her face so tightly it stretches her skin. Trying to be polite, I ask her where she's from.

Münzkirchen, she says, spitting out the word. Upper Austria.

I'm from Nußdorf in Vienna, I say, but she's clearly not interested. She glares at me fiercely.

You're here to work, Braunsteiner, not to make idle chit chat, she barks. You are going to help me with a unit of one hundred prisoners. They are filthy asocials, prisoner scum. They are enemies of the state and you will treat them as such. If I see you showing any sympathy at all, I will fail you. If I see you talking to them other than to give orders, you will be punished with twenty-five hard lashes. Do you understand?

I'm completely taken aback by both her abruptness and this threat. I only just manage to stutter a *Yes*.

We settle into a routine in which Mandl berates me continually, insisting that I need to be harsher, until finally, after four weeks of training, she sees me clipping a prisoner around the ear for being late to the roll call and gives me some praise.

That's the spirit, Braunsteiner! she says. The *Appell* is the most important part of the day. These bitches need to know they can never be late.

The majority of the work here is construction. The prisoners heave about huge planks of wood while Mandl screams at them.

Filthy sluts! You are never going home! Work harder, you whores! Work and be grateful, you pieces of shit!

Though Mandl's shouting plays on my nerves, the training makes me toughen up fast. To stave off her criticism, I follow suit and shout at the prisoners. I start to get used to it. Sometimes, I even give them a slap. Nonetheless, I can't wait until our training is over so that I don't have to spend my days by Mandl's side. Maria tells me that Binz is even worse. She saw Binz beat a small child of four or five years old for falling out of line.

I will never hit a child, says Maria. If she asks me to do that, I will leave, even if Binz beats me black and blue.

Hold tight, Maria, I say. Two more weeks to go and then we won't have these monsters breathing down our necks anymore.

Russell.

May 1959. Elmhurst.

It's love at first sight. The puppy wins your heart by tugging at the hem of your dress. Once she's latched on, she won't let go, and she tussles with your dress in a tug of war. You pick her up and kiss her on the top of her head.

Let's call her Mitzi, you say as she licks your face.

Mitzi is an eight-week-old English toy terrier. I'm not a dog person, but not long after you arrived, you started to agitate for a puppy and I didn't really have any reason to object. On the way home, the dog sits on your lap, craning her head upwards to look out of the window. We drive home through Flushing and Jackson Heights. I glance at you, my beautiful wife, cooing over the dog, and my heart swells.

I pull into Elmhurst and turn onto our street. Mitzi stretches upwards, poking her nose out of the top of the window and you laugh in delight. It's amazing how quickly you've settled into life here; it feels like you've been here much longer than a month. You already know the neighbours on both sides. Last week, when I came home from work, Linda next door was leaning over the fence admiring your green fingers as you planted out beans, tomatoes, lettuce and cucumbers, impressed with how quickly you've transformed our front yard into a vegetable plot.

When we reach the house, you carry the puppy inside carefully, as if she's a baby, and set her down. She runs around the living room, exploring, while you go to the kitchen to get her something to eat. She follows you, tail wagging.

Come and get it! you say, hitting the side of the dog bowl

with a spoon.

The noise startles the puppy and she runs out of the kitchen with a yelp. Both of us laugh. You run after her and deliver her back to the bowl. She soon starts to eat.

Back in the living room, I feel a lazy sort of contentment. The windows are open and the noise of the street carries in on the warm summer air. I go to pick up my trombone but only manage to play a few notes before you shout out to me to stop.

Put that down, Russ! You'll frighten Mitzi.

Sure honey, I say. Though I hope you're not going to ask me to give up my trombone. I don't think I can do that.

Of course not, you say, not entirely convincingly. Maybe you could just leave it until she's settled in.

You walk over to me give me a kiss. Everything's going remarkably well, even if I have to share you now with a puppy.

Hermine.

September 1939. Ravensbrück.

Maria's been given a dog. A one-year-old German Shepherd called Herbert. She chose his name but won't tell me where it comes from. I tease her that she named him after a sweetheart and call him *mein Liebster*. Maria blushes and tells me to stop.

Herbert is soft, with a young pup's bounce. He is hazel and black with big chestnut eyes. He's received basic training, so he's already obedient, though he's young enough still to chase after his tail. The incredible thing about guard dogs is how friendly they are off duty, but once they are working, their personality changes completely. The transformation is quite something to witness.

A month ago, I saw one of the guard dogs tear off a prisoner's breast. As soon as the dog was given the command to release, he let go of it, dropping the spoils onto the ground, a mound of fresh meat and nipple almost intact. It was such a shocking sight that I vomited. Nobody saw me, thank God, because everyone was staring at the prisoner. Afterwards, I could not stop thinking about the sheer brutality of it, imagining both the pain and what it's like to have just one breast. Each time I thought of it, I felt faint and brought my hands up instinctively over my own chest. Eventually, I found a way to block out the image by digging my fingernails into the palms of my hands at the same time as forcing my mind to think about something else.

Last week, another prisoner was set upon by a dog about Herbert's size. Both of her legs were shredded so badly she could no longer walk. Sinews curled out from her bones like ribbons. Two other prisoners had to drag her away. Again, I felt sick, but this time I managed to control my nausea, knowing that I need to learn how to suppress it, or I will not last here. Both prisoners who were attacked by the dogs had been caught while trying to escape. The first prisoner died from her injuries within a day; the second after a week. The dog attacks are savage, but Langfeld says that we simply cannot allow the prisoners to escape.

Maria's a natural dog handler. She loves Herbert more than most people and takes him everywhere with her, talking to him as if he is human, kissing him constantly. Her clothing is covered with dog hair, and she even lets him sleep in her room. She argues that the prisoners clean her room and her clothing, so it's not an inconvenience and, for the time being, Langefeld accepts this.

Maria conducts escape training with Herbert twice a day, morning and early afternoon, so he knows how to handle runaway prisoners. Sometimes I help her out with a role play, playing the prisoner dressed in a smock and headscarf. I set off at a run then Maria shouts, *Halt*! at which point I stop and stand stock still, not twitching a muscle. I look at the ground, knowing better than to make eye contact with a guard dog, even in training. Herbert circles me, barking, so close I can feel the heat of his breath. By now, my heart's pounding because I've seen what these dogs are capable of, but then he gets my scent and knows it's a game. He covers me with licks when I pull off the headscarf. Maria feigns consternation, but I know she's delighted that her beloved dog likes me.

After training, I suggest that we go for a walk around the lake. Before long, we pass the guards, who let us out of the camp gates. Within minutes, we're deep in woodland; orbs of mistletoe hang like baubles high in the trees. Herbert runs ahead, sniffing the ground.

It's good to get out, I say as we navigate the woods. It's a reminder that life exists outside the prison.

Yes, says Maria. It's good to get a break from it all. Sometimes, I find our work difficult. I don't agree with the way some of the guards behave. Take Binz, for instance. She beats the prisoners with no provocation when she could just use words.

I agree with you, Maria, I say. Though sometimes force is the only way with the worst of the prisoners. You don't have to look after the asocials. They're always fighting and they refuse to take orders. They're very hard to deal with. Sometimes, the only way to get them moving is to give them a cuff. And sometimes the prisoners need punishing, just like when you use the dogs on them.

Maria stops in her tracks.

That's totally different, Hermine, she says. The dogs are used to prevent escapes. That's completely different from using violence unnecessarily. The prisoners know that escape is against the rules. The thing I object to is unnecessary violence.

I agree with you, of course, I say, trying to appease her. It's just that violence *is* sometimes necessary with the more difficult prisoners.

Maria doesn't reply, which I know means that she disagrees with me. I don't want to argue with her, so I say nothing, but I don't see how she can possibly think that her use of force is necessary while mine is not, or that an injury caused by a dog is different from an injury caused by a guard. Her moral superiority is an affront. It's not worth saying anything though, because nothing will get Maria to change her mind once it's made up. However much I explain the difficulties of my job, she will never understand what it's like to work with the more difficult prisoners.

Let's go back, she says sharply.

She calls Herbert over, puts him back on his leash and walks several steps ahead of me.

Come on, Maria, I say, trying to smooth things over. Walk with me a bit longer.

Maria drops back to walk next to me. We continue in silence. When eventually I talk, I change the subject and ask her about her family. Maria lost her father in the Great War. He never came back; they don't even know where he died. She relaxes as

THE MARE: A NOVEL

she tells me about her mother and sisters, and then asks after my family. I talk about Nußdorf, the Lackners, Luise, Fritz and Mutti, and tell her how much I miss my father too. Those times seem so distant. I feel so much more grown up now. It feels like much more than a year since I left home. We keep walking and talking, and our friendship returns to its natural rhythm.

I'm happy to be sending so much money home, I say. It makes a huge difference to my family.

Yes, we should be proud, says Maria. The work's not easy here, but it's worth it to be able to send so much home.

We turn around and return by the lake. A few months ago, the lake was as blue as an opal. Now it is ashen, like a disused hearth. Reed beds bend and flex in the water under a pewter sky. I wouldn't dare to dip in a toe. It feels like the lake might swallow me whole.

Russell.

June 1959. Maspeth.

George and Molly meet us in Stokes. You've dressed up for the occasion in the blue dress you were wearing when I first met you. You look gorgeous; it brings back happy memories of our day on the lake. Molly's all dolled up too. She's in a red dress and wearing bright lipstick; her hair skims her shoulders in neat brown waves.

You look great, Molly, I say and she smiles. Hermine, this is George and Molly, my oldest and best friends.

They both say hello to you and shake your hand. Molly signals for you to sit next to her and you slide into the booth.

Now, how do we say your name properly? asks George. I'm sure to get it wrong.

It's Hair – me – nay, you say, smiling.

Such a beautiful name, says Molly. What does it mean?

It's the female version of Hermann, which means soldier.

Well, you don't look like any of the soldiers I've ever met, says George. You're far too attractive!

Molly laughs and taps George on the hand in faux reprimand. Your shoulders relax. George has always known how to put people at ease, even back when we were kids in school. Molly hands you a menu and runs through the selection.

This place does the best ice-cream in Queens, Hermine, she says. You're in for a treat.

The waitress arrives and Molly asks for a peach melba. You order a banana split and George and I both ask for hot fudge sundaes. Molly beams at you.

It's so good to see Russ finally married, she says. We were a little worried about him for a while. He was becoming quite the bachelor!

Oh, shush, Molly! says George. Russ is just very selective.

That's right, I say. I was just waiting for the right lady to come along and it was worth the wait. I'm a very lucky man.

You smile at me. This meeting's going well.

So, Hermine, do you like your new house? George asks.

I like it a lot. I love having my own garden.

She's quite the gardener, I say. Extremely green fingered.

I don't know about that, you say. Gardening is nice, but now I need to find some work.

What's your line of work? asks Molly.

I've done some domestic work and I've worked in some factories, you reply.

How about the knitting mills in Jamaica? says George. They're always taking people on.

That's a great idea, George, says Molly. I'm happy to come with you, Hermine, if you want to take a look.

Yes please, you say. I'd like that. Thank you.

The ice-creams arrive. You spoon banana heaped with whipped cream, nuts and hot chocolate sauce into your mouth.

I was a nurse before we had children, Molly says. Since then, I've been at home. The children may be getting older, but they still keep me busy!

How many children do you have? you ask.

Three: John, David and Susan. They're fifteen, thirteen and eleven. No time for nursing!

I wanted to be a nurse too, you say. But then the war happened.

George looks up from his ice-cream.

It must have been tough having the Germans invade your country, he says.

You look at me to see if this topic is OK and I nod at you. I know that George and Molly won't judge.

I was working in London as a maid when the Anschluss happened, you say. I had to return to Vienna. I couldn't find any good work there, so I went to work in a factory in Germany. It made parts for aircraft. I hope you don't mind that. I didn't have much choice during the war.

You look at them apologetically.

Of course, we understand! says Molly. It was a terrible time here too, straight after the Depression. There weren't many choices here either. We don't mind at all that you're German. The war ended a long time ago.

Hermine's Austrian, I say and Molly's cheeks turn red.

Of course, silly me! she mutters. Anyway, let's not talk about the war now. Russ is a very good man, just like my husband. You're lucky to have found him.

And handsome, says George with a smile. Don't forget that!

Molly sighs dramatically and pats your knee. You smile back at her, and in that instant, I know you'll be friends.

Hermine.

September 1939. Ravensbrück.

Germany is at war. Langefeld delivers a directive from above.

All orders from the state are to be obeyed, she says. We are supervising enemies of the Reich. We need to step up the work.

She announces that Ravensbrück will soon house a factory to make uniforms for both the prisoners and soldiers at the back of the camp.

The work we do here will help the war effort, she says. I must warn you that our numbers are going to swell with prisoners of war, as well as opponents of the Reich.

My assignment is to oversee the roller, a huge stone cylinder that is used to flatten roads. Prisoners pull it forwards over the newly dug track while other prisoners follow it, picking out loose stones. The work is slow because the roller is heavy. I'm careful to oversee from a distance because recently two prisoners picking up stones were crushed when the roller slipped backwards onto them. All the other prisoners started to scream and by the time I'd calmed them down enough to pull the roller off the prisoners underneath it, they were both dead. It's the first time anyone has died on my duty and it really shook me; I felt responsible for the prisoners' deaths.

That evening, Langefeld called me into her room and spoke to me kindly.

What happened today was an unfortunate accident, she said. You must not feel bad about it. I'm afraid accidents like this will sometimes happen due to the nature of our work. I find that it helps to remember that every prisoner at Ravensbrück is here for a reason. They are here because they are a threat to the nation. If they weren't here, they'd be out causing havoc. We're here to serve the Reich. We must learn to crush any feelings of sympathy. All the women here desire to harm the Reich. We must not weaken our resolve towards them. Your job here is very important. As the camp fills up, we need better roads. If a few prisoners die in the process, well, all I can say is that it is not your fault. You are doing your best.

Thank you *Oberaufseherin*, I replied. It is hard when someone dies, even if they are a prisoner.

The prisoners are not like you, she said. They are not good people. They are made of something different. Something not good. You must not take it personally if something happens to them. Think of where your duty lies.

I told her that my duty is to the Reich.

Your behaviour is very professional, Braunsteiner, she said. If you keep up your professionalism, I'm sure you'll go far.

Langefeld's speech put the prisoner deaths into perspective and made me feel much better. She is right. These women are dangerous. I need to care less.

Meanwhile, Dieter's been extremely busy. He's in charge of building the new factory, so his days are long. I look forward to Sundays when we walk into town and head to the bandstand. I lie on the grass, put my head on his lap and listen to the music, the squeezed chords of the accordion, the swell of trombone.

Russell.

October 1962. Elmhurst.

The days have drawn in. It's already getting dark outside. I close the front door and hang up my coat. Music streams out of the kitchen from the radio. Above it, I can hear the voice of a young boy.

I enter the kitchen. A boy is sitting at the kitchen table. He has tousled brown hair and is wearing jeans and sneakers and what looks like a home-knit sweater. At a guess, I'd say he's about ten. The maple syrup and butter are out on the table in front of him. You're at the stove cooking pancakes. Mitzi sits on the floor between the two of you, looking up hopefully. You flip a pancake onto the boy's plate.

Hi Russ, you say. This is Joe. Do you want a pancake?

Sure, honey. Why not?

I look at the boy curiously.

So, who are you, Joe?

He looks at his plate shyly and then up at you. You smile at him and nod.

Hello sir, he says.

His voice has a quiver.

Nice to meet you, son. So, what brings you here?

He looks at me nervously.

I'm sorry, sir, but I accidentally hit my baseball the wrong way. It cracked your living room window. I'm terribly sorry.

I already told you it won't be a problem, Joe, you say. My husband is a very kind man. You will not find kinder. Go check it, Russ. It's not that bad at all.

It's nice to hear you say that I'm kind. It puts me in a good mood as I go check on the broken window. The streetlamp lights up the cracks in the darkness, white against black. Splinters spread across the windowpane like a spider's web. I control my irritation as I hear you talking to the boy in the kitchen, telling him not to worry. I think to myself that it's you who is kind. When I go back to the kitchen, Joe looks at me sideways, with the look of a dog that's chewed at the furniture.

Don't worry, I say, trying to be kind. It's not a big deal.

Joe's face melts with relief.

Thank you, sir, he says. I'll do some work for you to pay for it. I could do some gardening or help you to fix things.

It's OK, son. It's the wrong time of year for gardening and besides, Hermine's got that well and truly covered. You just eat up your pancakes. That can be your job. Saying you like them can be your payment.

You smile at me broadly as Joe cuts into the stack and shovels chunks of pancake into his mouth.

I told you my husband is a nice man.

I smile back at you.

Thank you, Mr Ryan, Joe says. These pancakes are delicious, Mrs Ryan!

I watch the boy eating hungrily and, for a second, imagine what it would have been like if we had a son of our own. By the time we got married, it was too late for children; we'd missed that boat by quite some time. We don't ever talk about it. Even mentioning it seems like a loss.

When Joe's finished eating, I ask him if he'd like to see our colour TV.

Oh, yes, sir! he says, his face lighting up.

I draw the curtains in the living room to hide the cracked window and then switch the TV set on. An episode of *Bonanza* flickers onto the screen.

Look at the colour! I say. Isn't it great?

It's amazing, Mr Ryan, he says.

I work in television, I say with pride. I work on the production line checking all the parts work. Let me tell you, son, the colour revolution is coming. One day, all homes will have a colour TV.

We don't have a television in our house, he says. Not even a black and white one.

The boy's eyes scan the room and come to rest on my trombone.

What's in that case, sir? he asks. Is it a musical instrument?

It's my trombone.

Joe's eyes widen.

Can you play it?

Yes, I can. Though I don't play so often now because my wife seems to think it bothers the dog.

Would you play it for me? he asks, his voice full of excitement. I love music.

I want to oblige, relishing the chance to play in front of an audience; I only ever play now when you're out with the dog. You arrive in the living room doorway and survey the scene.

Can I play it, honey? I ask. Joe would like to hear. Could put Mitzi out in the back yard just this once?

Sure, Russ, you say. I'll put her out.

Once the dog's gone, I place the mouthpiece against my lips and the room fills with melody. I play one of my favourites, *Way Down Yonder in New Orleans*. Joe's feet start tapping, his eyes fill with admiration. When I finish, he claps. It makes me feel surprisingly good.

Amazing, sir, he says. I wish I could play the trombone. My mom says we don't have enough money for me to learn an instrument.

I could teach you if you like, I say. Though, you'd need to check with your mom first, of course. I don't know whether I'd be much of a teacher, but we could give it a shot.

Oh yes please, sir! he says. Would you really? I would love that.

I look across at you to see what you think. You're eyeing me quizzically.

Would that be OK, Hermine? You could take Mitzi out for a walk while I give Joe a lesson.

Sure, you say, in such a way that I'm not sure if you like this arrangement or not.

That night, I lie next to you in bed. It's cold out. Wind shakes the windows; the blankets are pulled high. I come close to you to share your warmth, resting my leg between your thighs.

You were so kind to that boy today, Hermine, I say.

It's you who is kind, Russ, you reply. Offering to teach him like that was a very thoughtful thing to do.

Do you mind me teaching him?

No, not at all.

It's nice to do something for a kid in the neighbourhood, I say, relieved that you approve of my gesture.

You roll towards me and look at me directly.

You would have been a very good father, you say.

Your words stir a deep feeling of longing within me, a feeling of longing that's tinged with regret.

You would have been a good mother too.

You wait a while, saying nothing, and then roll away from me.

I'm not sure about that, you say. I've never been particularly good with children.

Don't be silly. You're good with children. You were great with Joe. You'd have been a good Mom. I guess some things are just not meant to be.

I lean towards you to kiss you. You pull up your nightshirt and take hold of my hand. I tingle and spark as you place it gently on your stomach and then you move it slowly up your body towards your breast. You lean your face right in towards me and whisper softly into my ear.

You're all I need, Russ. I'm happy with just you.

Hermine.

January 1940. Ravensbrück.

The camp wake-up call jolts me awake from a dream in which I was walking through Döbling with Mutti, delivering piles of clean washing, huge flakes of snow falling onto our shoulders. I close my eyes as the dream evaporates, desperate to hold on to it, to see my mother again, but she is gone. I turn on the light. It's 5am and so cold in the room that my breath's forming clouds.

I get out of bed and splash cold water onto my face at the sink, put on my uniform and slip my feet into warm, fur-lined boots. In the winter, the *Aufseherinnen* wear black woollen capes, which wrap round us like the wings of a bat. I cock my hat, pull on my leather gloves and look in the mirror. I feel like a different person in this uniform, so competent and powerful. I know what I'm doing now. I've really grown into the job.

Maria's waiting for me outside with Herbert. Even the dog looks smart in his felt coat embroidered with the SS insignia. It's still before dawn. Stars dot the sky. We tramp across ground frozen solid towards the camp gates. Our torchlight catches the frost in bright sparks.

Breakfast is quick: coffee and bread rolls with ham and cheese. Dieter smiles as he passes me, touching my back. I bend into him, but he's gone already. He's so busy now, supervising building works as the camp extends. I won't see him again until dinner. Maria and I head across the square onto the camp road, which is lined with prisoner barracks, twenty in total, ten on each side. Linden saplings were planted recently along the length of the road. Their young branches bow under a thick layer of frost. Each guard manages a block. My block is number twenty; it's made up of the asocials, the most difficult prisoners. Langefeld only assigns the most capable guards to the hardest blocks, so this allocation means I'm doing well.

A prisoner is also put in charge of each block. The *Blockova* is responsible for making sure all the other prisoners are lined up in neat rows of five by the time I arrive. If someone is missing, I strike the front women with my whip and order the *Blockova* to search the building until the prisoner is found, removed and beaten, which is not always easy if she clings to the bed posts. All this takes time and delays the start to the day.

This morning, when I reach my block, the women are lined up neatly in their striped uniforms, staring forward, avoiding my eye. The *Appell* should take place in absolute silence but there is coughing among them, a sign there is typhus. I keep my distance; I don't want to get sick. The *Blockova* approaches. Her skin is covered with sores and her head is tufted with patches of hair. She is disgusting. I recoil as she hands me the list.

All one hundred women are present, ma'am, she says.

I enter the barrack for inspection and the fetid odour of faeces engulfs me. I cover my nose and mouth with a cloth as I gag, passing through the building as quickly as possible, checking the beds while trying not to breathe in the stench and the germs. This is the worst aspect of the job. Not only does it make me feel nauseous, but I worry about infection. I emerge into the winter air and gulp it in. I'm about to dismiss the women to work when a shriek reaches us from a block further down. A second and third howl follows, and then I hear a shout, unmistakably Binz.

The next person to look at me dies too! she screams. Nothing would make me happier than seeing another one of you die!

My prisoners stand frozen like statues, completely silent, not even a cough. I'm extremely irritated. There's enough death here without Binz adding to it. I signal to the *Blockova* that the

Appell is over. The prisoners head off to the road roller or out to the fields. A few of the women follow me to the clothing store, which I'm in charge of now. Thankfully, another *Aufseherin* has been assigned to the roller. On the way there, I pass Maria, who stops to tell me what happened. A prisoner from her block was late. Binz was nearby and took umbrage at the tardy prisoner. She pulled Herbert's lead out of Maria's hand and set him onto the woman. When Binz finally called Herbert off, the prisoner was still alive, so Binz beat the woman with the handle of her whip until she was dead. Two other prisoners fainted at the sight of their dead comrade, at which Binz set upon them. At this point, Rosa Schaefer, who was supervising the next block, started to vomit at the sight of so much blood. Binz was in such a frenzy that she raised her whip towards Schaefer, only just managing to control herself before she struck. Even in her rage, Binz knew that hitting another guard would likely see her demoted. Maria's furious that she manhandled Herbert.

How dare she? she fumes. He's my dog, not hers.

Binz is completely out of control, but what can we do? I say. There's no point telling Langefeld. She knows what Binz is like, but she can't control her; she contravenes Langefeld's orders almost daily now. She's a complete barbarian. To her, a whack to the face is no different to an assault resulting in death.

Our conversation is cut short by the barbarian approaching. I turn away sharply and Maria cuts behind one of the huts. When I arrive at the storeroom, the women are waiting, visibly shaken.

Calm down! I say as I set them to work.

Our job is to sort through the piles of civilian clothing and shoes that the prisoners arrive in, removing anything too stained or broken. The usable goods are cleaned and sent to the stores, ready to be transported back to the Reich. As the prisoners are working, I notice a Viennese accent among them. We're not meant to converse with our wards, but the accent so reminds me of home. I seek out the woman; she's wearing the red triangle of a political prisoner. I ask her name and she recites her camp number; the prisoners are not allowed to tell us their names. But I keep on asking until she reveals it.

My name's Anna Baum, she says. I'm from Währing.

That's two suburbs away from Nußdorf! I exclaim. You will come and help me today.

Baum complies and stands next to me at the counter, handing out prisoner uniforms to the new arrivals. I talk to her about how much I miss Vienna and tell her about my family.

I miss all the food, I say with a sigh. Strudel, Sauerkraut, delicious rye bread! This conversation is making me homesick.

Baum says nothing. She looks down at the prisoner uniforms and sorts through the pile.

Russell.
January 1963. Brooklyn.

The court clerk says *Austria* and you rise. You're wearing a new woollen suit that you bought for the occasion. Your fingers are wrapped tightly around a miniature American flag. Once everyone's standing, you raise your right hand and repeat the oath in unison with the other new citizens:

I hereby declare, on oath, that I absolutely and entirely renounce and abjure all allegiance and fidelity to any foreign prince, potentate, state or sovereignty of whom or which I have heretofore been a subject or citizen; that I will support and defend the Constitution and laws of the United States of America against all enemies, foreign and domestic; that I will bear true faith and allegiance to the same; so help me God.

You lower your hand and the sound of clapping fills the room. I smile at you while the clerk addresses the room.

Welcome, new citizens. I want to share with you the American's Creed written by William Tyler Page in 1917:

I believe in the United States of America, as a government of the people, by the people, for the people; whose just powers are derived from the consent of the governed; a democracy in a republic; a sovereign Nation of many sovereign States; a perfect union, one and inseparable; established upon those principles of freedom, equality, justice, and humanity for which American patriots sacrificed their lives and fortunes. I therefore believe it is my duty to my country to love it, to support its Constitution, to obey its laws, to respect its flag, and to defend it against all enemies.

These are powerful words, the clerk continues. As it says in the Creed, as new citizens, you may be subject to attempts to overthrow the government by our enemies. They may try to enlist you in their cause, both radicals of the right, including those like the Nazis and Fascists, and those of the left, including the Communists. I advise you to be scrupulous in avoiding either extreme, instead to pursue the middle course, a democratic course. This middle course is the American way.

Pride stirs within me throughout the clerk's speech. Pride for my country, pride for the patriots who serve my country, pride for the service I've given to my nation and, above all, pride for you, my American wife.

After the ceremony, we leave the court and head out into Brooklyn. The warmth of the building gives way to sharp cold. It's well below freezing. Our boots crunch on the snow-covered ground. We head across Tillary towards the Korean War Veterans Plaza. I want to pay my respects before we head home. We stop in front of the stone engraved with *Lest We Forget*. These words feel even more potent on such a momentous day. We stand in silence, our breath forming ice crystals.

No one talks much about the Korean war, I say. I had the easy job. All I did was keep the airplanes serviced, but the guys that flew those planes saw horrible things. That's if they even came back.

Low walls frame the Plaza entrance, engraved with the names of fallen heroes. Snowflakes start to fall through the pale winter light. You scan the list of American dead.

It's the same in Austria, you say solemnly. Long lists of people who died in the war. Sometimes, I think we should stop thinking about the past and let the dead rest.

Maybe, I say. Though it's a good thing to honour them. Come on, no more talk of war on your first day of citizenship. Let's go get some hot chocolate. I've got something for you.

As we walk along Cadman Plaza, I put my hand in my coat pocket and turn over the box that I've concealed there. We enter the first café we come across. It's long and narrow, with a black and white chequered floor. We go to the back where it's warmest and sit down at a round wooden table.

How does it feel to be American?

You smile and then shrug. I take the box out of my pocket and put it on the table, turquoise and tied with white ribbon.

American jewellery for my American wife, I say.

Your eyes start to well.

Oh, Russ! you say. It's too beautiful to open.

Go on, open it, I say. I chose it carefully.

You open the lid. Inside, a silver heart-shaped pendant rests on a black cushion.

Take it out, I say. Look at the back.

You take the necklace out of the box and turn the pendant over. I've had your initials engraved there in cursive: *HR*.

Oh, Russ, you say as you unclip the necklace. I love you so much. You couldn't have chosen a more beautiful gift.

Hermine.

July 1940. Ravensbrück.

I pull back the curtains and open the window. Birdsong pours in. It is 7:30am and I've had a good rest. All of a sudden, I remember what day it is and leap out of bed, full of excitement. Today is my twenty-first birthday and we're taking a picnic out onto the lake in row boats to celebrate. It's the first time I've ever been rowing and I cannot wait.

Dieter, Maria, Hans and Rosa meet me after church. We've arranged to rent boats from the small dock next to the Stadtpark. The slatted brown hulls bob in the water, surrounded by ducks. Dieter and Hans take one boat each and grab hold of the oars, insisting they row. Maria and Rosa go in with Hans, leaving me alone with Dieter. The sun warms our backs through the gentlest of breezes. The lake reflects the blue of the sky. The oars send out ripples across the lake's glassy flatness and ducks paddle furiously out of our way. Dieter steers us towards the south-east shore, where a passage leads through to a much larger lake. On Shwedtsee, you can see the camp from all angles, which reminds us of work, and I don't want to think about work on my birthday. He navigates us deftly into the channel. It's not long before the camp is out of view. Linden and birch trees line the channel on one side, summer meadows filled with grasses extend on the other. It's like being on holiday. The week's work lifts from my shoulders.

When we reach the end of the passage, it opens out into the next lake. There is a low bank here, perfect for picnicking. I hitch my skirt into a knot at my side and clamber out of the boat to guide it to shore, feet sinking ankle-deep into silt, soft as silk. The water is refreshingly cold. As I wade through it, my feet stir up fine particles and tannin swirls around the lakebed. Tiny fish dart through the shallows as a swan watches us from the banks. Dieter jumps out after me with a splash and hauls the boat up onto the sandy foreshore.

Quick, Hermi, he says. Let me give you your gift before the others arrive.

Dieter removes a square package from his pocket, wrapped in creamy white paper tied with blue ribbon.

Oh Dieter! I say, turning the gift in my hands. It's far too beautiful to open.

He smiles and gestures for me to go ahead. Underneath the paper is a dark blue box. When I open the lid, it reveals a gold brooch, circular and shining. I throw my arms around him. He leans down to kiss me, then lifts up my skirt, slides his hand up my leg and tugs at my underwear. I push him away.

Stop it! I say. The others will be here any moment.

Later, he says. When you come to my room.

I blush and look down at the box.

Thank you, I say. I love it! It's beautiful.

Just like you, Dieter says, his eyes piercing mine. That brooch belonged to my grandmother. She wanted it to be kept in the family. Maybe one day you can pass it on too.

The meaning of his words knocks the breath out of me. I try not to cry. We're interrupted by the splashing of oars as the other boat appears around the corner.

This way, shouts Dieter, waving them in.

Hans steers the boat towards the bank. Maria gets out and carries the picnic basket above her head to the shore. Dieter spreads out the rug, then Maria lays out the feast: bread, cheese, ham, apples and pears.

Happy birthday, Hermi! she says, wrapping me in a warm hug.

I feel so happy and loved.

You're so kind, Maria, I say. Always so thoughtful.

After lunch, we paddle in the shallows. Hans splashes Rosa,

who sprays him in return. Dieter swims out deep into the lake and calls for us to join him. Maria and I glide out towards him; the water licks at our chins. Beyond the silt, the lake is crystal clear. I dive down into it. Its cold layers squeeze me tight like an accordion. I come up for air and Dieter swims close to me, looping his leg round me while treading water.

You're a strong swimmer, he says. I like that you're strong. I can't wait for tonight. I'm going to make you feel good.

It's dusk when we land the boats back at the park. We're running late. Dieter and I have been invited to the *Kommandant's* house and need to be changed within half an hour. We leave the others to sort out the boats and run back to the camp, arriving sweating and out of breath. I hurry to my room. There's no time to wash, so I wipe the day off me with a damp cloth, and then slip on my dress and brush my hair up to hide the remnants of dampness. As I pin Dieter's brooch to my dress, I mull over his words. He told me that I'd pass this brooch on. Does this mean that he thinks I'm the one? I can't wait to tell Mutti.

Kommandant Koegel's house is styled as a mountain chalet. It sits high on the bank above the *Aufseherinnen* quarters, at the end of the line of SS housing. His house is built sideways onto the camp to give him an unrestricted view. The lower half of the building is painted light yellow with pine green shutters; the upper half rises high into a triangular peak, slatted with dark brown wood. SS men smoke and chat on the balcony, absorbing the fading warmth of the last of the light of day. I knock on the door. It's opened by a woman with hair pulled back into an immaculate chignon. She wears a long navy skirt and a light blue blouse with a large, elegant bow.

You are? she says.

Hermine Braunsteiner. One of the *Aufseherinnen*.

I'm Anna Koegel, the *Kommandant's* wife. Come in.

Frau Koegel is known to like fashion. She visits the camp hair salon each day while the rest of us work. The existence of a hairdresser at Ravensbrück owes itself entirely to her; she brought the staff here with her from Dachau. I prefer to go into Fürstenberg to have my hair done; it's a thousand times nicer to get out of the camp.

The first person I notice in the room is Binz. She's sitting at a table opposite the entrance, a glass of wine in her hand, talking to Langefeld, no doubt bending her ear. I walk away from them into the room. Being cornered by Binz would ruin my birthday. The hood of an enormous fireplace takes up the right half of the room, its hearth filled with a huge bouquet of red and white roses that are giving off a beautiful scent. I comment favourably on the flowers and Frau Koegel seems pleased. She tells me that she grew them herself, right here in her garden. I indicate the fireplace and venture politely that it must be warm here in winter and she delights in telling me that the whole house never gets cold as they have central heating, powered by coal. To the left of the fireplace is a doorway to the kitchen. Inside, three prisoners are preparing the food. Frau Koegel sees me looking at them.

Jehovah's Witnesses, she says. The best workers. They never steal or try to escape. But my husband can't stand them. He has a complete disdain for all religion.

I make a note not to mention I'm Catholic. I've buried my religion deep down inside. Dieter arrives a short while later, looking extremely handsome in his clean, pressed uniform. He comes to stand next to me and smiles at me when he sees that I'm wearing his grandmother's brooch. I feel so grown up, here at this party. Perhaps one day, Dieter will become a *Kommandant*, and I will support him with flowers and food.

After a few minutes, Dieter goes to mingle with the men. I spend the rest of the evening talking to Frau Koegel. After the initial pleasantries, she is full of complaints: she finds the food bland, the wine mediocre, Fürstenberg parochial, she much preferred Lichtenburg.

Worst of all, the Jews have started to arrive at the camp, she says, wincing. I cannot abide them. I try to keep my interactions with the prisoners to an absolute minimum, but they're always around, digging the garden, delivering food, cleaning the house. I find them so revolting with their horrible shaved heads and filthy uniforms. They make my skin crawl. The Jews are simply disgusting. I honestly don't know how you do your job, day in, day out. It would make me feel sick. The work here is unpleasant. I don't know how we do it.

I'm not entirely sure what work she thinks she does here, and after such a nice day, I don't want to discuss the camp. Sometimes I wish that I could go back into the world of civilians. I'd spend my summer rowing on the lake. But I guess I am lucky to have a good job, and if I hadn't come here, I'd have never met Dieter. I long for later when I can go to Dieter's room.

Russell.
July 1964. Maspeth.

The cuckoo clock on the wall snaps open behind you and the small wooden cuckoo starts to call. Tension rises in the room as we wait for it to finish. When it finally stops, Lelyveld leans forward in the armchair and addresses you once more.

Mrs Ryan, can you confirm that you were a concentration camp guard during the war?

You cast your eyes downwards and pick at your nails.

You've got the wrong person, I say. My wife was a guard in a prison, not a concentration camp.

He waits and then he rephrases the question, turning it into a statement of fact.

Mrs Ryan, you were a concentration camp guard at Ravensbrück and Majdanek. It's in your interest to tell me the truth.

You exhale slowly. It sounds like air escaping from a punctured tyre. Why aren't you answering him? What is this man talking about? What have you not told me about your past?

Hermine.
August 1940. Ravensbrück.

I find the perfect present for Maria's twentieth birthday in Fürstenberg, a book called *Dog Training, Handling and Behaviour*. I hope she will like it.

I wrap the book carefully in brown paper and tie it with orange ribbon. After dinner, I return to our housing, collect the present and walk to Maria's room.

My dear Hermi! she says. Come in!

Herbert is lying on her bed. He opens one sleepy eye and immediately closes it, which makes us both laugh. Langefeld is so lenient; any other *Oberaufseherin* would insist that a dog live in a kennel. I hand over the present and Maria unwraps it, squealing in delight.

Oh, Hermi, you're so clever! I couldn't have chosen better myself. You're such a good friend!

She kisses me hard on the forehead. Her breath smells of melted butter on toast. We sit together on her bed next to Herbert and look through the book.

Look at that dog! she says. My, he's a beauty! Now that one is sitting well! Oh, I didn't know that!

Her delight makes me more and more pleased with the gift.

Later, our conversation turns to home. I received a letter from Luise last week telling me that Mutti is well. Maria's mother has a chest cold but is otherwise fine. She asks me how things are going with Dieter and I tell her the truth: that one day I hope we will get married.

He's so devoted to his work and to his country, I say. And he's so good in the bedroom.

My comment embarrasses her.

Sorry, I say. But seriously, I can't imagine ever meeting anyone I could love more.

Dieter is perfect for you, she says. He will make a good husband and father. You are so lucky. Look at me. I just have Herbert.

You will find someone to love too, Maria, I say. There's someone just like Dieter out there, who will fall over himself to marry you. You are such a good person, so phenomenally kind.

Maybe, she says. Until then, it's just me and my dog.

Russell.

July 1963. Coney Island.

The carriage clicks up the track in steep ascent.

I'm scared, Russ! you say, clasping tightly onto the bar.

It pushes tight into our stomachs, holding us into the ride. We pause at the top for a split second and then tip over it into steep descent, plunging downwards, hurtling furiously along the track. My stomach hits the roof of my mouth as the car reaches the bottom and then curves back up again over the next hill, lurching to the right, tipping us sideways. Both of us scream. I look across at you. Your eyes are shut tight. We drop again and you let out another loud scream. At last, the ride pulls back into the station.

That was awful! you say. Never again!

I can't stop myself from laughing.

How about something a little milder, honey? The Wonder Wheel?

You look across at the big wheel and shake your head. Its cars are rocking and spinning as it rotates.

OK, I say. Let's go and find something less stomach churning.

This is your first trip to Coney Island. We're here to celebrate your forty-fourth birthday. The day is warm for May and the beach has filled up already with sunbathers; lots of people splash about in the sea. We've brought our swimsuits too, but first I want to show you the funfair. Along the boardwalk, we come to the house of mirrors.

How about this, Hermine? I say. It's full of weird mirrors. When you stand in front of them, they make you bend. It's kinda fun.

Anything's better than another rollercoaster, you say. Let's go in.

We walk round the room and look at mirrored versions of ourselves, elongated, compacted, twisted and warped.

You giggle as you stare at yourself, squat and wide.

I look terrible, Russ. Like a short, fat girl!

This one's much better, I say.

While my top half is lifelike, my bottom half is extended, making my legs long like a giraffe's. You join me, turn sideways and admire yourself.

I like my legs like this, you say. Like a movie star.

You already look like a movie star! I reply. You don't need a mirror to make your legs look great.

You smile at me, clearly pleased by my comment.

It's not flattery, I say. You're beautiful, Hermine. Nobody would ever guess you're forty-four.

The next mirror makes our torsos short and pot-bellied, while stretching our necks.

Would you still love me if I looked like this? I ask you, pointing at the abomination in front of me.

You throw your head back, laugh and shake your head. I pull you towards me and our contorted reflections kiss. Back on the boardwalk, we stop to get cotton candy. You twirl the pink sugary threads round your fingers and put them into your mouth as we walk. The pier juts out into the sea ahead of us. We walk to the end and sit on a bench. The day's getting hotter. You take off your sweater. Underneath your shirt, I can see that you're wearing the red swimsuit you wore when we first met. It brings back memories of us picnicking on the pier at Wörthersee, the day that I gave you the seeds. A gull flaps down to the railing and shuffles along carefully with its feet. It eyes the remains of your cotton candy and you shoo it away. It's then that I notice the brooch on your shirt, round and golden. I've not seen it before.

Is that new? I ask, reaching out to touch its smooth metal surface. You look away from me, out over the sea.

No, you reply. It's very old. I found it recently at the bottom of my suitcase when I was tidying up. I'd forgotten about it. It was a birthday present from a friend a long time ago.

I feel a strange pang of jealousy about your former life, one full of friends and family I will never know. You know everyone in my life in New York.

Who gave it to you?

My friend, Maria, you say, matter-of-factly.

Another pang. A friend close enough to give you a brooch and you've never mentioned her.

You haven't told me about Maria. Who is she?

She was my best friend during the war. You would have liked her. She was clever and kind, just like you. I worked in the factories with her and then at the camp.

My heart quickens at that word. My discomfort must be visible because you add quickly, I mean prison. In German, the word is *Lager*. It means prison camp. I've told you before that I worked at the women's prison at Ravensbrück. Maria was there with me.

We haven't discussed your work as a prison guard. I don't like to picture you inside a jail.

Yes, you've mentioned Ravensbrück, I say. But you never really told me what it was like there. It always feels like you don't want to talk about it with me.

Can you blame me, Russ? It was a long time ago now. I was very young and it was horrible work. I especially don't like to talk about it here in America. People wouldn't understand it. Remember, I'm from the side that lost the war.

I run my fingers across the brooch. It's warm to the touch.

I understand, I say. And it's not about sides. I don't care which side of the war you were on. It means nothing to me. If you don't want to talk about it, that's fine. I'm just glad to hear you had a good friend back then. Did you stay in touch with her after the war?

I tried to find her in Vienna, but she never came back. I called on her family, but they'd heard nothing from her since just before the end of the war. I dread to think what happened to her. The Russians took over Ravensbrück. We were so frightened of what they would do to us. They were complete barbarians. Maybe they took her back to a gulag in Russia, maybe they killed her. Either way, I'm sure she is dead. Poor Maria. We were very close. I don't like to think about what happened to her. Could we talk about something else?

Your voice is quavering. I feel terrible for asking you to remember such a difficult time on your birthday of all days.

I'm sorry, I say. I won't ask you about it again. Come on. Let's cheer ourselves up with a swim.

We get up and walk out onto the beach, picking our way through the sunbathers to find a spot next to the water. I take out our towels, unroll them and lay them flat on the sand. The sea's not been warmed yet by the summer heat. I don't want to enter, but you run in ahead of me, diving straight in. You plunge under and when you emerge, you are ten feet further out, swimming towards the horizon with powerful strokes.

Hermine, I shout after you. Wait for me!

The water's great! you call back. Come on, get in!

I follow in your wake. You're far braver than me, always taking the lead.

When we arrive back home that evening, both of us still hold a glow from the day. You make us some dinner and I take out my trombone. I play *The Memphis Blues*, relaxed and upbeat; it reflects how I feel after such a nice day. Mitzi curls up on the floor next to the sofa; after many years, she's finally got used to the noise. Later, we head out for a movie. Dusk paints the sky a soft salmon pink. *Cleopatra* is playing at Maspeth Theatre. Molly's been raving about Elizabeth Taylor's performance, but I don't think it can possibly live up to the hype.

Hermine.
January 1941. Ravensbrück.

Koegel and Langefeld have been preparing for weeks. Even though it's the middle of winter, tubs of red flowers have been put out everywhere. All the camp roads have been swept meticulously clear of snow just for today. *Reichsführer*-SS Himmler is visiting along with his entourage. The fuss around his visit is so great that you would think it was the *Führer* himself. For two weeks now, we've practised marching for hours every day; drill after drill until our feet ache, up and down the camp path, between the lindens, over and over, again and again.

By the time Himmler arrives, we've been waiting lined up outside the SS headquarters for more than an hour in the snow, boots shining like mirrors, uniforms ironed stiff as boards. Himmler chats briefly with Koegel, then walks in front of our lines to inspect us. We stand stock still. He stops a few paces away from me. The air catches his breath in small icy puffs. I glance at him nervously and am taken aback by how small he is; he's much shorter than Dieter and not nearly as well built. It shouldn't surprise me that someone so powerful is so unimposing; it's said that the Führer himself is a very small man. My heart pounds as I avert my gaze, fearful that Himmler might single me out, but he walks straight past me, moving on quickly down the line. When he reaches the end, he turns to Langefeld and raises his arm.

Heil Hitler! he shouts, then he turns towards Langefeld and says loud enough for us all to hear, Your *Aufseherinnen* are well disciplined. Well done.

Langefeld glows visibly.

Heil Hitler, *Reichsführer*! she says. *Aufseherinnen*, at ease!

We all breathe out, relieved that we've passed this most important of inspections. With that, they walk on, and we do not see Himmler or his party for the rest of the day.

As a reward for our work, Langefeld's arranged for a movie screening to mark the occasion. A projector's been set up in the SS headquarters. The movie she's chosen is *Jud Süß*, a classic tale of justice. A row of seats lies empty at the front for Himmler and his associates, but they've already left. The rumour is that the *Reichsführer* has a mistress living nearby. Dieter's saved me the seat next to him. The lights are turned out and the film starts to play. The screen fills with the face of the predatory Süß. I grasp at Dieter's hand and I'm still gripping it tightly when the movie comes to an end. When the lights are turned on, he looks at me, agitated, and leans in towards me so close that his stubble scrapes at my cheek.

Give a Jew your little finger and he'll take the whole hand, he says. They would take over Germany given half the chance. All of them are like that Jew Süß. They must be stopped.

How? I ask.

I overheard Himmler tell Koegel that the senior command is coming up with a plan for the Jews, he replies. I'm not sure what it is, but let's hope they put it into action soon.

Russell.

March 1964. Maspeth.

Our new house is a short walk from the expressway, on the right, a little along from where the road starts to slope downwards into a hill. The move has taken us from Elmhurst to Maspeth. You wanted a nice backyard for Mitzi to run around in, so that's what we got. Inside the new house, it smells of fresh paint. We got a painter to go in before us to save time as our leisure time has become increasingly precious. Both of us have been working long hours to pay for the house. We've hardly crossed paths for weeks.

You open the back door and Mitzi shoots out down the steps into the yard like a bullet and then runs around exploring. It's a good-sized grassed area, surrounded by beds. I feed off your delight as you survey the back yard, knowing you're already making plans for the garden. I'll suggest flowers and you'll overrule me, insisting on vegetables. That is the pattern of our married life.

Hermine.
July 1942. Ravensbrück.

Summer in Ravensbrück. Birds stab at insects mid-air while prisoners toil in the heat, covered in sweat. Dry heat has ground all the mud into dust. There is much to do. The Reich is taking more and more prisoners, so the camp is expanding, creating ever more work.

Langefeld's been transferred to Auschwitz to set up a women's camp. Koegel's replaced her with Maria Mandl, who struts about Ravensbrück like a puffed-up cockerel. The power has gone straight to her head. Worse still, she's chosen Binz as her deputy, a formidable team that brings about change. The first development is an increase in prisoner beatings, which are so numerous now that we can no longer manage them by ourselves. Binz solves this by calling for volunteers among the prisoners, offering them extra rations. Desperate for food, many step up.

Today, our assignment is to flog a consignment of the Jehovah's Witnesses because they refuse to do anything that supports the German war effort. The latest order they've rejected is collecting rabbit fur from the hutches as the angora wool is used to line army clothing. They're principled beyond measure. Koegel and Mandl agree that the only way forward is to beat some sense into them. I must say I agree. Nobody else in the camp gets any choice about where they will work, including the *Aufseherinnen*; we work here too and we have to do as we're told, often doing unpleasant jobs.

By the time I arrive in the *Strafblock*, the beatings have already started. There are fifty women to get through, so it will take quite some time. The *Strafblock* contains rows of isolation cells for the worst of the prisoners, plus three identical rooms for the punishments, each bare apart from a large wooden block over which the prisoner is beaten and a tap in the corner to clean down the flagstones.

As I enter the room, I hear a sharp intake of breath, then a broken voiced, *Thirteen*, as the prisoner counts the lashes aloud.

Blood seeps out from the lines criss-crossing her buttocks.

Count louder! screams Binz.

A quavered, *Fourteen*.

The woman is unconscious before nineteen.

Binz deals the final blows and then ends with her personal signature, a sharp blow to the head with the handle of the whip.

I can do whatever I want to you! she shouts like a lunatic. Your god is not here!

Binz un-straps the prisoner and pushes her roughly off the block. The woman's head cracks on the flagstone. Blood trickles out of her ear. Binz turns on the tap. It splutters to life with a hiss, shooting out a jet of cold water, which flows around the prisoner. A puddle of water forms around her head; blood mingles with it, swirling around it like red paint.

I look at Binz in disgust. We're meant to be beating the Jehovah's Witnesses as punishment so they will work, not killing them, but Mandl is in charge now, and under her, Binz can do whatever she pleases. All of a sudden, Binz looks up at me, piercing me with her eyes. I look away fast, hoping she didn't catch any sign of my disapproval. I know she'd have no qualms about flogging me too if she thought I was questioning her authority.

Leave the water running, Braunsteiner! she barks. Let that bitch drown. Bring in the next one!

I head out to the corridor to fetch the next prisoner. A cockroach scuttles along the wall in front of me, feeling along the brickwork with red-brown antennae. The prisoners hold their heads down in prayer, surprisingly calm given what they've just heard. In some ways, the strength of their faith is admirable. My faith is not that strong. But mostly it's stupid. These women would rather be beaten to death than pick wool from rabbits, which is the easiest job in the camp.

Russell.

May 1964. Maspeth.

The plaza in front of the Queens Veteran Foundation fills up with veterans holding umbrellas. A fine mist of drizzle gives the sidewalk a sheen. George and I hold umbrellas above you and Molly. You're holding bouquets of red and white carnations tied with blue ribbons. George and I stand aside to make room so you can step into line to lay the flowers next to the stone plaque.

Days like Memorial Day make me dwell on my country. It's been a hard year. The nation's still reeling from Kennedy's death. Johnson's pouring more and more men into Vietnam. I close my eyes and say a prayer for the servicemen, both dead and in battle. You lay your flowers, come back under my umbrella and take hold of my hand. Your coat is covered with droplets of rain. George shelters Molly and we move away to make space for the other veterans. As we're about to leave, I feel a tap on my shoulder and turn around. I recognise Jerry Moretti instantly, even though I haven't seen him in years.

Russell! he says. I thought it was you!

Jerry! I reply. It's good to see you. How are you?

I'm good, he says. You?

I'm doin' fine, I reply. This is my wife, Hermine. This is George. George went to school with me. This is his wife, Molly. Jerry and I served together in Korea. He serviced airplanes too.

Pleased to meet you all, Jerry says with a smile.

Likewise, says George, holding out his hand.

Jerry shakes it and then turns to me.

So, what are you up to these days?

I work for RCA testing colour televisions. What about you?

That sounds really interesting, he says. My job's not nearly as exciting. I teach electrical engineering nearby at Queen's College.

That's great! says George. My son David's studying engineering there. Have you come across him? David Allen. Everyone says he looks a bit like me.

Jerry examines George's face.

Well, maybe you do look a bit familiar, he says with a smile. But unless he's taking electrical engineering, I won't have taught him. Though, I might have seen him on campus.

Well, there's a thing! says George. Do you live around here?

Not too far away. Jackson Heights. I came here today to pay my respects, but I better get going home. My wife's unwell. I left her at home. I need to go check on her.

Good to bump into you, Jerry, I say. Sorry to hear your wife is sick. You better get back to her. Let me give you my number and we can catch up sometime for a beer. I'd love to hear all your news. Do you have some paper?

Jerry reaches into his pocket, pulls out a packet of Lucky Strikes and hands it to me.

Write your number down on the back of this, he says. I'll get in touch when Brenda's feeling better.

Molly passes me a pen and I scrawl down my number on the back of the packet.

You should think about giving these up, I say. You know they're not good for you.

I know that, he says. But they help with the stress.

Jerry holds out his hand and I shake it. He shakes hands with George again and says goodbye to the ladies. As he heads off up the street, George says, He seems like a nice guy.

He's a good man, I say. I hope he gets back in touch.

It's still raining. You turn towards George and Molly.

Would you like to come home for lunch with us? I can cook you something Austrian.

Well, that would be lovely, Hermine, Molly says. George and

I love your cooking.

Molly takes you by the arm and I let go of your hand. I'm so happy that you two have become such good friends. You walk together ahead of us, leaving me talking to George. I tell him all about all the developments at work.

We're behind the curve, George says. We still have a black and white TV.

So, how about you? I ask. How's work?

Accountancy's just totting up numbers, he says. But it's fine. It pays the bills.

And the kids?

They're all doing well, Russ. John's started dental school and, as I told your friend back there, David's at Queen's College. He's getting good grades and Susan's doing OK too. She's in her final year of high school. Molly's just hoping she'll meet someone nice.

They're good kids, I say. You should be proud of them.

Oh, we are, Russ. We are.

Our conversation turns to Johnson's 'Great Society' speech that's been all over the newspapers.

Kennedy sure left big shoes to fill, I say. Johnson does seem to be filling them.

I like his ideas, George says. He gives me hope for our country.

When I open the front door, Mitzi runs out, barking and flicking herself around and around in circles. She's five years old now, but she still behaves like a pup.

Calm down, Mitzi! you say, pushing past me to pick her up.

Easy, Hermine, I say. No need to shove.

I wait until you ladies have entered, then lead George into the kitchen and take two bottles of Rheingold out of the fridge. We head into the back yard. The dog follows us, wagging her tail happily. As we drink our beers, George throws a ball back and forth. Mitzi runs to fetch it, skidding to stop at George's feet. He tickles her under the chin.

There's no doubt who's got the best life in Queens, he says with a chuckle. It's definitely this dog!

Hermine.
August 1942. Ravensbrück.

Dieter's been so busy for the past two months that we've hardly crossed paths. He's in charge of building a new factory in the forest south of the camp. The plant will use female prisoners to produce parts for the engineering company, Siemens. The construction of the factory is very hard work. First, they cleared and levelled the forest, then they laid a track to connect to the main train line, and now they're building the factory itself. The strenuous labour is making many of the prisoners critically weak, which annoys Dieter greatly. In the process, he's lost more than three hundred workers.

What use is a workforce if it cannot work? he asks bitterly. I train them and then they just die.

Recently, Dieter asked Koegel to provide his workforce with extra rationing, explaining that each death causes delays, but his plea fell on deaf ears.

It is of no consequence if they die, Koegel told him. They are *Untermenschen*. Just replace them.

Dieter shakes his head. Each new replacement is weaker than the last, plus it takes time to train them; it's a colossal waste of energy and time. All the digging has churned the mud into a quagmire, which is having a knock-on effect on my stores. The prisoners ruin good shoes and we don't have enough to replace them. It's got to the point where I have to turn prisoners away barefoot. Dieter is irritated with me because without shoes the prisoners are even less efficient. I explain to him that resources are scarce, but he shows no understanding of the difficulties I face. He's in a constant bad mood. I find myself starting to resent him. On the few occasions I do see him, he talks endlessly about his damned factory. I cannot wait for it to be completed so that our relationship can get back to normal.

Russell.

May 1964. Maspeth.

By the time you call us in for dinner, the sun has started to set, casting long shadows over the grass. I say grace and then Molly passes round the dishes of potatoes and beans. I announce proudly that the beans are from our garden, all your hard work.

You're so good in the garden, Hermine, Molly says. I'm envious. I can't grow a thing!

Thank you for the wonderful food, says George. Delicious as always.

You smile at them both across the table.

After the meal, George and I retire to the sofa, while you and Molly do the dishes in the kitchen. I turn on the TV. It's a news report about Vietnam. The Viet Cong has sunk a vessel carrying jeeps in the Saigon River, killing five US sailors. George shakes his head.

The Viet Cong seem impossible to beat, he says. It doesn't seem to make any difference, however many men we send there.

I wish I could go over there and help, I reply.

Are you kidding me, Russ? It's seven shades of shit out there in the jungle. Our boys are doing us proud, but Vietnam's a hellhole.

Doing your duty for your country is the most important thing, George.

I agree with you, Russ. But we've already done our time for our country. It's the next generation's turn.

Hermine.
August 1942. Ravensbrück.

The factory's complete and at long last Dieter's in a better mood. He insists that I come to its opening and gives me a private tour before the others arrive. He's rightly proud of his creation; he built the whole thing in less than ten weeks. The woods are silent apart from the buzzing of the electrified fence that circles the factory. He opens the door and shows me inside. The hall is cavernous; it contains hundreds of rows of tables, stacked with machines.

These machines wind copper onto spools, Dieter explains. For field telephones. If it all goes to plan, we hope to expand. I'd like to run this factory, of course, but Siemens want their own people here.

Dieter feels raw because Siemens installed its own Director, Herr Grade. Grade came out from the company's headquarters in Berlin last week to choose his workforce out of the prisoners. He picked young women with good eyesight and long, steady fingers. Dieter does not like Grade. He says an outsider will have no idea how to handle the prisoners. Dieter tried to talk to Grade about the importance of maintaining discipline among the prisoners and how he uses punishment, but he was sure that Grade was not listening.

When we step back outside, *Kommandant* Koegel is waiting. Grade stands next to him, a fish out of water in a civilian suit and shoes caked with Ravensbrück mud. Dieter shoots me a look.

The prisoners line up for the *Appell* in the clearing in front of the factory. Their foreheads glisten with beads of sweat. It's

8am, but the sun is already strong. Grade steps forward to address the prisoners.

Your working day is eleven hours with a short break for lunch, he says. If you wind more than your quota, you will receive a token for the factory shop. If you wind less, we will be displeased.

Koegel scowls and steps forward in front of Grade, blocking him completely. He starts to shout.

If you wind below your quota, you will feel my stick!

He reinforces this message with a rain of imaginary blows. The prisoners shake. I look towards Grade to gauge his reaction, but his face is unflinching; if Koegel's behaviour surprises him, he conceals it well. Dieter's face gives away nothing either, but I know how unimpressed he is by this display. Neither Koegel's brutality nor Grade's humanity will get optimal results.

Russell.

July 1964. Maspeth.

Lelyveld looks at you, waiting.

After a while, you say, Yes, I was there.

My chest tightens. I remove my arm from your shoulder. You've told me about Ravensbrück, but you've never once mentioned anywhere called Majdanek. I stare at your face, but it gives nothing away.

What was Majdanek, Hermine? I ask. Please will you tell me.

You do not answer. My head starts to pound. It feels like my brain is pulsing, pushing itself hard outwards against the bones of my skull. Still you say nothing. Lelyveld turns towards me and speaks.

Majdanek was a concentration camp in Poland, Mr Ryan.

The words pound me with the force of a punch. Concentration camp! This cannot true. I look from him to you, waiting for you to deny it. You cast your eyes downwards. Though you can't bring yourself to look at me, finally you speak.

I was posted to Majdanek for a year, Russ. But for eight months of that time I was sick and in hospital. I got typhoid again and again. I can hardly remember it. That's how sick I was. I was barely there; that's why I've never told you about it. For most of the war, I was working in Germany. I've told you before how awful that was. After the war, I just wanted to forget it.

I look at you blankly. My mouth has gone so dry I can't speak. What else is there that you haven't told me? What else have you tried to forget?

Hermine.

September 1942. Ravensbrück.

Our new *Kommandant*, Fritz Suhren, arrived last week from Sachsenhausen. He's a slim man with the kind of light, freckly skin that blisters at the slightest ray of sunlight. Though he's smaller than Koegel, Suhren's already proven himself to be more than his match. Dieter approached him yesterday to ask for increased rations for his workers in order to reduce the attrition rate. Each time he takes the men out to work, more collapse, making his job impossible.

Suhren listened to him silently and then snorted with laughter. He pushed his face right in towards Dieter until they were almost touching, and then burst forth with furious sarcasm. The vein in his neck pulsated outwards, fat as a worm.

Your puppies want more food, do they? Well, tell them, this is a prison camp not a vacation camp! They work until they drop! Do you understand me?

This morning, Suhren *reduced* prisoner rations. Dieter is furious. Suhren's response defies logic.

Productivity is going to drop even more, he says to me that evening in bed. One day, when I am in charge, I'll run things properly with you by my side.

A wave of delight washes over me. Hearing you talk about our future like that feels so good. I would do anything to make this wish come true.

Russell.

June 1964. Maspeth.

Your eyes are watering from chopping an onion. You wipe away tears with the back of your hand. The radio's tuned to WNYC, a news report about Chaney, Goodman and Schwerner, three civil rights activists from New York who've gone missing in Mississippi. They were last seen two days ago, trying to get African Americans to sign up to vote. Their station wagon's just been found all burnt-out.

George's son John knows Andrew Goodman, I say. They met at Queens College. John told George that Goodman's a decent young man.

You put some oil in a pan, put it onto the stove, toss in the onions and give them a stir.

I'm just glad John and David didn't go with them, I say. They're both involved in the civil rights movement, forever attending protests and rallies. I see why they do it, but I don't agree with their methods. I don't think rioting and lawlessness is the best way. It's brave of those men to go to the South, but altogether foolish. It feels like they've been playing with fire.

You say nothing. You just stir at the pan.

When the news report comes to an end, the radio crackles as a song starts to play. The tune is immediately recognisable as Nina Simone's *Mississippi Goddam*. This song's been getting more and more airtime as tensions rise. Anger pumps hard through her lyrics: *hound dogs, school children, picket lines, boycotts, a country full of lies*. The piano and double bass keep up the fast beat as Simone cries out furiously for equality.

I want to engage you in conversation about this; it's a serious topic affecting our country.

It's a complete mess down south, don't you think? I say. George is terribly worried about these missing men. So am I.

The onions glisten in the heat of the pan.

At last, you reply. Yes, it's a mess. I bet Molly's relieved that John and David didn't go there.

Yes, she is, I say. I dread to think what's happened to those boys. I hope they're found safe.

You open the refrigerator and take out a packet of ground beef, wrapped in brown paper, open the packaging out and crumble the meat out into the pan. The smell of your cooking is making me hungry. You turn to me abruptly.

I hope that those men are found safe too, Russ. But I think John and David should stay out of it. I'm not sure they're doing the right thing.

Hermine.

October 1942. Ravensbrück.

Langefeld's back. Mandl's taken her place at Auschwitz. But she's returned visibly thinner and full of neuroses. She pulls at her skirt, straightening creases that are not there. There's a rumour going around that Langefeld had an argument with *Kommandant* Höss and that's why she's back at Ravensbrück. A week after her return, she calls a meeting of the *Aufseherinnen* and tells us that while she's been away, there have been changes that she does not like.

The beatings must stop, she says. There's absolutely no point thrashing the Jehovah's Witnesses. We all know it's pointless. They're not like the Jews or the Sinti; they will never submit. Much better to put them to work in the fields; at least that way they are productive. From now on, there will be no more beatings without my permission. Do I make myself clear?

She looks firmly at Binz, who coughs overtly and then rolls her eyes in open defiance. Binz's power increased exponentially under Mandl. She runs the *Strafblock* now and is not going to give up her domain willingly. Langefeld looks at her directly, confronting the challenge. The two women stare at each other for quite some time, but it is Langefeld who looks away first. She tugs at her skirt.

While I don't like Binz at all, I agree with her in this instance. If we let the Jehovah's Witnesses get their way, other groups of prisoners will follow and we'll lose all control. It's hard enough as it is to control more than a hundred women each and to get them to work. If we don't have strong discipline, who knows where we'll be. Whatever happened to Langefeld at Auschwitz has made her weak. She needs to toughen up and lead by example. This is not just about productivity. It's about setting a precedent.

Russell.

July 1964. Maspeth.

Lelyveld looks up from his notepad, raising his eyes from me to you.

Mrs Ryan, he says. There are witness accounts that say you were brutal, that you beat and kicked women with no provocation, that some even died as a result of your force.

You grab at me fiercely, shouting, *That is a lie!* And then you break down into huge, gasping sobs. I put my arm back around your shoulder to try to protect you. My voice shakes with anger.

Get out of here! How dare you come here like this and upset my wife with these lies!

Lelyveld looks taken aback by my anger, but he does not move.

Mr Ryan, he says calmly. I am only repeating what's been said by the witnesses.

I'm about to lose my temper entirely. This whole thing is ridiculous.

What witnesses? I shout. These people are lying! My wife would not hurt a fly!

Hermine.

October 1942. Ravensbrück.

You need a strong stomach for this job. Rosa's off her food and she's got very thin. I tell her she must try harder not to be weak. The problem is caused partly by the position of the staff canteen next to the bath house. Each time a new batch of prisoners arrives, we're exposed to them lining up, filthy and naked, waiting to be showered and shaved, while we're trying to eat. This view is hardly conducive to digestion. We all agree that it would be far better if the canteen was moved outside the gates, so that we could separate work life from leisure. Despite this, I really look forward to mealtimes. We can take the weight off our feet, sit down and chat. It's convivial and the food is surprisingly good. If you arrive early enough, there's a choice between Schnitzel and some sort of stew, served with bread and butter and piping hot tea. It's almost as good as Mutti's home cooking, most probably helped by the fact we're all hungry from work. The five of us always sit together: Maria, Rosa, Hans, Dieter and me.

Today, as we're eating, I tell them about the spotted woodpecker I saw this morning in the trees near the Siemens factory on my way back from dropping off the prisoners. I heard the distinctive toc, toc, toc and followed it into the woods. I found it half-way up a tree, pied black and white, flashing its blood-red rump as it hammered the trunk.

I knew she was female, I say. Because she lacked the male's distinctive splash of crimson plumage on the back of her head.

I turn to Dieter to tell him my theory that the crisp autumn air carries the woodpecker's sound better, which is why the knocking is so sharp and harmonious at this time of year, when I realise that he's looking away. His gaze rests on the bath house. Aware that I'm looking at him, he looks back towards me and says, *Hm, hm.*

Maria and I continue to discuss the woodpecker's call. When I glance over at Dieter again, his eyes are back on the bath house. I follow his gaze and see he's looking at a prisoner. She's standing there naked. Her chestnut hair skims down to her buttocks. Her body is curved, her eyes are dark brown, and she has a very full mouth. There is no denying that the prisoner is beautiful, even as she stands there shivering to the bone. She holds one arm tightly over her breasts, the other is wrapped protectively around a young child, who is also naked and hugged tight to her leg. I cannot tell from this angle if the child is a boy or a girl. I stop talking and the others turn to see where I'm looking. Dieter's eyes jerk back to the group. He puts his fork down and his cheeks turn bright red. The feeling is visceral, like being punched very hard in the stomach. I feel too weak to stand, but I manage to pull myself up, leaving my plate on the table, more than half full.

Shortly afterwards, Dieter comes to my window and shouts up at me, begging me to come out to talk to him. I cover my head with a pillow, blocking him out. Maria comes to my door.

Couldn't you just talk to him, Hermi? she begs. He's a good man. He just made a stupid mistake.

I shake my head.

How can you say that, Maria? My father didn't look at other women like that. Do you know how humiliating that was for me? Everyone saw it. How could he do that after he keeps mentioning marriage? It's not just embarrassing, it's also disgusting. That woman is an *Untermensch*, prisoner scum. Looking at her like that not only contravenes the rules of decency, but it also contravenes the rules of this country.

I start to cry. Once I've started, I cannot stop. Out floods a tide of grief and disgust.

Russell.

July 1964. Maspeth.

The low hum of traffic reaches us from the Long Island Expressway. We lie side by side on a picnic rug in the corner of Elmhurst Park. We got here early to avoid the day's heat. The temperature has been up in the nineties for five days now. The nights have been extremely uncomfortable with the added humidity. My office is air conditioned, but the knitting mill has been unbearably hot this past week. A woman passes nearby, pushing a buggy and holding a dog tied onto a leash. Perhaps we should have brought Mitzi. We left her at home in the backyard. Although, it's nice to just sit here and relax without her running around. I like it when it's just the two of us, me and you. I reach across you to take hold of the newspaper, open it and start to flick through.

The Reds are making gains in Vietnam, I say. The Fourth of July message says that we cannot rest on past accomplishments.

I turn the page.

Oh, this annoys me, I comment. Yet another article about people protesting the war. They don't want the war, but they don't understand what will happen if Vietnam goes. It'll be a domino effect. One by one, all the other countries will fall. And then what will we have? Communism, that's what.

You roll over onto your front and look at me pleadingly.

Russ, please, for one day can you not talk about the Vietnam war?

You roll over again, so your back is towards me. I continue to read, quietly this time. It's hard for me not to talk about the war. For one thing, it's in the news the whole time. For another,

I am a veteran. You sit up and take an apple out of the basket.

Hey look, Russ, you say, pointing at a tree not far from us. Do you remember the bird we saw when we first met in Velden? The one in the park by the lake? That bird there is similar; it has the same behaviour.

I look at the tree. A small bird hops up and down the trunk, prying the bark with its beak. I remember the bird and I remember that day. You showed me your bird book, which is when we first kissed. I feel a warm glow.

It's a *Spechtmeise*, you say. In English, you call it a nuthatch.

How on earth do you know that, Hermine? You're so clever! You take a bite of the apple.

I got a book out of the library a while ago, you say when you finish your mouthful. I look up the birds when they come to the feeder and learn their names in English. The nuthatch is one of my favourites. I like it even more than the blue jay now.

I put the newspaper down and lie on my back looking up at the sky. Cumulus clouds billow above me. You never fail to impress me. You notice things I don't even see.

Hermine.

October 1942. Ravensbrück.

I spot her on the way to the Siemens factory. Though her head is shaven, I recognise her instantly; it's the arch of her lips. She's eyeing an apple core in one of the pig troughs. Stars line my vision. Without even thinking, I hear myself scream.

Hey you!

The women all stop and stare at me, eyes widened like surprised cows. I shout at her again and she points to herself in a ludicrous gesture. My head pounds as I reach for my whip. I crack it down hard onto her leg; her skin splits open and starts to pour blood. It's the first time I've whipped one of the prisoners with real venom. It comes much easier than I expected; I'm so full of hate. She drops to her knees. Time seems to slow. A leaf falls through the air between us in the complete silence, tumbling and curving until it comes to rest on the ground in front of her. She stares down at it, not daring to look up.

On your hands and knees, stinking pig! I shout.

I whip her again, hard across the back. She screams and drops forward onto all fours. I remember the way Dieter looked at her. The complete humiliation. This is the stupid bitch who's ruined everything for me. I point to the pig trough.

I saw you looking for food in the trough, I shout at her. Go on, put your snout in it and eat!

The woman is trembling. I whip her a third time and scream at her to *Go on!* She crawls over to the trough and pushes her face into the swill. When she comes back up, she is retching. I push her face back down with my foot. When I remove it, she emerges, choking. She splutters and then vomits.

I can hear the sound of continuous ringing in my ears. I do not feel satisfied. She's not suffered enough.

Now roll in the mud! I order.

The prisoner crawls away from the trough and does what I say, rolling on her back, this way and that. Sobbing breaks out behind me, interrupting my thoughts. When I turn around, the women look away. Several are shaking.

You bunch of good-for-nothing filthy pigs! I scream. Get back to work! And that includes you!

I give the prisoner a final kick and then indicate for her to get up. She peels herself off the ground and limps to the back of the line. The rest of the women shuffle in silence towards the factory. I look down. The leaf that fell earlier remains next to my foot; it is spattered with blood. I stamp on it, grinding it hard with my heel.

When all the women are inside the factory, I turn around and head back to the camp, pausing to sit on a tree stump to give myself time to calm down. Orange fungus clings to the stump's side, clustered in layers, like tiny crabs. I touch its smooth surface; it's unexpectedly warm and soft, like candle wax. My breathing slows and I begin to calm. I think about what I have just done. Whipping the prisoner did not make me feel any better; in fact, the whole thing has made me feel worse. I behaved just like Binz, with no self-control. It's then that I hear the woodpecker again. The sound takes me straight back to the bath house, to Dieter's revolting display of lust. It dawns on me that this is not about the prisoner at all. It's all about Dieter. Even if she dies, his act will remain. Anger rises within me. Why would he do that to me? He told me that he wanted to marry me. He gave me his grandmother's brooch. Dieter's the one who has ruined it all; he's made a complete fool out of me. I will never be able to look at him again.

When I get back to the camp, I go straight to Langefeld's

office. She's looking out of the window at the ridiculous aviary that she had built. A parrot squawks loudly.

You know this was my idea? she says, indicating the structure containing peacocks and other exotic birds. Birds have a calming effect, which helps when you work in a place as difficult as this, don't you think, Braunsteiner?

I look from Langefeld to the birds. Her eye is twitching. She's far too nervous to do this job. I could run Ravensbrück better than her.

I would like to put in for a transfer, *Oberaufseherin*, I say. I've worked very hard here and I've learnt a lot, but I think it would be good for me to progress and get some other experience.

Langefeld scratches her face, dragging her fingernails across the skin of her nose. She leans forward and speaks in a conspiratorial whisper.

A transfer may not be a good idea, Braunsteiner. The other camps are not like here. Auschwitz is like nothing I've ever seen. The prisoners that can't work there are put into chambers that are filled with up with gas.

Her breath smells vinegary. The smell of it combines with a vision of gas. I've heard rumours about gas chambers. I push the image that's formed in my mind away. Outside the window, a peacock fans wide its feathers in a vivid display of colour and light.

It needn't be Auschwitz, *Oberaufseherin*, I say. But I would appreciate the opportunity to move somewhere else. It's time I moved on. I'm ready to take on a more challenging role.

Langefeld taps at her desk.

I admire your ambition, she says. I'll see what I can do.

Russell.

July 1964. Maspeth.

Lelyveld scratches furiously into his notepad.

This is a mistake, I say. My wife was a prison guard. She wasn't high up. Why aren't you in Germany chasing after the people who set up those camps? They are the ones who are responsible, not my wife!

He looks at me intently.

Mr Ryan, he says. Three different witnesses have made the same claim. They say that they saw your wife commit atrocities. This information comes from Simon Wiesenthal in Vienna. He's a reliable source.

Who's Simon Wiesenthal? And what on earth would he know about my wife?

He's the man responsible for tracking down Adolf Eichmann, Lelyveld says. As I said, he's a reliable source.

I lean forward and put my head in my hands. This makes things much worse. I followed the Eichmann trial when it happened, the entire furore. I don't understand why this man Wiesenthal would want to come after you. Eichmann was a senior Nazi. You are nothing like Eichmann. This is completely insane.

You turn to Lelyveld and start to beg.

On the radio, all everyone talks about now is peace and freedom. All of this happened fifteen years ago now. I was punished back then. I was in prison for three years. I'm an American citizen now. During the war, I was just a warden for women in prisons. I was not important. I was very low down. Mr Lelyveld, please don't write about this. What can you possibly want from me now?

I look at you in disbelief. Prison for three years? Is that true? I need to get this man out of our house so I can talk to you in private. What else don't I know about you?

You need to leave now, Mr Lelyveld, I say. And let me tell you something. I worked in Korea for the US Air Force during the Korean War. We had prison camps there too, you know. Prison camps run by Americans who worked there. They were doing the same job. Maybe you should go and knock on their doors.

That may be the case, Mr Ryan, he says. But we're not talking about Korea. That's not why I'm here.

I try to change tack.

My wife is a decent person, I say. She's never upset anyone. She's not capable of cruelty. She wouldn't hurt a fly. Ask anyone round here. She's very well liked. I think you should leave now. I need some time alone with my wife.

Lelyveld stands. He reaches towards me and holds out his hand. I leave it hanging until he withdraws it.

Mr Lelyveld, I say as he walks to the door. This is not a news story. If you turn it into one, you might sell a few newspapers, but you'll ruin our lives.

He pauses for a second and then turns towards me.

There's a large Jewish community here in New York, Mr Ryan, he says. I can tell you that this is a very big story. I suggest that you speak to your wife when I've gone and ask her exactly what it was that she was doing during the war. If you want to contact me again, my telephone number is on my card.

Hermine.

October 1942. Ravensbrück.

My transfer request is granted four days later.

You're going to Majdanek, says Langefeld. It's a camp in the General Government, the German-occupied zone of Poland. I warn you, it's a much harsher environment that Ravensbrück.

I'm not afraid of that, I say. I'm physically and mentally strong as well as hard working.

The camp mostly holds men, but there is a small section for women and that is where you will work, she continues. The prisoners are mostly Jews and Slavs, a tough crowd. You are one of our best workers, Braunsteiner. You will be missed. You will leave first thing tomorrow by train. *Kommandant* Koegel expects you there in three days. There is no need to continue with your duties today. You're free to pack and say your goodbyes. If you don't like it there, you can always come back. You will always be welcome here.

Thank you, *Oberaufseherin*, I say. But I won't be coming back.

The thought of the distance between me and Dieter brings great relief. For the first time in two weeks, I feel happy as I leave Langefeld's office. Outside the *Aufseherinnen* quarters, prisoners dig at the hardening ground. They scurry round the *Kommandant*'s house, no doubt preparing the beds for next year's roses. In the three years I've been here, the gardens have grown. The trees that were planted when I first arrived are now twice my height.

As I enter the *Aufseherinnen* house for the last time, I look around. I'm furious with Dieter. This has been my home for three years. He's the one who's making me leave. I fold all that I own into my suitcase: my uniform, home clothing, a few photos and books. By the time I have finished, only one item remains: the small navy box containing Dieter's brooch. It sits on my desk. I cannot bring myself to open it or to put it into my case.

Maria enters the room and surveys its emptiness. There's nothing left out apart from the box.

What's happening, Hermi? Is everything alright?

I tell her about the transfer and she starts to cry. This makes me cry too. I don't want to leave her. She's such a dear friend.

I don't want to go, Maria. I sob. But I can't stay here while Dieter is here. Each time I see him, it breaks my heart even more.

I don't think Majdanek will be a nice place, Hermine, she says. There may be women there, but it's not a camp for women. It will be much more tough. Couldn't you go back to Vienna instead?

I don't think so, I say. I don't think we can just leave this work. Besides, the money's too good. What work would I get in Vienna?

I think you could leave if you wanted to, she replies. Other guards have left service.

Hardly any, I say. And I don't know what else I'd do for the money. The beer factory pay is so low, and who knows if it's even still up and running.

She nods at me silently, eyes full of tears.

I'll write to you regularly, I promise, I tell her. If it's not too bad, you could ask to move too.

Maybe, she says, but I can see in her face that she will not follow me to Majdanek. She likes her life here.

After Maria's gone, I sit at my desk, pick up the box and turn it over in my fingers. I think about the day that Dieter gave it to me, my birthday, how happy I was then. I open the box and look at the brooch. It feels like my heart is being wrung out. I go to slam the box and the brooch against the wall but stop myself short. I need to be rational. I do not have much. This brooch is my most valuable possession; one day I might need it to sell. I snap the box closed and shove it down the lining of my case.

Russell.

July 1964. Maspeth.

The room feels dangerously charged, as if someone has thrown a grenade between us, as if we are about to explode. You look at me, frightened. *Concentration camp. Jail.* I'm trying to reconcile these words with the woman I know as my wife. I've seen images of the camps in the newspapers, just like everyone else. An image of you in prison guard uniform enters my mind. I push it away. I cannot allow myself to place you there. That cannot be you. You lie sprawled on the sofa, sobbing and shaking all over, completely distraught.

I only did what everyone else did back then, Russ, you gasp. I was no different.

Your body convulses. You lock your arms over your head. I've never seen you so upset. Suddenly, I remember that you are my wife. Where is my loyalty? What am I thinking? I should be protecting you. But there are so many things I need to know. I sit down next to you and speak to you gently.

I love you, Hermine, but you told that man things you've never told me before. You need to tell me absolutely everything. There can be no more secrets.

You start to wail.

That's not fair, Russell! I'm not keeping secrets. It was wartime. I was conscripted. I just did my duty like everyone else. I don't talk about it because it was horrible. I'm ashamed of it. I just wanted to forget it.

My face is covered in a thin film of sweat.

Hermine, I say. You need to tell me everything, all of it.

Where you were, who you were with, what you were doing. I can't help you unless I know all the facts.

You slump backwards on the sofa and pour it all out.

I worked in a women's camp north of Berlin. It was called Ravensbrück. You know that already. Like I've told you, I was just a guard. I was transferred to Majdanek in 1942. It was a camp in Poland. I was there for less than a year and most of the time I was sick. Very, very sick, so sick I could not move. The last place I worked was a small camp called Genthin. It was back in Germany, near Ravensbrück. All I did was guard prisoners, just the same as prison guards now.

Why haven't you told me all this before? I ask.

I told you I was a prison guard when we first met, Russ. I told you about Ravensbrück. I never went into detail about the rest because you never asked. It's not something I wanted to talk about. I don't even want to talk about it now. I tried to put it all behind me. That doesn't mean that I'm hiding things from you. You haven't told me details of all the work you did in the war.

Hermine, I say. I was just fixing airplanes, doing air force stuff. This feels kinda different.

Your face tightens.

That's not fair, Russ! Can't you see? It *is* the same thing! I didn't get to choose where I worked. I did what I was told, just like you. If you had been me, you would have done the work too.

I stand up and pace round the room, trying to make sense of it. It's true that I've never asked you for any details about your work. I sensed right from the beginning that you didn't want to talk about it, so I left it alone. I know that wartime is wartime and that everybody just gets on with their job, but of all damned things, why did that have to be your job?

Honey, I say. What did you do in the prisons? What was your role?

I told you already, Russ, I was a guard. I watched over the women prisoners.

What else did you do?

You blink away tears.

I told you already! I did what prison guards do now.

I don't really know what prison guards do now. You're gonna have to tell me.

You sigh hard, clearly not wanting to expand on your story.

Honey, what did you do?

I made sure the women got up, got dressed, did their work. I counted them to make sure there were none missing. I made sure they got back to their barracks in the evening. That's all.

Hermine, I say. You told that reporter that you spent time in jail. Is that true?

You look at me dolefully.

Yes, Russ, that's true. After the war, in Austria, they tried people who worked in the camps. Everyone who had worked in the system was sent to jail, even though we were just doing our job like everyone else. I was put in prison just because I'd been there. It's as simple as that. Afterwards, an amnesty was granted for all of us who'd been imprisoned for that reason. The amnesty pardoned me. I was told I didn't need to declare it, that the slate was wiped clean.

Why haven't you told me any of this? Going to prison is a pretty big deal.

I didn't tell you because if I had you wouldn't have married me. You would have thought I was a criminal. And the slate was wiped clean. I didn't need to tell anyone anything.

You burst into tears again. Your nose starts to run.

I'm not a criminal, you wail. I'm a good person. If I'd told you that I'd been to prison, Russ, you wouldn't have married me. I wouldn't be here. I would not be your wife.

The weight of this hits me. Whatever happened to you in your past, I love you. You are my wife. You start to sob again, gulping in huge gasps of air. I kneel before you, ashamed of my doubt.

I'm so sorry, Hermine, I say. Shhh! Shhh! You need to calm down. I love you. I wish you had told me all this, but of course

I know you're not a criminal.

You look at me through swollen red eyes. I take your head in my hands and pull your face right up close to mine, so close that when you exhale, I breathe in your breath.

Everyone was involved, Russ, you say softly. We were just the easy ones to blame. I've already been punished for something that was never my fault. I don't know why this man is coming after me all over again. It's going to ruin everything. I've never had anything. You're all that I've ever had and he's going to take you away from me.

Hermine.

October 1942. Lublin.

The journey to Majdanek takes three full days. I share the carriage with nine other *Aufseherinnen* chosen by Else Ehrich, the new *Oberaufseherin* of Majdanek. Ehrich tells us that we should all feel very proud because we are the first female guards to be chosen to work there, the cream of the Ravensbrück crop. I do feel proud. Even though I put in a request to be transferred, the fact is that I still had to be chosen.

We travel through Berlin and Frankfurt, sleeping upright, propped against each other and the wall of the train. Weber, Witthuhn and Ernst spend hours discussing what they imagine our conditions will be like. I stay out of the conversation. My mind remains focused on Dieter's betrayal, which still cuts like a knife.

The train crosses into Poland. Gone are Germany's mountains, hills and plains. The land here is flat, dull and grey; it melds indistinctly into the monochrome sky. I fall asleep and wake up as we pull into Warsaw. We disembark at Central Station and change trains. The last leg of the journey lasts nearly four hours. It's uninspiring, kilometre upon kilometre of flat plains. Finally, we arrive at Lublin station. An SS man is waiting for us, wearing the grey-green uniform and skull-and-crossbones *Totenkopf* cap of the Death's Head battalion. He doesn't make eye contact or offer to help us. It's a far cry from the gentlemanly reception Maria and I received from Herr Schmidt in Fürstenberg.

Which one of you is the *Oberaufseherin*? the SS man barks.

When Ehrich steps forward, he looks at her with undisguised disdain.

Your accommodation has not been built yet, he says. I'm taking you to a hotel while *Kommandant* Florstedt works out what to do with you. I don't understand why he can't put you in a communal barrack like the rest of us. Why should women get preferential treatment?

Erich glares at the SS man. She snaps at him sharply.

We did not ask for special treatment. *Kommandant* Koegel knows many of us personally from our service at Ravensbrück. Perhaps he thinks we deserve better conditions. At least he is civilised, not brought up in a farmyard.

The man ignores her and turns on his heel. He stalks off, black boots clipping sharply against the cobbled street. We follow him away from the station into Lublin, passing rows of cream and orange houses until we reach the hotel. Once inside, Ehrich organises us into rooms.

You're in with me, Braunsteiner, she says.

It's the first time she's spoken to me directly. At Ravensbrück, we kept our own crowds. I follow her into the room. It's not far off freezing. Icy October air pushes through cracks in the windows and wall. Ehrich paces the room, hands balled into fists, venting her spleen. I nod in appeasement as she tells me she's furious about this delay.

Why haven't they prepared for us? she mutters angrily. They knew we were coming. They've had plenty of time to get ready for us. The women's camp opened here two months ago. Did you see how that man looked at us, so high and so mighty, with so much contempt? Did you hear his accent? He's nothing but a jumped-up farm hand. He would not have got away with that kind of behaviour at Ravensbrück. The men there treated us with the respect we deserve. I will speak to the *Kommandant* about this as soon as we get there. Believe me, I will not be spoken to like that!

Russell.
July 1964. Maspeth.

You press your body against mine, the body that I've held and loved as my wife, the woman I've known to be gentle and kind.

Hermine, I say. I need to phone Lelyveld back. I'm sorry, but I need to ask you some more questions so that I'm totally clear. Can you tell me about Majdanek? Was it a prison or was it a, a..?

I can't even bring myself to say the word.

It was a *Lager*, you say quietly. In translation, I guess you could say that means a camp.

Does that mean it was a concentration camp?

A long pause and then, Yes, Russ. It was.

I feel physically sick. I can't stop the images: twisted bodies, gas chambers, emaciated men. Surely, it can't have been like that in the camps for women? It must have been different wherever you were.

Oh my God, Hermine! When I think of concentration camps, I think of people dying. Were there gas chambers there?

You sigh and look down at the floor. When the admission comes, it is plaintive but honest.

Yes, Russell. There was a gas chamber there, but it was nothing to do with me.

This knowledge crushes me like a lead weight. I sit silently under it, not knowing what to do or to say. When I do not respond, you start pleading.

Russell, you must believe me. I was hardly there at Majdanek. I told you before, I had typhus many times. I was off sick for most of the time. My job there was the same as at Ravensbrück.

I just looked after the women. That's all that I did. I didn't design those places. It was wartime. I didn't have a choice about it. I just did what I was told. Try to understand it from my point of view. What else do you think I could do?

You start to cry again and cling on to me tightly.

Please, Russ, you sob. Please, please try to understand.

I'm trying, Hermine, I say. Really, I am. It's just that it's a very big shock for me to find out that you were in a concentration camp. I need some time to take it all in. I also need to ring that journalist back. If this ends up in the newspapers, it will destroy us. I'd better call him now. Have you told me everything? Is there anything else you think I should know?

No, you say quietly. That's everything.

Confession over, your body goes limp.

I take Lelyveld's business card out of my pocket and say a quick prayer. I need to stop him from writing an article.

Hermine.

October 1942. Majdanek.

After three days of waiting, a different SS officer arrives in a truck. He's tall, at least 190 centimetres. We gather at the front of the hotel. He scans us and then flashes a huge smile.

My name's Georg Wallisch, he says. I've come to take you beautiful ladies to the *Lager*. Jump into my truck!

This officer is so much nicer than his colleague who collected us from the train. The opposite, in fact. He looks at us directly and helps with our luggage.

Your quarters haven't been finished, so you cannot stay in the main camp, Wallisch tells us. In fact, the whole camp is still under construction. It's very muddy, which makes it extremely hard to walk around, so we're putting you outside the main camp until your accommodation's built.

We drive out of the centre of Lublin. The town gives way to flat open fields, empty apart from the odd labourer. Trees line the road, their branches stripped bare. A hooded crow sits on a fence post; its dark head on top of its grey and white body looks like it's been dipped in black ink. The truck pulls off the road into a site surrounded by a double fence of barbed wire. Wallisch leaps out of the driver's seat and comes to the back of the truck to let us out. He's whistling cheerfully.

This is the Old Airfield Camp, he says. The Clothing Works is based here. You ladies will be living and working here for the time being. It's a short walk from here to the main camp of Majdanek. Once your barrack's completed, you'll move into the camp.

As he pulls open the truck's tailgate, he winks ostentatiously at Erna Pfannenstiel. She blushes and smiles. Wallisch's cheer has put us all in a good mood. He leads us through the old airfield, past the clothing works, towards a large stone building that is painted bright white.

Your housing, he says as he opens the door.

The building stinks of boiled sausages.

This is the dining room for senior SS officers, he says. You're welcome to use it, though there is also a kitchen over there to the side if you want to prepare your own food.

Another SS officer walks over to greet us. He is short, stocky and balding. What's left of his hair is slicked backwards onto his head. Wallisch salutes him and then heads back outside.

Good morning, ladies, the SS man says. I'm Hermann Hackmann, the *Hauptsturmführer*, your compound leader. I will show you your rooms.

Hackmann leads us upstairs and points along a corridor, indicating a passageway lined with four doors.

I believe that at Ravensbrück, you had your own accommodation. Here you must share. There are three rooms and a bathroom on this floor. My SS guards share seven to a room, so this is the height of luxury; only my officers get their own room. I will see to it that you all get extra blankets. It gets very cold here at night.

Ehrich chooses a room and picks Hildegard Lächert and me to lodge in with her. Lächert has a reputation for having a terrible temper, but it's pleasing to be chosen by Ehrich herself. The room's walls are bare stone. There's no stove or side lamps, just an overhead light bulb, which flickers and blinks. In the absence of cupboards, we push our suitcases under our beds. Ehrich is clearly displeased. She heads back into the corridor, clears her throat loudly and calls down the passageway.

Hauptsturmführer, it's important that my *Aufseherinnen* get good rest between their work shifts. I hope we will not be in this temporary accommodation too long.

Of course, *Oberaufseherin*, Hackmann replies. Believe me, I'm just as keen as you are to get you out of here.

Russell.

July 1964. Maspeth.

I dial Lelyveld's number. After three rings, he picks up.

Mr Lelyveld, it's Russell Ryan. You came to my house this morning. I need to talk to you.

A pause.

Sure, go ahead.

I take a deep breath and embark on my speech.

I've spoken with my wife about all of this, er, all of this affair, and I can explain. She told me it was a conscriptive service. She had no choice in the matter. She just did her duty like prison guards do now. She was not in charge of anything. She's completely innocent, as God is my witness. My wife's a good woman, Mr Lelyveld. There's no more decent person on this earth.

The sound of typing comes down the line, followed by Lelyveld's voice.

Mr Ryan, we have witness accounts that say your wife hurt people badly.

I try to keep calm, but my voice starts to quiver. I suck in air through my teeth.

Who are these witnesses exactly? Where did you find them? How do you know these people are telling the truth? I sure don't believe them.

Lelyveld replies calmly, Three women in Tel Aviv identified your wife to Simon Wiesenthal. They called her the Mare of Majdanek because she stamped people and kicked them to death.

I take in a sharp breath and raise my voice into the receiver.

What the hell, Mr Lelyveld! She did *no such thing*! She did no such thing! Those women are lying. They're just swinging axes. They just want to punish someone who was doing a job.

This conversation is not going the way I had planned. I try to swallow, but my throat has gone dry.

Mr Ryan, do you know what your wife was doing at Majdanek?

Yes, I do. She says she was sick for most of the time she was there. You've got the wrong person, Mr Lelyveld. You need to leave us alone.

He pauses again. The typing sound stops.

How well do you know your wife, Mr Ryan? Did you even know she was a concentration camp guard?

Something inside of me snaps.

You have absolutely no idea what you're talking about, Mr Lelyveld! I shout, unable to contain my anger. I know my wife perfectly well. It's you who doesn't know her. Besides, what would you know about any of this? Have you ever served your country? Have you been to war?

Hermine.

November 1942. Majdanek.

The walk into the camp takes less than twenty minutes from the airfield. Ehrich has asked me to accompany her to meet *Kommandant* Florstedt. Koegel left for Flossenbürg a week or so ago. It's an unexpected honour to be asked to go with her. Despite the cold, the walk is pleasant. Thick frost crunches under our boots. Ehrich tells me about the ambitious scope of Majdanek, how it's going to be an enormous work camp.

This camp will provide labour to keep Germany fed and supplied as the Reich expands, she says. We need *Lebensraum* for the *Volksdeutsche*, living space for our countrymen. The Treaty of Versailles forced us to cede land to the *Untermenschen* and our frontiers have bled continually ever since. The Jews and the Slavs are filthy and uncivilized. They breed like rabbits. It's right that they're being moved out. Of course, Braunsteiner, you are Austrian, so you are *Volksdeutsche*. Your place is in the Reich.

In the surrounding fields, crows pry at the hoar-hardened ground, searching for food frozen into the land. We pass a sign marked with a skull-and-crossbones, warning in German that all intruders to the camp will be shot. The camp comes into view. It is vast and surrounded by a double layer of barbed-wire fencing. Huge wooden guard towers space the perimeter evenly, manned by armed guards. Inside the camp, row upon row of wooden barracks for the prisoners extend in the distance. Ehrich sweeps her arm towards the camp in an arc.

A step up from Ravensbrück, she says with evident delight.

We stop at the outer gate checkpoint. The guard on duty stands upright in the pale winter sun. He checks our passes and opens the gate. Inside, a long black road leads to the prisoner entrance. To the right of this road is a little white house. Ehrich tells me it belongs to the *Kommandant*. We reach the SS headquarters and wait seated outside *Kommandant* Florstedt's office for about fifteen minutes. When he finally opens the door, his appearance surprises me; he looks like an ageing fox, with small sunken eyes, a pointed nose and dry rufous skin. Florstedt addresses Ehrich and they chat for a while about the camp and the condition of the workers. Then he turns towards me.

Aufseherin Braunsteiner, Florstedt says. I've heard very good things about you.

He picks up a square black box from his desk and opens it towards me. Inside the box, a cross-shaped medal rests on top of purple silk. In its centre, there's a circle imprinted with a swastika. The medal's attached to a ribbon banded with black in the middle and flanked by strips of white and red on each side.

Kommandant Koegel gave me instructions before he left that I am to give you the War Merit Medal 2nd Class for your service, Florstedt says. *Oberaufseherin* Ehrich, be so good as to pin this to the *Aufseherin*.

Ehrich is smiling. She must have known. She lifts the medal from the box, undoes the clasp, and attaches it to the buttonhole of my jacket.

Well deserved, Braunsteiner, she says. You've done very good work.

I cannot believe that this medal's for me. I am bursting with pride. I thank him and tell him I will do my best for the Reich.

Hard work leads to greatness, does it not, *Oberaufseherin*? says Florstedt.

Indeed, *Kommandant*, Ehrich replies. *Aufseherin* Braunsteiner is destined for good things.

I feel a rush of joy. I'm not sure which is better, the medal or Ehrich's fine words. Florstedt taps loudly on his desk, interrupting my thoughts.

I'm afraid I must share some less happy news, he says. The movement of people out of the Reich is taking place very fast and we are extremely short staffed. I've asked for more

Aufseherinnen to be sent here from Ravensbrück, but it may take a month or more for them to arrive. Right now, we have two thousand female prisoners. You are only ten guards, so you will be managing two hundred women each. I appreciate that this is far from ideal. However, the male guards are under just as much pressure. Can I count on you, *Oberaufseherin*?

Yes, *Kommandant*, Ehrich says.

She smiles broadly, seemingly undaunted by this very high ratio of prisoners to guards.

Braunsteiner, she says, turning towards me. As soon as more guards arrive, I will need a deputy. Can I count on you?

Of course! I say, full of delight.

This day could not be going any better.

And now to your barrack, says Florstedt. I'm afraid it's still not built. We're working hard to get it completed, but the prisoners are weak and slow and there is always the issue of communication. The Polish Jews, the Lithuanians, the Russians, the ethnic Poles, they're all very stupid. Hardly any of them speak German, which is incredibly frustrating. I will see that you have prisoner translators wherever possible, but sometimes there are better ways to be understood than language, if you know what I mean?

Ehrich nods vigorously and I follow suit. Florstedt pauses for a moment. His expression is pained. He's not quite sure how to phrase what comes next.

One final thing. How can I put this? It is most unsavoury. You will have to excuse the smell over the next few days. We have run out of oil for the crematoria and we have a backlog of bodies. The bodies will be burnt in the Krepiec forest. Once the crematoria are back up and running, the whole process will become smooth again, but right now, we must resort to pyres. I'm afraid that means there will be a bad smell. That is all. Heil Hitler!

As we walk back to the airfield, I thank Ehrich profusely for all her support.

Hermine, she says. When it's just the two of us, you may call me Else.

Russell.

July 1964. Maspeth.

I buy the newspaper first thing this morning, before anyone else is out on the streets. The benches in Garlinge Triangle are empty. My heart pounds as I sit down and start to leaf through. By the time I find the article, I'm in a full sweat.

Former Nazi Camp Guard is Now a Housewife in Queens.

Nausea hits me as I process the title; they're calling you a Nazi! I put the paper down on the bench next to me and take some deep breaths. I summon the courage to read what comes next. When I pick the paper back up again, words spin out at me: *guard, prison, death camp, Majdanek.* That asshole journalist has gone and given out our home address! People will be able to find us at home. Why did he do that? My chest tightens. I struggle to breathe; it feels like I'm being choked.

Everyone we know will see this: my family, my colleagues, George, Molly, the neighbours, all of New York. I read the article over and over until I make myself stop because I'm gasping for breath.

When I get home, you're upstairs, taking a shower. I put the paper on the kitchen counter and wait. You come down the stairs and enter the kitchen. Your hair is wrapped up on your head in a towel. When you see the paper on the counter, your eyes widen with panic and your breath picks up speed. I hold my head in my hands. It is heavy, like a huge chunk of stone.

I don't think you should read it.

What does it say, Russ? Is it that bad?

Yes, I'm afraid it is bad.

You walk to the counter and reach out to the paper, pick it up carefully and flick to the right page. The colour drains from your face. You drop the paper onto the linoleum, scattering sheets all over the floor, and then lean against the counter and retch.

Oh my God, Russell! you say. He's written the word Nazi in the title. I'm not a Nazi. How can he write that? It's simply not true. I was never a Nazi. I didn't ever join the party.

You sit down opposite me and reach out for my hands. I hold onto your fingers, trying to work out what we should do.

I need to know what the rest of the article says, you say. Would you read it to me?

I'm not sure I should do that, honey. I don't think it will be good for you to hear.

You have to, Russ. I need to know what it says.

I pick up the papers and sort the pages back into order, clear my throat and repeat the headline out loud. I look up at you. Your face is ashen, but you signal for me to continue. I read you the article. You listen quietly, wincing as it mentions Majdanek, Simon Wiesenthal, your previous prison sentence. You gasp when it details where we live, and again when it questions your citizenship. When I finish, I put the newspaper down. Tears roll down your cheeks.

I'm sorry, Hermine, I say. It's not good. This is not going to be good for us.

I don't know what else to say.

Why are they doing this to me? you splutter. Why aren't they chasing the people who ran the camps, not small people like me, who had no power? The reporter talks about taking away my citizenship. Can they do that, Russ? What would happen to me if they did that? Would they take me away from you?

The mention of you being taken away from me is too much to bear. My eyes well up. This is all so unjust. I need to pull myself out of this sorrow so that I can fight for you.

They can't take you away from me, I say fiercely. I promise that I won't let them do that. You are my wife, Hermine. I am your husband. I'm going to protect you.

Hermine.
November 1942. Majdanek.

The numbers arriving at the camp keep increasing. Majdanek holds nearly ten thousand prisoners now. Transports arrive almost daily from Poland swelling the numbers, for the most part, with Jews. We cannot keep people who are unable to work: children, pregnant women, the elderly and weak. There are a lot of people who do not fit the criteria. The numbers are becoming almost impossible; we don't have enough room for them, let alone enough food. No sooner does one load arrive than we get the next. There aren't enough guards to deal with them all. It is beginning to feel overwhelming.

Today, more than two hundred Jews arrive mid-afternoon. Ehrich chooses Lächert, Ernst, Meinel, Wöllert and me to assist with the selections. The first selection is easy. People who cannot work go to the left and those who can work go to the right. The main difficulty is the women with children; they become hysterical and refuse to separate. Many of these mothers are good for work, so there is no need to send them to the gas yet. Lächert pulls them apart and kicks any child or mother who resists going to the correct line. I hate this part of the job, but it must be done.

The adults in the right-hand line are taken to the bathrooms, where they undress. Then they're brought back to the rose garden naked and lined up for the second selection. The name rose garden is a misnomer; where once there were flowers, now it is bare. Once the prisoners are lined up, we walk among them, inspecting their bodies for signs of weakness. If there is any doubt, I make them run, as this is a good way to determine whether they have the strength to cope with hard labour. Those who cannot run back and forth along the length of the garden five or six times are sent to the left.

Today's selection is in progress. It has started to snow. Huge flakes fall onto the women as they run, melting on their bare skin. In a strange sort of way, it's remarkably beautiful. Before long, the ground is covered with muddy brown footprints in the white snow. One of the prisoners collapses in front of me while she is running. She pulls herself back up and tells me in heavily accented German that she is fine. Her legs look strong, so I give her a second chance, but she slips over again. I tell her to get up and go to the left.

The prisoner looks at me from the ground with eyes full of hatred and spits out the words, How can you live with yourself? God will punish you for this! You are going straight to hell!

I'm completely taken aback. This is the first time a prisoner has dared to speak to me with such disrespect. Who does this woman think she is? Ehrich must have heard her too because she strides at the prisoner and whips her hard across the back.

Don't let an *Untermensch* speak to you like that ever again! she says. She's making a fool of you.

Anger courses through me. I need to prove myself to Ehrich if I am to become her second in command. I aim my boot at the woman's face and kick hard. It hits the prisoner's nose with a crunch. In my fury, it's easy to do. The snow around the prisoner is spattered with blood. She puts her hands to her face to protect it and lets out a low moan. I will not be treated like a fool, least of all by a prisoner. I stamp down on her head. There's a loud cracking, like the sound of a walnut breaking open. Blood pours out from her ear. I lean down towards her and scream into her face, Your God has left you, filthy Jew!

Enraged, I turn to the rest of the women and point towards the crematorium, which is up and running again. Smoke twists upwards from its tall brick chimney, puffing ash into the sky.

The women freeze in panic, fear emanating from them in a silent scream. My body tingles with a strange sense of power. They are clearly petrified by me.

Who wants to be next? I shout. There are far too many of you. The only way any of you will ever leave Majdanek is through that chimney!

The prisoners start to whimper and wail.

Good work, Braunsteiner, says Ehrich. You show these bitches who is the boss.

Ehrich's approval makes up for the fact I have killed a prisoner. Though, she was going to die anyway, so what difference does it make?

Two other prisoners drag the corpse away to one side. It trails bright red blood behind it in a line, as if someone's run a paint brush over the snow. Behind Ehrich, an SS man climbs up a ladder onto the roof of the gas chamber, wearing a gas mask. He balances himself carefully while he twists the lid off a canister and deposits it neatly into a hole in the roof. An icy wind curls around my legs and I shiver. We've been promised new accommodation with a stove; I hope we're moved into it soon to get out of this cold.

Russell.
July 1964. Maspeth.

Since the article came out, I've gone over it all again and again, forwards and backwards, asking you more and more questions, twisting and turning, pulled in all directions by the force of your answers. It's been like being on the Cyclone at Coney Island, desperately grasping onto the bar, climbing upward in a steep ascent, and then rolling over the top and hurtling downwards, screaming as I lurch this way and that.

Were you a Nazi?

No. I never joined the National Socialists.

I lurch to the left.

Did you see the gas chambers?

Only from the outside. That wasn't my job.

I jerk to the right.

Did you see people dying?

Yes, people were dying all the time, but what could I do?

My head slams backwards into the seat.

Did you ever use force?

Sometimes I had to. There was no other way to control them. There were so many of them, and we were so few.

Pale-faced and shaken, I reach the ride's end and then get back on it to start all over.

Who did you live with?

The other guards.

Were there men there with you?

Yes, but we lived separately.

Were those men Nazis?

They were in the SS.

My stomach churns. You were working with Nazis. How can this be happening?

Were you in the SS?

No. None of the women were in the SS. I wasn't a member of the National Socialists.

So, you weren't a Nazi?

I told you that before, Russell. I never joined the party.

You promise me, hand on heart, that you were not a Nazi.

I keep telling you, no. I promise you that I was not in the party.

I pause to breathe. The ride stops and starts up yet again.

Did you see the starvation?

Yes, Russell, I saw it.

How did that make you feel?

I felt bad, of course, but what could I do? There were too many of them. There was not enough food. It was not a nice place for us either. It's not like we had lots of food.

But couldn't you have helped them?

Oh my God, Russell. You are so naïve. How could I have helped them? They were prisoners. We were *at war*. What do you think I could do?

The car jolts to a stop. I cannot get off it. It sets off again.

Were the women you were guarding Jewish?

Lots of them were but there were also Poles and Slavs, gypsies, other criminals.

But they weren't really criminals, were they? They were just people the regime didn't like.

It's easy to say that now, Russell. We didn't know that. We were told that they were criminals. I believed what I was told, just like you believed what your government told you during the war. What do you think I was supposed to think? That my government was lying? If you had been there, you would have believed it too.

The ride jerks to a halt. I try to imagine it, to put myself there.

What would I have done? Would I have refused to do that work? Would I have stood up to the regime?

You come straight back at me.

You tell me, Russell, if you had been me, what would you have done? What do you really think you would have done?

I'm at a loss for an answer. I want to say I would not have done it, but I know too much about war to be able to say that. You were young. You were doing what you were told to do by your country. But what took place in those places was so inhumane. It's hard to hold the two things in one hand.

At last, I say, Honestly, I just don't know.

Well, I do know, Russell. If you are capable of being truly honest with yourself, you would know that you would have done it too because *everyone* did what we had to, even though it was hard. We had no choice.

Couldn't you have refused to work there?

Don't be ridiculous, Russell. It was during the war. I needed the money. What other job was there for me to do? You are trying to make me feel bad about it, but I was serving my country. I was serving my country, just like you served your country too.

I'm not trying to make you feel bad, I say. I'm just trying to understand it. I'm finding it very hard to understand.

That's exactly the problem, you reply. Nobody can ever understand what it was like there unless you were there. It was a hell on earth. I did not enjoy it. I did what I had to until I could leave.

What would I have done? The question goes through my head on a continuous loop. I'm under no illusion. I know I had much easier options than you. How were you to know what Hitler was planning? I go over it again and again and again. Who am I to take the high moral ground?

At the same time as this internal examination, the external pressure starts to mount. Our doorway is pelted continually with eggs. People appear outside the house, climbing the steps, peering in through the windows. I close the curtains and lock the front door. You're far too frightened to go out. You call in your resignation at the mill, unable to bring yourself to go into work anymore. The mill owner and a good portion of the workforce are Jewish; you're worried that you're going to be attacked. I'm worried about it too. I've become completely paranoid about what people are saying. Friends and neighbours have started to abandon us. George is about the only person I can talk to, but he hasn't called. Why hasn't he called me? I feel so alone in this. The only person left to turn to is you.

Hermine.

December 1942. Majdanek.

Tomorrow is *Heiligabend*, the day before Christmas. I do not feel festive at all. In fact, I feel miserable, sick, depressed. Last week, I had dysentery and now I am running a fever. Beads of sweat trail down my forehead like ants.

We've been moved into a shared apartment within the clothing works. It's still in the old airfield, but it's nicer than the block we were in before. There are only two of us per room now and the rooms all have heating plus a wardrobe, so at least now we can hang up our clothes. I'm still in with Ehrich. Lächert is now sharing with Ruth Ertl. I can't say that I miss her; she loses her temper so easily, frequently snapping at other guards. This doesn't seem to bother Ehrich, who likes Lächert immensely; they go horse-riding together in their spare time. Ehrich and I have become good friends. She will never replace Maria in my heart, but I enjoy her company. Recently, she's been dropping hints that I'm going to be promoted. I hope that does happen, not only for the recognition, but also so that I can send more money home.

Luise sent me a letter saying she's going to spend Christmas with Mutti, Erika, Inge and their children. Dieter and Josef's wives and children will be with their own families as the men are away fighting. Fritz is engaged to a nurse called Berta. Berta's father was killed a few months ago. Hearing all this makes me feel so distant. I wish I could spend Christmas at home. Instead, I'm stuck far away in the middle of Poland, up late washing my clothes in freezing cold water. My hands are so chapped now that they are raw. I don't know why they don't make the prisoners do this for us here. It's even worse than when I did the washing in London; at least the water there was hot and the soap was good. Here, the soap is awful; it smells bad and doesn't lather properly. Worst of all, there's the issue of lice. When I rub my clothes together in the bucket, they float to the top, their tiny legs sweeping through the dirty water in circles until eventually they drown. I've asked Ehrich several times to get permission from Hackmann for us to be able to use a laundry in Lublin. We'll get sick if we can't clean our clothes properly and there's a lot of sickness here already. Last month, a typhoid epidemic swept through the camp. The new *Aufseherinnen* barracks are not far off completion, but I'd rather stay here at the airfield, even though it means sharing a room. The sanitation is terrible in the camp. There are far, far too many people.

Ehrich comes into the washroom and gives me a look of pity when she sees what I'm doing. None of us enjoy washing our clothes.

Else, I say.

Her first name still sounds strange tripping off my tongue.

Please will you ask Hackmann to let us use the laundry? Look at these lice.

I thrust the bucket towards her. It slops onto the floor. She looks in it and pulls a face of disgust.

Alright, she says. I'll ask him. I was just about to a couple of days ago, but it wasn't the right time.

She's referring to the last time we saw Hackmann, outside the clothing works, just after closing time. Ehrich had lined up the prisoners, ready to escort them back to the camp as Hackmann was passing. Just then, one of the prisoners coughed and spat out a globule of phlegm. Hackmann stopped in his tracks and turned red as an apple. He pulled out his baton and struck the prisoner hard across the face. The strike made a hollow *thwock*, like the sound of a bat hitting a ball. The prisoner slumped to her knees.

Hackmann waited a second, then screamed, Lick that back up!

The prisoner looked at the ground, quaking in fear. It was

clear that she did not speak German and did not understand Hackmann's instruction. One of the other women in the line spoke to her in Polish. The prisoner stuck out her tongue and scraped at the dirt, ingesting the globule along with some mud. While she was down, Hackmann hit her again hard across the back, which made her fall sideways. She curled into a ball, holding her hands to her face instinctively, expecting a further assault, but he decided to leave her. Instead, he marched up and down the line, screaming at the women.

None of you filthy bitches get to spit! This is a workhouse, not a fucking whorehouse!

He turned to the woman who had translated into Polish.

Go on! he said. You who are so helpful with German. Yes, you, stupid bitch. You tell them that!

The prisoner-translator spoke to the group in Polish. When she had finished, Hackmann put his baton under her chin and thrust it upwards.

Now you tell these fucking filthy sluts, in your fucking filthy language, that I will show them what I mean.

The translator's voice shook as she relayed his words. Hackmann then made a great drama of hacking and coughing. He spat a huge lump of phlegm onto the ground at the feet of the translator, removed the baton from under her chin and shoved her head downwards.

Lick that up, bitch, he said. It's delicious and German.

The translator stared at the lump of green phlegm, which had picked up bits of grit from the ground at its edges. Her whole body went into spasm. Hackmann raised his baton and struck her hard on the shoulder, causing her to collapse, and then turned to Ehrich, all puffed up, clearly pleased with himself.

Sometimes a demonstration works better than an explanation. He sneered and then he leant down to the woman and screamed in her face.

Lick it up!

The woman obeyed. I could see that she had vomited into her mouth, but she didn't release it; she swallowed it back down. Hackmann strutted off like a peacock. For all his ridiculous bravado, I knew he was right. These women are disgusting. Spitting spreads diseases and typhoid is rife.

Back in the washroom, Ehrich steadies my bucket.

Hackmann thinks he impresses me, she says. But he couldn't be more wrong. He says spitting is disgusting, but then he does it himself, right in front of us. He's no better than a pig. But anyway, yes, I'll ask him about the laundry. Come on, let's go to bed. We don't want to be tired tomorrow for *Heiligabend*.

Russell.

August 1964. Maspeth.

Finally, George has come round. He called me this morning and
said he'd drop by, but he doesn't arrive until past four o'clock.
When I open the door, he greets me with a smile that is a little
too wide. I look behind him for Molly, but she is not there.

Hey Russ! he says, overly cheerful. Sorry, buddy. Molly couldn't
make it. Susan's got herself a boyfriend and she's bringing him
home tonight for the first time. A guy named Ronald. She met
him in high school. Molly's busy cooking up a storm.

It's the first time that George has ever come here alone.
Though it is, of course, possible he's telling the truth, I think
it's unlikely. I try my hardest not to show I'm upset.

Good for Susan, I say, matching his false cheerfulness with
my tone. That's a shame about Molly. Hermine will be sad she's
not come.

I try to gauge his reaction, but he keeps on smiling, giving
nothing away. We go into the living room.

How's Hermine doing? he asks. How's it been for her, since,
since…you know.

He can't quite say it. Nobody can.

Since the article, you mean?

He nods.

She's OK, I say. Bearing up.

George takes a seat in the armchair, while I take the sofa. I
know that you're listening in from the kitchen.

So, where is Hermine? George asks politely.

She's in the kitchen preparing some food. We'd hoped you'd

both stay and eat with us, but it's OK. I understand.

George looks at his feet, clearly uncomfortable.

How are you doing, Russ? he says at last. This must be very hard for you.

Yes, George, I say. It's been absolutely terrible. It's terrifying, by which I mean I feel genuinely terrified. People keep trying to get into the house. We've had things thrown at us. We get shouted at. Once something like that gets into the papers, it's difficult to persuade people that it's not the truth. Both of us are finding it very hard indeed.

George throws me a look of genuine concern.

I'm sorry to hear that, Russ. To have all this in the papers is a terrible thing.

I point my head in the direction of the kitchen.

When she comes out, you will be kind to her, won't you? She's feeling awfully afraid.

Good lord, yes, Russ. Of course, I will.

Hermine, honey, I say loudly. George is here!

I want you to come out so that you can see that George is here and being supportive, but you stay in the kitchen, so he calls for you too.

Hey, Hermine! Aren't you going to come out and see me?

When you walk into the room, you are wearing an apron covered with flour. Your disappointment that Molly's not here is written all over your face. Tears fill your eyes. The sight of you so obviously upset makes me feel so bad. I'm on the verge of crying myself. George is not stupid. He can see the state you are in.

I'm so sorry, Hermine, he says. Those damn paper men are causing a whole lot of trouble for you. Hopefully, it'll blow over soon. I hope you're OK.

I'm sorry, you say. I can't talk about it. It makes me feel very unwell.

You run back into the kitchen.

She's really struggling, I say. She thinks that everyone hates her. You don't think differently of her, do you?

George pauses a while and then says, I'm going to be honest with you, Russ. This whole thing has been quite a shock to us. We've found it hard to comprehend. My boys didn't want me to come today, but I thought I should see you.

I look at him quizzically.

What's this got to do with your boys?

Well, they're so into the civil rights movement, equality, you know. Everything like that.

I feel my face getting hot.

What the hell's this got to do with the civil rights movement, George? What are you talking about equality for? This is about a complete stranger accusing my wife of things she did not do!

George straightens his collar and takes in a breath.

I'm sorry. That didn't come out right. Let me try to say that again. I'm trying to explain to you why it's taken me a while for me to come to see you. The truth is that I didn't really know what to say to you. We've all seen the pictures of what happened in those camps. It stands for everything we fought against during the war.

The words hit me hard. Even George is turning against me.

So, you think she's responsible for all of that, do you? I say bitterly. That it was us versus her?

George shifts in his seat, pulling at his pants. He looks incredibly uncomfortable.

That's not what I said, Russ. Of course, I know that Hermine was not responsible for everything that happened. Look, I don't want to upset you. I just needed some time to think about what all of this means.

What it means, George, is that she happened to be given a role in those camps during the war. That was the position she was assigned to. She had no choice and none of it, *none of it*, was her idea. We got assigned to the US force; she got assigned to work in prison camps. You're my oldest and dearest friend. You know me like no one else does. You know both of us. You know that we're good people.

George stands up and comes to sit next to me on the sofa. He puts his hand on my arm.

Russ, he says gently. I know you're a good man. I'm trying to be supportive. Really, I am. But you've got to realise that not everybody around here knows you like I do. Put yourself in the shoes of most of the people who hear about this. The newspaper article said she was a Nazi. It talked about Simon Wiesenthal. He's the guy who tracked down Adolf Eichmann, for heaven's sake. It just doesn't look good to a lot of folks. You've got to admit it, if this wasn't you we were talking about, it wouldn't look good.

But it is me we're talking about. It's me and my wife. Hermine's a good woman. She wouldn't hurt anyone. She wasn't a Nazi; that's a downright lie. Have some faith in me, George. Have some faith in my wife. Don't just believe what you read in the papers. The people who are accusing her of these things are just searching for someone, anyone, to drag through the mud.

I understand what you're saying, Russ. I'm just trying to explain to you what other people might think.

Other people aren't you, I reply. I don't care about them. Well, maybe I do, but most of all, I care what you think.

He looks at me dolefully and then says, I'm so sorry. Is there anything I can do to help?

Actually, yes. There is something you can do.

George looks at me, worried, clearly wondering what it is that I'm going to ask him to do.

I got a lawyer this week, I say. He's called John Barry. He told me to collect written statements from people who know Hermine, to say that she's of good character. Will you write me a statement?

George looks relieved. He replies straight away.

Of course, Russ. I'd be delighted to do that. Will you tell Hermine that I'll do that for her?

Yes, George, I will.

We sit there in silence. The clock ticks on the wall. At last George speaks; he changes the subject.

Did you hear that they found Chaney, Goodman and Schwerner in Mississippi? Fourteen feet under, dug into a dam? Those poor boys had been beaten and shot. God rest their souls. I hope the murderers are brought to justice. I don't agree with the death penalty but, in this instance, I think they should get it.

There's something about the way George said the words murderers, justice and death penalty that make me feel extremely uncomfortable. Maybe I'm being paranoid, but it feels like he's equating these things with you. We both stare at the carpet. An awkward silence takes over the room.

Well, George says eventually. I'd better get going. Molly's making dinner and I don't want to be late.

I show him to the door. Though George's visit should have brought me some comfort, it's made me feel worse.

Hermine.
December 1942. Majdanek.

It's my day off. Thoughts of food consume me. I can't think about anything else. The food here is horrible; the diet is heavy on turnip and potatoes and what meat we do get is stringy and tough. I lie on my bed, salivating at memories of Mutti's goulash. Ehrich comes into the room and I tell her about all of the food that I crave.

You need a good German meal, she says. I have a plan. At the first possible opportunity, let's go to the *Deutsches Haus*.

The *Deutsches Haus* is a restaurant, café and club on Krakauer Straße, a favourite venue of the Majdanek guards. On the ground floor there is a dance hall, which the *Aufseherinnen* can go to unaccompanied; however, Ehrich suggests that we go with some SS guards to gain access to the first-floor club.

It's much nicer upstairs, she says. I'll ask Hackmann. Who shall we ask to come with us?

Ehrich suggests Lächert, Ernst and Pfannstiel because they're the most fun, but not Wöllert; she finds her annoying. Ehrich looks at me wryly when I request that Johann Fischer is among the men.

Fischer, eh? she teases. Well, I suppose you Austrians must stick together.

Fischer is from Baden bei Wien, twenty miles south of Vienna. He's tall, well-built and nice looking, with dark hair and a very nice smile.

Later that evening, a prisoner-messenger comes to our room with a package for me containing the mittens that I asked Mutti for when I first arrived. They're lined with soft rabbit fur; she must have paid a lot for them. Enclosed is a letter full of Christmas greetings and news from Nußdorf. I lie on my bed and read it multiple times, wishing that I could go home even just for one week, but that will not happen; we are far too busy here. Outside, the wind howls around the block, making the windows chatter like teeth. I'm so glad to be inside, warmed by the stove.

Russell.
September 1964. Maspeth.

You're out at work when I find it, hidden away at the back of your drawer. I feel a wave of terror, then anger, and wonder again if I'd made a terrible mistake.

You've taken a job cleaning the local shopping mart on a Sunday. Though it's much lower paid than your job at the mill, it's not such bad work. You're in there alone, so there's no one to bother you. While you are out, I spend the morning doing chores: walking the dog, tidying the kitchen, and then heading upstairs to sort through the pile of ironed clothing that you've left on the bed. I put away my shirts and pants, hang up your skirt and fold your sweaters neatly onto the shelf. Then I sort through the underwear, first mine and then yours. Your drawer is next to mine. When I go to open it, it jams; something's preventing it from moving forwards. I don't want to force it, so I go back downstairs and fetch a kitchen knife to prise at the blockage.

After some gentle manoeuvring, I manage to get the drawer to budge. When I discover the cause of the problem, I'm delighted; it's the turquoise jewellery box that I gave you on the day of your citizenship, your engraved pendant. My skin tingles as I remember your tears of happiness and the look on your face when I gave it to you. Carefully, I take the drawer out of its casters so that I can straighten out all the clothing I've dislodged. As I empty the drawer onto the bed, two more boxes fall out, one black and one navy. I look at them, wondering what's inside. I don't want to pry; however, curiosity gets the better of me. I pick up the navy box first and open the lid. Inside is the brooch that your friend gave you during the war. It conjures up another nice memory of you on Coney Island, cotton candy twirling in your hand. I sigh contentedly as I put the first box down and pick up the second one. This box is longer and flatter. My fingers find the catch and gently open the lid. Inside, a cross-shaped medal rests on purple silk, attached to a ribbon of black, white and red. I've not seen this before. I lift the medal out carefully and then turn it over. My stomach shrinks into a tiny, tight ball. In the centre of the medal is a small, raised swastika. I put the medal down on the bed, unable to hold it, but then brace myself to look at it again. The blood drains from my head. I sit down on the bed heavily, feeling faint. You told me you were not a Nazi, and I believed you, so why have you got this Nazi medal? Why did you lie to me? I married you in good faith. I brought you to America. I've given you a nice house, a dog I never wanted, a comfortable life. I've defended you against the accusations of other people. Who are you? What other remnants have you hidden of your secret past?

I pull out all the other drawers in a frenzy, emptying the contents onto the floor, searching desperately for any more clues. I take out your suitcase and shake it to see if it rattles, prying at the stitching, looking for a hidden compartment, but there is none there to find. I search through your pockets and rifle through your bag, but all I can find are pencil stubs, a lipstick, a packet of gum. These remnants of your life all look so normal, so ordinary. I look at the medal again and feel a surge of anger. Fists balled, I pound at the bed clothes, pouring out rage. I've defended you at work and in our community, at great personal loss. Nobody speaks to me anymore other than George, and even he feels distant, like a satellite tracking ever further away. You've made a complete fool of me. Exhausted, I kick at your clothing and sit down on the floor.

When you come home from work, I'm waiting for you at the

kitchen table, holding the box on my lap. Mitzi runs out to meet you, but I do not move. You call for me when you come in the door, but I say nothing. When you walk into the kitchen, I stare at the table. Normally, I would get up to greet you, but today I stay in my seat.

What's wrong? you ask, worried.

I take the box out from under the table and place it in front of me.

I found this in your drawer, Hermine. Why have you got this horrible thing?

Your voice quivers with panic.

It's my war medal, Russ. I got it for service to my country.

It's got a swastika on it, Hermine. It's a fucking Nazi medal.

It's the first time I've ever sworn at you. I don't normally swear, but the words tumble out as my voice gets louder and louder until I am shouting.

You told me you weren't a Nazi, Hermine, so what is this thing? Why have you got it?

You start to cry and then choke out words through your tears.

It's my war medal, Russ. I got it for service to my country, for doing my job.

My voice bristles with anger.

Do you know what I think of when I see this? I think of soldiers dying. I think of D-Day. I think of Hitler, yes, Hitler. And now, because I know that you worked in the camps, I think of the gas chambers. That's what I think of when I look at this medal. How am I meant to believe you and defend you when I find this? Who the hell are you? What made the Nazis give this to you?

I'm not a Nazi! you shout and you snatch the medal out of my hand. I've already explained all of this to you.

It's the first time you've ever shouted at me. I look at you, my wife and yet a complete stranger. Who is it that I'm married to?

That was the symbol of my country back then! you say

angrily. It means something different now, but not when I got it. Americans were given medals too. Your medals must have something on them. What is it? An eagle? A president's head? This was given to me as a reward for following orders, working hard and doing my duty. I was proud to get it, just like everyone is proud to be given a medal by their country. You want to know why I hid it? Because we lost the war, which makes everything our side ever did wrong in your eyes.

A lot of the things your country did *were* wrong.

You slump down on the linoleum, shaking with tears.

You're like everyone else, blaming everything Germany did on me.

That's not what I'm doing, I say defensively. I just don't know why you've got this…this thing.

Do you want to know why I kept it, Russell? Because it's the only time in my life that I've ever been given anything for good work. Do you think that when I worked as a maid or in a factory that anybody was ever kind enough to say well done? Do you think when I clean the shop here, I get a thank you? I can't help that I was born Austrian, not American, or British or French. How easy it is for you to judge me. Your history is different to mine.

You get up off the floor and slam the medal into the trash can.

There, you say. It's gone. It's worth nothing, like all of my past.

I go to get up but feel immediately dizzy, so I sit down on the floor next to you. Why is this happening to me? I've been a good citizen. I've lived a good life. You've turned my whole world upside down. My body fills with waves of emotion: anger, despair, self-pity, regret. I don't sleep properly. I worry about intruders. People at work won't talk to me anymore. I worry endlessly about money; how we'll manage to pay the mortgage as well as a lawyer. I'm living in an ongoing nightmare, and now I'm worrying about who you really are. I've loved you from the moment I met you, but this is tearing me apart. Why can't I just believe you when you say all you were doing was following orders? What if it was more than obedience? What if those awful people had your support? I try not to let myself think about it because it makes me feel sick. Tears prick my eyes and my shoulders start to heave. Would I have chosen you if I knew who you really were? You put your arm round me.

I'm sorry, Russell, you say. I know this is hard for you, but I cannot be made to feel ashamed of everything my country did. It's not fair. I'm not responsible for everything that happened. I thought you of all people understood that, but now it feels like even you are turning against me. I'm genuinely sorry for all the trouble I've caused you, but I'm a good person. Please don't think the worst about me. I was in the wrong place at the wrong time. It was only six years of my life. All the rest of my life, I've been kind. If I could erase those years, I would, but I can't. I can't stay here with you if you're going to doubt me.

Your arm clasps round my shoulders, supporting me as I slump on the floor.

Part of me wants you to disappear, but I also can't bear the thought of you leaving. You're all that I have now; everyone else has gone. Without you, I have nothing.

I'm trying hard not to doubt you, I say quietly. Finding that medal shook me a lot. I don't know what's real and what's not real anymore. I feel like I don't know who you are anymore. I worry that you married me to get away from your past. I'm completely lost. I don't even know who I am anymore.

Hopelessness swims in the blue of your eyes.

I married you because I love you, Russ, you say quietly. Look at me. There's nothing different about me. I am still me.

Hermine.
January 1943. Lublin.

Ehrich's asked Hackmann to book a room at the *Deutsches Haus* this evening to celebrate my promotion. I've been made *Rapportführerin*, which means that I'm now second in command of all the female prisoners. As Report Leader, my job is to keep a record of the prisoners, so we know where they're all working, who is sick, who has died. The promotion's not an enormous surprise, but it's pleasing, nonetheless. The job is very busy. There are currently 3,923 female prisoners, though the numbers change daily due to new arrivals and deaths.

I choose a blue floral dress with a white collar, stockings, and some low brown heels, all of which I found in the stores. Ehrich's wearing a maroon dress with a pink collar and cuffs. She's had her hair done into soft waves. We wait at the camp gate. The men stand on one side, the women on the other, stamping our feet to try to keep warm. I'm wearing my mittens, which helps with the cold. Stars blink down at us from the black sky. The guardhouse floodlight sweeps over frosted ground with a bright yellow beam. A horse-drawn carriage pulls up; the horses' breath turns to crystals as they stomp on the hoar. It's a beautiful scene, as if in a fairy tale.

Ladies, says Hackmann. Your carriage awaits.

We climb in and the men wait for the second carriage. The journey into Lublin takes fifteen minutes; the carriage buzzes with the excitement of the evening ahead.

Have you ever seen a man more handsome than Kurtz? asks Lächert. He is magnificent!

It's true that Kurtz is attractive. He's tall with dark hair, blue eyes and sharp cheekbones, but I find him too quiet. I prefer

Johann, whose conversation is easy.

As we pass through Lublin, the horses' feet clop against the cobbles until we pull up in front of a creamy white façade. The entrance to the Deutsche Haus is grand, an enormous porch supported by four thick-waisted pillars framing an oversized wooden door. Inside, an attendant leads us up a huge wooden staircase to a private club room on the first floor. The men arrive shortly afterwards, looking extremely handsome in their uniforms.

In the club room, a table is covered with a fine white cloth, porcelain plates, silverware, and crystal glasses engraved with the SS insignia. The staff spread out a feast, plates piled high with roasted pork hock, Schnitzel and Bratwurst, huge bowls of braised cabbage, carrots and fried onions, Spätzle, Bratkartoffeln, rye bread and butter. I'm sitting between Johann and Kurtz. Hackmann places himself between Ehrich and Lächert, opposite me. The wine starts to flow and before long, the whole room fills with conversation and laughter. The men bore us by talking about war until we plead with them to change the subject. Johann keeps filling up my glass and I am quite tipsy by the time the dessert arrives, an enormous Black Forest cake, apple strudel and Quarkkäulchen, sprinkled with sugar and cinnamon. By now, Wallisch and Hackmann are singing and Ehrich has the blush of too much red wine. Wallisch suggests that we go downstairs and Johann leans towards me and asks me to dance.

The dance hall is in a high-ceilinged room with shiny wooden floorboards and deep red velvet curtains that hang ceiling to floor. At the far end, a band plays on top of a platform. Johann grabs my hand and pulls me towards him. His breath smells of garlic and wine.

You're beautiful, Braunsteiner, he whispers. I want to kiss you. Later, you should come back to my room.

By the time we get back to the camp, it is past 2am. I hang back with Johann, so the others don't see us going into his barrack. Tomorrow is Sunday and I'm not on duty; it doesn't really matter if we don't get much sleep.

Russell.

October 1964. Maspeth.

The Colt 45 is loaded. I've put it in the side drawer next to the bed, along with spare ammunition. It slots in neatly, next to my Bible. I wonder what the good Lord would think of that. I've never been a gun man; even during war time, I just fixed up airplanes and jeeps. I cannot imagine shooting a man, but things have got so bad lately that I figure I need to be able to defend us in case of intruders. We've had dog shit spread all over our front steps. The front door keeps getting pelted with eggs and some jackass keeps painting a swastika on the garage. As quickly as I clean it off, it reappears. The whole thing's made me extremely jumpy, and you won't go out by yourself anymore. You'll only walk Mitzi if I come along too. You tell me the gun makes you feel much safer, but I'm worried that if someone breaks in, I will freeze, unable to shoot. I'm looking at the gun inside the drawer when I hear a knock downstairs at the front door. Adrenaline surges through my veins. I grab the gun and rush down the stairs. A figure is standing behind the glass in the door.

Who's that? I call out. What do you want?

My name's Jimmy Vitale. Can I talk to you for a moment, Mr Ryan? I'm friendly, I promise. I live a few houses down. I wanted to talk to you about the neighbourhood watch, about keeping your property safe, about keeping the whole street safe. Would you open the door?

Hang on a minute, I say.

I go to the sitting room and hide the gun under a cushion.

Vitale is slight and Mediterranean looking. He's wearing

slacks and a brown plaid shirt. He smiles at me kindly and holds out his hand. I shake it and then he looks down at his feet. The floor underneath him is spattered with eggshells. Vitale may look Italian, but when he starts talking, his accent's pure Queens.

This is no good, Mr Ryan, he says, pointing at the eggshells.

I'm sorry, I say. The newspaper articles are full of lies, but that doesn't help us much once they've been published.

I take the newspapers with a huge pinch of salt, he replies. To my mind, most newsmen are assholes. Look, Mr Ryan, I'm not here about that. All I want to do here is keep this street safe. There are lots of families living here and we've all got kids, I've got four of them myself, and we've also got cars that we don't want to be damaged. So, a few of us got together to keep a look out for each other in the neighbourhood.

He takes a step back and kicks away eggshells.

I'm sorry for what's happening to you, Mr Ryan. Really, I am. We're going to keep an eye out for the thugs that do this.

Thank you, Mr Vitale. That's very kind.

No problems, Mr Ryan. If we see anything, we'll call the police. You do the same.

He holds his hand out again and I take it and pump it up and down. Back inside, you ask me who was at the door. When I tell you, your shoulders relax. You've been holding yourself tight for more than a month now. Your muscles have calcified round your body in self-protection, like armour.

Come on, I say. We've all been stuck in the house far too long. Let's take Mitzi out and get some fresh air. It'll do us both good.

After some resistance, you take out your coat, wrap your head in a scarf and put on some sunglasses.

You look like a movie star, I say, trying to cheer you up. Or Jackie Kennedy.

Don't be silly, Russ! I just don't want to be recognised.

I get Mitzi out of the kitchen and attach her to the leash. She bounces around excitedly, desperate to get out. Outside, I hold your hand as we walk. When people approach, you look down, but no one bats an eyelid and we reach the park unnoticed. Trees frame the park with Fall colours: russets, umbers and yellows. Wind rustles the leaves. We go to our usual spot, and Mitzi runs about while we sit down and watch her. For the first time since the article came out, I feel a strange sort of peace.

After a while, you say, It was nice of that man to come by the house. At least there are some people here who are still on my side. Everyone else here seems to side with the Jews. Nobody believes me once they start to talk.

I'm on your side, Hermine, I say.

Are you really, Russell? I'm never quite sure if you are.

That's not fair, honey, I say. You know that I'm on your side.

You sit quietly for a minute and then say, I'm so sorry, Russell, that this is happening to us. I'm so sorry for bringing this upon you.

I lie back on the grass and look up at the sky. Clouds move like jellyfish through the pale blue. This past month, we've talked things over and over. You've explained what happened carefully and I've listened to everything you've said. You've told me what went on in the camps and I know that what happened there is not your fault. You were young and impressionable, your head was filled with propaganda and poison, you thought you were doing the right thing. It's unfair to hold you responsible for the crimes of a nation. Of all the people, why did they have to come after you? I roll over towards you and take hold of your shoulders.

I know you're a good person, honey, I say. Don't worry about me. You've already got enough to worry about. When we married, I promised I'd take care of you, and I take that vow seriously. That's what I'll do.

Hermine.
March 1943. Majdanek.

This is the sickest I've ever been. I ache all over my body. It feels as if someone is reaching down inside me and twisting my guts. The doctor gives me medicine to combat the typhus and slowly, slowly my fever comes down. Once I am well enough to take in my surroundings, I realise that I'm in a room by myself. The wallpaper has small orange flowers on it and the bed sheets are freshly laundered and crisp. The nurses leave my windows open to let in the air; the breeze carries in the soft smell of spring from the tree-lined streets outside the hospital. I hear the distinctive warbling of a nightingale. The sound is better than medicine. My heart lifts to hear something so pure and so different from the sounds of the camp. The wildlife at Majdanek consists of insects, rats and carrion birds; the only sounds their scuttling, squeaking and cawing. The thought of going back to Majdanek utterly depresses me. I pretend to feel unwell for several more days to avoid returning to work.

When I get back, I find that in my absence, the *Aufseherinnen* have been moved from the Old Airfield into the camp. Our new accommodation is barrack thirty-eight, an L–shaped building made of dark stained wood positioned next to the SS men's barracks, so I'm now right next to Johann, which makes my nightly visits much easier. Unlike the men, who share seven to a room unless they are officers, in the new barrack the *Aufseherinnen* each get our own room. This has caused griping among the male guards, who don't see why women should get better treatment. I'm just thankful that Johann is an officer and has his own room.

Our barrack is heated with brand new stoves, which is welcome as there is still snow on the ground. Ehrich tells me that in my three weeks away, I missed some early issues with the plumbing; the water kept backing up in the toilets and sinks. Due to this, and the fact that sickness is rife, Hackmann finally gave in to Ehrich's request that our washing be sent to a laundry in Lublin, so at last there is an end to us having to wash our own clothes. This is the biggest single improvement in my life this year.

The camp is extremely crowded now. Female prisoner numbers are over 4,000, meaning we have more than 260 women each to guard. To cope with all these women, a new section has been set up in Field V, and we're now expected to work there as well as on work details. Our workload is impossible. The overcrowding is causing significant issues. The sanitation in the women's camp is terrible; it's making a very large number of prisoners sick. There's not enough food to feed all the prisoners and fights break out frequently among them for food. So many prisoners have diarrhea now that they cannot keep up with the washing, which forces them to remain in soiled clothing. The stench is revolting. I feel permanently sick.

Our biggest problem is how to accommodate all these prisoners. Each prisoner barrack contains between 500 and 800 women; they sleep on bunks stacked three high. Each bunk houses three, sometimes four women, and even though they are emaciated, the beds cannot always take the combined weight. When the top section fails, it drops onto the second, which often causes the whole structure to collapse. Last week, this happened twice. Five women died and four were so seriously injured that they had to be sent straight to the gas chamber. Lächert screamed at the women not to share so many on a bunk.

It's simple physics! she shouted. There are too many of you on the beds. Some of you will have to sleep on the floor.

The floor is piled thick with mud, shit and piss. Of course, they don't want to sleep there. When I think back to Ravensbrück, it feels like a dream. With conditions like these, it's no wonder that typhus spreads so quickly.

Russell.

March 1965. Maspeth.

I went into the office this morning on a Sunday to get a few things done with no one else there. That way, I avoid all the whispering. This whole thing has made my life impossible. When I come home, you're still out at your cleaning job. I'm glad that you're working. It gets you out of the house and I think that is good for you. Mitzi runs up to me at the front door, jumping about, excited to see me. Her exuberance annoys me. I push her away, sit down on the sofa and turn on the TV. Mitzi jumps up on the seat next to me. She's not allowed on the furniture, but I know that you let her do it when I'm not here. It irritates me how you coddle this dog, letting her break all the rules. I hate the way you feed her from the table and let her jump up onto our bed. The whole thing's intolerable. I shove the dog off the sofa onto the floor. She yelps in surprise and then I feel bad. What's wrong with me? Everything's getting to me. My patience is frayed.

The past few months have gotten harder and harder. More articles have appeared in the newspapers, which has made things even worse. Nobody knows what to say to me. The neighbours are avoiding us; they just stay away. The worst thing is that George has stopped calling. That's the thing that hurts most of all. We've been best friends ever since elementary school. I thought our friendship was unconditional, but I guess I was wrong. I could really do with someone to talk to. I wish that my mother was still alive.

The news starts on the TV. It's a report about a group of young people who sat down on the floor in the middle of the White

House and refused to leave until they met President Johnson, demanding to talk to him about civil rights. It took seven hours to remove them. A sit-in they're calling it. Normally, this would interest me, but I don't feel like watching it. I turn off the set. My body's a lead weight. I struggle to move my arms up from my lap. Mitzi looks up at me from the floor with quizzical eyes, wondering if I'm still in a bad mood. I wish I could speak to someone about what's happening to us. How could George abandon me like this? Where the hell is his loyalty? If this happened to him, I'd be there by his side.

I pick up an old copy of the *Reader's Digest* that you've left on the table and read the first paragraph of a story over and over, but can't take it in. Wearily, I put it back down and go to pick up my trombone, but it doesn't feel right. Since Joe stopped coming over, it just serves to remind me of his absence. I hold onto it forlornly, unable to play, and then get up and go out into the back yard. Mitzi follows me, wagging her tail. The loyalty of dogs. She's already forgotten that I pushed her away.

The garden's coming into Spring. The tiniest of buds have appeared on the tree. I walk over to it and lean my hand against its trunk, solid and firm, and feel completely exhausted. The grass round the tree has started to shoot up. I ought to cut it. I sit down on the grass and lean my back against the tree. It's reassuringly solid. The earth below me feels cool and firm. Above me, a bird feeder sways in the branches. Usually, you fill it, but you must have forgotten with all that's going on. I stare at it hanging there, empty and pathetic, completely useless. Just how I feel. Mitzi lies down next to me and rests her head on my shoe. I put my hand on her head and she curls herself into me.

I'm sorry Mitzi, I say. I shouldn't have been so mean to you earlier. I'm just feeling blue. Come on, girl, I'll take you out for a walk. It might snap me out of this funk.

Mitzi follows me back into the house. I clip on her leash and take her into the street. As soon as we're walking, my mood starts to lift; the self-pity evaporates with each further step. To Mitzi's delight, I keep walking and walking. The walk is doing me good, so we keep going, heading north through Elmhurst into Jackson Heights. The sky above fills with the rumble of airplanes flying low as they come into La Guardia. I look up and wonder where all the people on them have come from. Are they all leading happy lives?

I realise that my ramblings have taken us all the way to St Michael's Cemetery. I haven't been up this way in a long time. I lead Mitzi in to have a look around. Rows of gravestones line the grassed areas. I hold the dog close to me as we walk past the graves, stopping to look at one of them. On it is engraved the name Hannah Brown, underneath the dates 1900-1925. The gravestone next to it is engraved with William Brown 1896-1945. Such short lives. Beyond these two graves is another smaller one, chiselled with Maisie Brown 1925. I guess that Hannah most likely died in childbirth. I wonder whether William and Hannah were happy. As I'm thinking about this, I hear a cough behind me and turn around.

Hello Russell, a man says. I thought it was you.

It takes me a moment to recognise Jerry Moretti, my fellow engineer during the Korean War.

Hi Jerry, I say. Sorry, I didn't recognise you at first. I wasn't expecting to see you here.

I was going to say the same thing about you. What are you doing up this way?

Oh, I'm just out for a walk with the dog.

Did you walk all the way here from Maspeth?

Yes, I did. I needed a long walk. What about you?

Jerry's expression is pained.

I came here to see Brenda, my wife.

He stands there in silence while I process this comment.

Do you mean..?

She died early this year.

Oh, Jerry, I'm so sorry for your loss.

She was sick for a long time, he replies. Cancer. The last time I saw you on Memorial Day, I didn't want to tell you how ill she was. It didn't seem the right time or place. Not in front of your friends. By then, she was very unwell. It was a bit of a miracle that she survived as long as she did. I buried her in January this year.

I'm so sorry, Jerry. Are you doing OK?

Jerry's eyes well with tears. He takes a cigarette packet out of his pocket, removes one, lights it and takes a long drag.

It's been very difficult, Russell, he says. She was the love of my life.

I put my hand on his shoulder, not knowing what to say.

I'm sorry, he says in between puffs. I still get upset.

That's OK. I can't imagine how hard that would be.

I meant to get in touch with you. I kept your phone number. I just... well, life's been quite hard, and I never really found the right time.

Don't worry about that at all, I say. By the sounds of things, you've had a hell of a year. Would you like to go get a coffee? I could sure do with a cup of Joe.

Yes please, Russell, he replies. That would be really nice. I'm in need of the company. I've felt so alone. There's a Horn and Hardart not too far from here. How about that?

Sure thing, I say. Let's go.

I follow Jerry out of the cemetery. On the way to the coffee shop, he tells me about his wife's illness and decline. Her death weighs on him heavily. Though I try to cheer him up, he can't see a future without her. When we reach the coffee shop, Jerry takes a seat. I tie Mitzi's leash to my chair and then go to the service counter, push coins into the machine and pour us two cups of coffee.

I'm glad I bumped into you, Russell, Jerry says. It's really helped me to talk about Brenda. Thanks for listening. I haven't spoken to anyone properly in a long time.

I'm glad it's helped, I say. I really am so sorry for your loss.

What about you? he asks politely. I've been so busy telling you about me. You haven't told me anything.

I stare at some crumbs on the table and wipe them off with my sleeve. Jerry's loss puts my situation into perspective.

I've had a difficult year too, I say, eyes on the table. Not as bad as you, I'm sure. I suppose you've read about it in the papers.

I look up at him. He's looking confused. He clearly has no idea what I'm talking about.

What with everything going on, I've hardly picked up a paper in the past year, Jerry says. What's happened?

I lean forward and rest my chin in my hands.

You must be the only person in New York that doesn't know, I say. I don't really know where to start.

I explain the journalist's visit and all the consequences that it's caused. When I finish, I look at Jerry for his reaction. He's staring back at me, wide-eyed as a bug.

That's a big thing to happen, Russell, he says. You must have been shocked to find all of that out.

The whole thing's been terrible, I say.

What are you going to do? he asks, full of concern.

I'm going to fight for her, Jerry, I say.

When Jerry replies, he sounds surprised.

But what if the stories are true?

Both his tone and the question annoy me profoundly, unleashing a wave of defensiveness so powerful that, in that one moment, all of the doubts that I've had disappear. The knowledge that I'll stay with you sets firm within me, like hardened cement. Jerry might not understand it. Perhaps nobody else will ever understand it, but I'm choosing to stay.

I'm Catholic, I say coldly. We do not divorce. Besides, nothing my wife did during the war was her fault. She didn't get to choose where she worked. Nothing that happened was down to her; she was in the wrong place at the wrong time. That's the fact of the matter. She's a good woman and I love her.

He looks at me carefully, choosing his words.

Love is a powerful thing, he says. I hope it works out for you.

I take a last sip of coffee and stand up to leave.

Hermine.
April 1943. Miesbach.

I contract typhus again. Because it is less than a month since my last bout, the doctor instructs me that as soon as I can travel, I will be sent away to recuperate in Stadelberghaus, a rest home in Miesbach, a small Bavarian town thirty miles southeast of Munich. Ehrich will come too because she's also been sick. Florstedt signs us both off work for a month. I never thought I'd be so pleased to be unwell; it's such a relief to be back in humanity.

The rest house is owned by Kurt and Petra, a friendly couple, who have the broad earthy look of the country. Both husband and wife are quick to smile. Petra is an amazing cook.

You girls are far too thin, she says. What on earth do they feed you at that camp? I'm going to put some meat back on your bones.

She makes us Schweinsbraten and homemade bread rolls and plies us with real coffee. All the while, we moan about the camp food. I ask Petra how she gets such good coffee and meat during wartime. She smiles at me mischievously and says not to ask about the coffee. That is her secret, but she's more forthcoming about the meat; they are allocated extra rations for recuperating guards and they also keep pigs.

So, you see, she says merrily. You girls are helping us just as much as we're helping you. You're an important part of the war effort. My job here is to build you back up.

My room overlooks an open green field through two large windows. Early each morning, a brown and white speckled bird with glossy black wings lands on my windowsill. It's larger than a blackbird and almost identical in shape to a woodpecker, but with a wider beak. I watch it preening itself in delight. I mention the bird at breakfast, but Ehrich is not interested. However, Petra overhears.

That's a *Tannenhäher*, she says. If you like birds, I will take you on a walk to look at them when you are stronger. There are lots of birds here. I'll organise a boat trip round Schliersee. There's an island in the middle of the lake which is perfect for picnicking. You girls will love it.

Picnicking by a lake makes me think of Dieter, which tugs at my heart. Even though I'm seeing Johann, Dieter sometimes surfaces in my mind. I haven't told anyone about him, not even Ehrich, though she has confided in me that she has been sleeping with Florstedt.

But Florstedt's married! I say, unable to disguise my disgust.

The thought of Florstedt pumping away at her with his blotchy red skin is quite revolting.

Oh Hermine, don't be so naïve, Ehrich says. All the married men at the camp have girlfriends and he gives me such beautiful things: pearls, silver earrings.

She unbuttons her blouse to reveal a fine string of pearls.

The only man who has ever given me jewellery was Dieter. I think about the brooch and feel a pang of something between anger and regret.

What about Johann? she asks. He's not married. Everyone knows that you're in his bedroom every night. You better be careful that you don't get pregnant.

I feel myself blush.

I *am* being careful, Else, I say. I like Johann a lot, but I don't want to marry him. I know what strong feelings are and my heart is not there.

Russell.

September 1967. Maspeth.

I'm waiting at the counter, when I hear his voice next to me, asking politely for a pound of hamburger.

I'll be right with you, Mr Allen, the butcher replies. I just need to finish serving this customer. I won't be a minute.

We stand there in silence, side by side. The air hangs between us, weighed down by the absence of words. The butcher hands me my package.

There you go, Mr Ryan, he says. That's seventy-eight cents.

I reach into my pocket and pass him the coins. As I turn to leave, I catch George's eye and he nods.

Russell.

George.

I take a deep breath and walk out the door. I manage to make it just past the window before I lean heavily against the wall, legs shaking like jello, breath fluttering like the wings of a moth. A young boy who's passing stops to help me, concerned.

Are you OK, sir?

I'm fine, son. I just feel a little weak and need to catch my breath. You don't need to stop.

The boy looks at me quizzically and I wave him away. The last thing I want is extra attention. There's a bench a little further up the sidewalk. I make for it slowly and sit myself down. I glance back along the street and see George coming out of the butchers. He looks in my direction and then turns to walk the other way. I know that he's choosing the long way home, so he doesn't have to come near me. The street pulses before me and my head starts to spin. George's desertion is the worst thing that's happened to me, worse than having to defend you in public, worse than the trash that gets thrown at our door, worse than the names we get called in the street. It's like the dull ache of a splinter, a constant pain in the background, always there, just under the skin. I'm absorbed in this feeling when I feel a hand on my shoulder. I hear George's voice and my heart pulses wildly inside my chest. He must have turned around and come back this way.

Russell, he says. May I sit down here next to you?

I go to reply, but I can't find the words. I start to cry. Embarrassed, I wipe the tears away with the sleeve of my jacket and indicate for George to take a seat. He sits down and both of us look forward, unable to look each other in the eye.

I'm sorry, Russ, he says. I wasn't expecting to see you. I didn't know what to say to you back there. I'm sorry. I should have been in touch.

Tears roll down my cheeks. I cannot control it. They pour right out of me, there on the street.

I needed you, George, I say. But you were not there. Of all people, I thought I would have had your support.

He hands me a handkerchief and I take some deep breaths.

I don't know what to say, Russ. I wanted to help you, but I didn't know how. The whole thing's been very hard to comprehend.

You should have asked me about it, I say. Because I can explain it. I know the truth. Just because you read things in the papers doesn't mean that they're true. You should have had some faith in me.

I've tried, Russ. Believe me, I've tried.

It doesn't feel like you tried very hard. Why didn't you come and talk to me about it? Hermine's being scapegoated. It's not her fault that she was living in Germany then. She just had the bad luck to end up working in a camp. And now, the Jews are trying to pin everything on her; she's caught in their trap.

George takes a sharp breath.

You shouldn't talk about the Jews like that, he says. Not after everything that happened to them.

I feel as sympathetic as the next person to the Jews, George. I'm just telling you the truth. What's happening to her is a witch hunt. She worked in those places. That's what it was for her: work. She didn't invent those places. She's not responsible for Germany's crimes.

I get that, George says.

Do you really? I reply. It doesn't feel to me like you do. None of us can possibly judge her for what happened. I've thought about it a lot. If we'd been there in her place, we'd have done the same thing. If you'd been there, or I'd been there, or Molly had been there, we would all have complied.

I don't know about that, says George. I think Molly would have refused.

Good God, George! It's easy to say that from the comfort of being here now. Can't you see that? How can you possibly know what she would or wouldn't do in a position where she's frightened and she's told that the people in front of her are the enemy? None of us have ever been put in that kind of situation. None of us have been tested in that way.

I hear you, Russ, but I can't agree with you. We all make our choices, however hard they may be, and we bear responsibility for those choices. I know for sure that Molly would have said no. I'm pretty sure that I'd have said no too.

My head boils with anger. How can George be so judgmental? So pompous and self-righteous? Where did he get his over-inflated sense of self-worth?

Just listen to yourself, George! Are you seriously telling me that you and Molly would have stood up to Hitler? That's what you really think, is it? You'd have stood up to him even though it would have got you both shot? And your kids shot too? Where the hell is your empathy? If not for Hermine, at least some for me. Think about it properly, George. Imagine what it was like for her. Put yourself in her shoes. Germany was being run by the Nazis. What choices do you think she really had, George? She did what she was told to do, just the same as our boys are doing now in Vietnam. I know you don't think it's fair when *they* come home and get criticized. We used to talk about that lots. How is it any different for Hermine? She was loyal to her country, same way our boys are now, same as Molly would be if she was put in the same situation. It's grotesquely unfair. I can't believe that you can't see that.

I lean back heavily. The slats of the bench push into my back through my jacket, their ridges dig into my skin. George sits there quietly, mulling my words.

I don't know, Russ. It's all very hard.

Yes, it is hard, George. That's exactly the point. It's not straightforward. That's what happens during a war. It's easy to judge when you're on the side that won. What if we'd lost? It's not like our forces didn't kill innocent civilians. It's not like they're not doing that now!

George remains silent, so I continue.

When I married Hermine, I took a vow: for better or worse. That was my promise. Right now, it feels like the worst it could possibly get, but I understand the position she was in back then. She's my wife, George, and she's a good person. I promised I'd stand by her, and God help me, that's what I'm gonna do.

George shifts in the seat, and then he stands up.

You're a good man, Russ, he says. You've always been a good man. You've always been loyal. It's an admirable thing. I've got to go now. Molly's waiting at home. You call me if it all gets too tough.

George walks away down the street and I watch him go. I wish I had told him what I am thinking: it's already too tough.

Hermine.

May 1943. Majdanek.

I've been back from Miesbach for less than two weeks and already I'm bedbound, this time with diarrhea. Yesterday, it was so bad that I had to sit in the washrooms all day, next to the toilet as the cramps twisted and squeezed at my guts. I lie on my bed, head pounding, covered in sweat, and look out of the window. My barrack is right at the edge of the camp. I can see prisoners toiling up and down between the perimeter wires, picking the grass. Hour after hour, they stoop and they pick. How is it they're well and I'm not?

Johann's face appears at my window.

Are you alright? he says, smiling at me through the glass.

I don't want him to see me looking like this, so I wave him away. He looks concerned but obeys my command. Later, Ehrich comes by, bringing some bread.

Try to eat something, she says. It will make you feel better.

Thank you, Else, I say. Could you leave it there on the table at the end of my bed? I can't eat anything now, but I'll try later.

She straightens the bed sheets and wipes at my forehead with a damp cloth.

You've had a bad run, she says. First typhus, then this.

It's because of the prisoners, I say. They have such poor hygiene. I cannot go near them without becoming sick.

I know, she replies. The overcrowding here makes it impossible. We need to send more of them to the gas chambers.

Ehrich leaves and I chew over her words, feeling quite drained. It doesn't matter how many prisoners we gas, more

201

just keep on coming. I long for my mother. What I would give to be back at home in her care. This place is horrible; it's all prisoners, disease and death.

Russell.

March 1971. Maspeth.

For God's sake! I don't believe it! I shout at the TV.

Mitzi comes scuttling into the room. You call out from the kitchen.

What's going on? Are you OK?

I'm watching the news, I call back. It's the My Lai trial verdict. They've convicted Lieutenant Calley and given him life.

You enter the room and look at the TV.

They've made him the fall guy, I say. They're sacrificing him so his superiors can go free. It's a disgrace. It's exactly the same as what's happening to you.

The TV footage turns to outside the courtroom. Kids and hippies are chanting and holding up banners painted with slogans: *End the War! Social crisis at home! Bring the troops home!*

Conscientious objectors, I say. None of them know what it's like to fight for their country, what it's like to put your life on the line. They have no idea of the sacrifices we made, and they get angry with our boys now when they come home from war. I cannot stomach it. It really disgusts me.

I switch the television off. You come and sit next to me. Your presence is soothing, like warm milk.

There's plenty of trouble right here in America, you say. Maybe that's why people still want to chase after me. It's a distraction from what this country is doing.

Should we all refuse to go to war in case sometime in the future the whole thing gets seen in a different light? I ask. All we seem to do now is prosecute and blame. Our country should be thanking Calley for his work and leaving him in peace. If they're going to prosecute anyone, it should be the people who make the policies instead of those who are made to carry them out.

Hermine.

June 1943. Majdanek.

At last, I manage to eat without cramps. Both Johann and Ehrich have been bringing me food: hot toast and soup, mashed turnip and carrot, even some fruit.

Take your time, says Ehrich. Build yourself up.

I stay in bed, finding any excuse I can to stay in my room. When I close my eyes, I see Miesbach, the fields and the lake. I imagine Petra's home cooking and the coffee, oh, the coffee, how much I'd give to have just one cup of her coffee instead of the slosh we get here. Memories of Miesbach meld into memories of home. I see Mutti standing over the stove, stirring the pot. I yearn for her and long for my sister, for Nußdorf, Vienna, our apartment, the brook. I think about Vati and my heart fills with sadness. Misery wraps me in a tight cloak.

That evening, I take out some paper and write a long letter to Mutti. I leave out the fact that I've been unwell because it would just make her worried. Instead, I keep the tone light, which helps to bolster my spirits. I write cheerfully about Johann and the *Deutsches Haus*. As I finish the letter, tears prick my eyes. I tell her how much I love her and how dearly I would love to come home. But for that, I'll just have to wait. Things are so busy here. It's inconceivable now that I'll be given a break. As I fold the letter into an envelope, Johann appears again at the window, holding a glass.

I've got something for you, he says. Fresh lemonade!

When I open the window, dry Majdanek heat pours into the room. Johann passes me the glass of cloudy liquid; it slips down my throat, at once syrupy and tart.

Where did you get this? I ask. What a treat!

One of the guards traded some goods from the stores for lemons in Lublin. I don't know the details and it's best not to ask. I just know that it tastes really good.

We both know that trading goods from the stores is forbidden, so I ask no more questions. Instead, I thank Johann for being so thoughtful. Dieter was never this kind to me. I wish I liked Johann more. What was it about Dieter that drew me so much? Why can't I like Johann that way? He's a much nicer person. He leans his face through the window towards me.

Your turn to give me something, he says.

I kiss him softly.

You're beautiful, he says with a smile. I hope that the lemonade helps you to get better.

Don't you worry about me, I reply. I'm a strong woman. One or two more days and I'll be back in the camp.

Russell.

March 1971. Maspeth.

The Jewish Resistance Assault Team are damned fools. They threw some sort of firebomb into a house a few streets away, mistaking it for ours. The idiots got the right number but the wrong street, not that I'm complaining that we haven't been bombed. The couple whose house it is have been doing interviews with all the newspapers. The story goes it was 1:30am and the couple were still awake because their baby was sick. The husband heard a window breaking downstairs in their living room, followed by an explosion. He ran downstairs and put out the fire. The maniacs had also poured petrol into their basement, but luckily that did not ignite. The family have three young children and an elderly neighbour living above them. Much has been made of how all of them could have died. Our names have been mentioned as if we're somehow responsible, which is ridiculous; the culpability falls firmly at the feet of this group. The newspaper articles have printed our address, which of course makes me worried that they will come back for us. I toss and I turn, unable to sleep.

The next morning, the telephone rings. The sound of the voice comes as a surprise. It's George. He hasn't called since I can't remember when.

How are you, Russ? he asks.

We're fine, George, I say with a snip in my voice. How are you?

George ignores the snip and carries on.

We're fine. Look, Russ, I'm sorry I haven't been in touch.

A pause. He continues.

I read the newspapers. It's a terrible thing. I just wanted to check you're OK. Is there anything I can do to help?

Yes, George, I say. You guys could come around here and give us some support. We've been deserted by everyone and we're finding it tough. The whole thing is ludicrous. I feel sick that my country is doing this to us. I'm American through and through. My great-great-grandfather was born here. I've fought for my country in two wars. Hermine's my wife. They should leave us in peace.

Another silence and then he says, Sure, Russ. I will.

I know that he won't, but I say nothing because at least he has called.

Hermine.

June 1943. Majdanek.

This morning, we have a major incident. A Polish Jew's managed to escape. When the alarm is raised, Florstedt orders a complete inspection of the barracks and the perimeter fence; sometimes missing prisoners throw themselves onto the electric wires. While the search takes place, the rest of the prisoners are summoned to an extra *Appell*, which lasts five hours. None of us like these additional roll calls, though at least it's more pleasant now than in the winter. The *Aufseherinnen* pace up and down the prisoner ranks, ignoring those who collapse. When word comes back that the wires are clear, the search party sets off into the surrounding area. The camp dogs track the girl down in a back street in Lublin. I'm in the camp office when she's brought into the room. She looks about twenty. Her body is slight and her hair has got longer than we normally allow it, a clear oversight. Both her legs are bloodied where the dogs must have bitten her. She's wearing civilian clothing, a red sweater and brown skirt, which she must have stolen from the laundry or stores. Another oversight. We need to review our systems. The girl speaks no German, so I send for a prisoner-interpreter to assist with the interrogation. Through the interpreter, the girl tells us that she should not be here.

This is a huge mistake, she bleats. My mother was not Jewish and neither am I. I'm Polish and I have done nothing wrong.

She glares at me defiantly. I don't like her look. I instruct the interpreter to inform her that she has done something very wrong. Attempting to escape is a serious crime, the most serious in fact; it is punishable by death. I tell her that we will

209

wait for *Oberaufseherin* Ehrich to make a decision. That knocks the smug look off her face.

Ehrich arrives twenty minutes later and informs me that this girl is to be hanged. Five of the male prisoners are erecting gallows in the centre of Field V. As soon as it's complete, she'll be hanged in front of the rest of the prisoners so they can see what happens to people who try to escape. The prisoner-translator hears this conversation and turns pale.

At this point, another prisoner enters the room. She requests shoes for rock duty, explaining that her shoes have been stolen while she was asleep, an annoyingly frequent occurrence these days. I'm about to send her away barefoot when I come up with a better solution. I instruct the prisoner-translator to tell the escapee to remove her shoes and hand them over. She looks at me, horrified, and remains mute. I raise my whip at her in warning, at which she mumbles something, and the escapee takes off her shoes and holds them out to the shoeless prisoner. At first, the second prisoner refuses the shoes. Losing patience, I grab them and throw them at her hard. The shoes hit her chest, then fall to the floor with a thud. I'm astounded by this prisoner. Shoes are a precious commodity. Is she completely stupid? She should take them gratefully. I turn to the interpreter and shout.

Tell this stupid woman that this Jew here has no more use for these shoes! It's as simple as that. If she feels so much solidarity, I will happily arrange for a second noose!

The interpreter translates and the second prisoner bends down to pick up the shoes. As she turns to leave, she mutters something quiet in Polish to the escapee. It is clearly some sort of message of condolence. This irritates me so much that I kick the prisoner in the stomach and scream at her to get out, and then I call for some scissors and order the interpreter to trim the escapee's hair close to the scalp. At this point, a small balding man with a puffed-out face and fat neck appears next to me. I recognise him as Enders. Normally, he oversees the crematorium; he must have been called here because he speaks Polish. As he speaks to the prisoner, his jowls wobble and shake. The prisoner replies in a short, quiet sentence and Enders translates.

She says she prefers to hang than be in this hell, he says with a pained expression on his bilious face.

The sight of Enders' oscillating chins combined with the insolence of this response makes me laugh out loud. Who the hell does this prisoner think she is? Some kind of martyr for the Jews?

Well, you can tell her that she is in luck! I snort. Her wish to be hanged is about to come true and her death will serve as a warning to others.

Once the gallows is up, we call the rest of the prisoners into the yard. Lächert marches up and down, shouting, and the prisoners cower before her.

If I see so much as one of you closing your eyes, she screams, you will receive twenty-five hard lashes of my whip! This is a lesson. There is no escape from Majdanek. You are all going to stay here until you die. If you want to speed up your death, you can jump on the wires!

Enders and two other SS guards escort the escapee to the gallows. To my surprise, she's still wearing civilian clothes. I'm not sure whose decision that is, but it doesn't seem right to me; she should die as a prisoner, not as someone who looks like they're free. She is barefoot and her hands are tied behind her back. As she walks towards the stool that has been placed directly under the noose, the sun comes out from behind a cloud, casting its rays across the dismal crowd. Lächert approaches the girl and strikes her hard across the face with her whip, creating a huge red welt on her skin, and then pushes her roughly up onto the stool. Brückner parades through the lines, beating any prisoner she catches looking away.

The escaped girl looks out across the assembled prisoners from on top of the stool and starts to shout loudly in Polish. The prisoners look up at her with wide open faces. Some of them smile. Lächert goes completely berserk. She runs at the girl and kicks the stool out from beneath her. The girl falls sharply and writhes against the rope, her shouting replaced by strange rasping chokes. It takes longer than I expect for the girl to stop twitching. Eventually, she dangles there still, bare feet flexed downwards. Two prisoners standing in front of the gallows faint, giving Lächert exactly the excuse that she needs; she sets upon them both with her whip and her feet, hitting and kicking first one then the other until both prisoners are pulp. As we leave, I find Enders, desperate to know what it is that the girl shouted.

She said that Poland is not lost and that all Poles will be free again, he reports.

Of course, this last-minute freedom cry has the opposite effect of a warning. Instead of crushing the prisoners as intended, it offers them hope. Ehrich is furious. She orders the corpse to be left hanging through the night. The next morning, as soon as it's light, she makes all the prisoners file past the dead girl and look at her face. Her corpse is tinged grey and ravens have pried out her eyes. As the prisoners walk past, Ehrich screams at them that there is absolutely no question of Poland ever being free.

From now on, she shouts. The slightest sign of insubordination and it's straight to the gas chamber. I hope I am making myself very clear!

Russell.

September 1972. New York.

Witness memory is unreliable, says Barry, our lawyer. It's almost impossible to recall events clearly after so many years. They are likely to muddle things up. They will talk about one person when they mean someone else. It will be hard for them to build a case against you. I put your chances of deportation at next to nothing. No one's ever been deported for something like this.

The Justice Department is trying to deport you on the grounds of war crimes. Last year, Barry advised us that you should give up your American citizenship in order to avoid a trial in the Federal Courts, which is what brings us to the Immigration and Naturalization Services building on West Broadway. The courtroom is stuffy and crowded. I sit next to you in the front row. Barry's on the other side of you. The room is filled with prosecutors, defence, onlookers and the press. There's not enough air for all these people; it's far too hot.

Vincent Schiano, the bull-doggish prosecutor, calls the next witness to the stand, a Polish immigrant called Jakub Kowlaczyk. Kowlaczyk is an elderly man. His shoulders are rounded, his back stooped. He walks slowly to the stand and wipes at his face with a handkerchief, body bent over, dry as a stick. One of the clerks rises to open a window. Air filters in, creating a welcome breeze. Schiano steps forward.

Mr Kowlaczyk, what did you do in the camps?

I worked as a horse.

Schiano glances around at various puzzled faces.

Can you explain to the court what you mean by that?

I pulled the wagon that distributed food, the vats full of soup. I was strapped to it with other men, just like a horse. We pulled the wagon from the kitchen in field III to the women's camp in field V.

My stomach churns. The thought of this weak old man strapped to a cart fills me with horror. His story is going to be difficult to hear. Schiano continues the examination.

I thought that the men and the women were kept apart at Majdanek. Is that not correct?

For most of the time we were separated, but I worked in the kitchen and we delivered the food to the women's field. That is how I got to see the female guards.

Kowlaczyk turns his face towards you.

Do you recognise Hermine Braunsteiner, Mr Kowlaczyk? Schiano asks.

Kowlaczyk's face twists into a look of pure hatred, the force of which is surprising from such a frail man.

I would recognise her anywhere. She was one of the worst.

Your body tenses. I take hold of your hand.

Can you describe what you witnessed?

One day, we could not enter Field V because there were so many people there. It was chaotic, full of women and children. The guards were loading the children onto trucks. The women wouldn't let go of the children because everybody knew where the trucks were going. An elderly woman was holding onto a small child of maybe two or three years old, perhaps her grandchild, I do not know. Braunsteiner shouted at this woman to give up the child. The woman refused. She bent her body around the child in protection. Braunsteiner started to hit her again and again with her whip until she fell to the ground alongside the child. Braunsteiner beat them until they were both dead. She left them there, face down in the dirt. It was me who picked them up and loaded them onto the cart to take them away. I will never forget it.

My gut wrenches. I close my eyes and see a vivid image of you in a uniform, carrying a whip. I open my eyes. The press reporters scribble furiously, pen nibs scratching noisily on notepads. You slip me a piece of paper. On it is written: *That is a lie!*

Schiano walks in front of the stand and asks Kowlaczyk if he has any other examples.

Yes, I saw her whip two women to death. They were in the zone between the two fences, clearing the grass. When the women thought Braunsteiner wasn't looking, they put some of the grass into their mouths. Nobody had enough food at Majdanek. We were all desperate. I was in a line of men shovelling coal near the fence. Braunsteiner whipped them to death. I saw the whole thing.

I'm overwhelmed by a feeling of complete revulsion. I think I might vomit. I pull my hand out of yours to cover my mouth. I've heard so many stories. Why is this one affecting me like this? I concentrate intently on holding onto the contents of my stomach and manage to suppress the urge to be sick. When I remove my hand from my mouth and wipe it across my brow, it's cold and clammy. What is wrong with me today?

Schiano continues, How many times did she whip them?

I don't know. It went on for a long time. By the end of it, both women were dead.

You pull the paper back from me and write on it again: *Another lie!*

My heart sinks. Even if I can make myself believe you, no one else will. Barry stands and walks towards Kowlaczyk. The comparison between the two men is stark. Barry is large and square, young looking for middle age. When he holds himself upright, he dwarfs the old man. I pull myself together. I don't want anyone to see signs of weakness and interpret it as doubt.

Mr Kowlaczyk, you say you saw two unarmed women being beaten. Did you go over to help them?

A gasp escapes from the spectators. Kowlaczyk looks at Barry, mouth agape.

I don't know what you mean, he says.

You say you watched this happen while you were digging coal nearby. Why did you not go over to help the women?

That was not possible.

But they were women and you are a man. You had a shovel. You could have used it to protect them. Why didn't you help them?

The court room is silent, not even a breath. At last, Kowlaczyk speaks.

You do not understand the nature of the camps. If you did, you would not ask me that question.

I know human nature, Mr Kowlaczyk, Barry says. Men help women, even at times of great personal risk.

A murmur swells in the press corps. One of the reporters looks at Barry. His jaw has gone slack. Kowlaczyk opens his mouth to say something, but nothing comes out. He slumps backwards. Schiano calls for a break in proceedings and then leads the old man gently out of the courtroom by the arm. The sound of conversation swells as people stand and file out into the corridor for the break. We stay in our seats. It's less hostile in here than out there mixing with the crowds. This session has gone particularly badly. I feel a wave of despair. Obviously, people will side with the old man. His stories do not paint you in a good light. You reach for my hand again and I let you take it. Your face looks how I feel: tired and worn. Your voice quavers.

He's making me sound like a monster, Russell. I'm not a monster. He's mistaking me for someone else, or else he's lying. I did not beat people to death. When will this be over? I want to go home.

Your palm sweats against mine. I want to go home too. I want my old life back, my life before you, but it's too late for that now. I'm an outcast in my own city. You seek my affirmation, desperation strangling your voice.

I said I'm not a monster, Russell.

I know you're not, honey, I say. I know it's not true.

What else can I say? I'm in far too deep now. There's no going back.

After the hearing, we head home and have dinner. I take Mitzi for a quick walk and then we get into bed. You face away from me into the wall. Though you're lying completely still, I know you're awake.

Hermine, can I ask you something? I say softly.

Yes, Russ.

Did the guards have whips?

Yes, we had whips.

I pause and then ask the next question.

Did you use yours?

It was a prison, Russell. I was supervising more than 250 women all by myself. Can you imagine that? They were rough. They jostled. I had to protect myself from them. But I didn't do the things that man said with my whip. I didn't kill people. I would never whip a child. Surely, you must know that's not true. He must have been mixing me up with Orlowski. She was a barbarian. I was not.

I never said you were a barbarian, I say defensively.

Then why are you asking me about whips? What do you think I am going to say? That I loved whipping people? That I whipped people to death? It's a lie, Russell. Do you have any idea what it feels like to be asked questions like that? When I started at Ravensbrück, I was only twenty years old. It was just a prison. I took the job because it was convenient. How was I supposed to know how things were going to turn out?

I understand that, honey.

You roll over to face me and stare at me fiercely.

No, Russ. You don't understand, because each time you hear a new story, you ask me more and more questions. Instead of doubting and judging me, why don't you put yourself into my shoes? Why don't you ask yourself how you would have controlled 250 sick, hungry women? Why don't you ask yourself how you would have made them work? What do you think you would have done? Offered them candy and apples? Stroked them with a kid glove?

My insides tighten, squeezed by your words. Perhaps I am judging you too harshly. How can I ever know what I would have done without having been there?

I'm sorry, Hermine, I say at last. Some of the stories are extremely difficult to hear.

Think about how hard it is for *me* to hear those stories, you say. They are about *me*. Everyone believes the stories told by the prisoners. No one wants to listen to my version of events. I count for nothing because I was a guard. You know what, I could have died in Majdanek, too. More than once, I nearly died from typhus. But I'm not allowed to say how difficult it was because no one believes me. No one is listening. Not even you.

I am listening, I say.

Then stop asking me questions that are designed to make me feel bad. You are meant to be my husband. Where is your loyalty?

You turn away again. We lie next to each other in silence. Though I try my hardest to clear my mind of the stories, they keep coming back. When I close my eyes, I see emaciated women in ragged clothing eating grass. I see children being forced into trucks.

Hermine, I whisper. Can I ask you one last thing? I'm not trying to make you feel bad. I just need to know. Were you there in that field when the children were put into the truck?

I looked after the women, not the children, you say. You know I like children. How many times have we had Joe round to our house? Think about the times I made him pancakes, hot chocolate, lemonade.

The thought of the tousle-haired boy sitting at our kitchen table, chatting to you, tugs at me hard. I miss him badly. I really loved teaching him the trombone. He wasn't my son, but he was the next best thing. I cannot bear the thought of you manhandling children. It is the one question I need you to answer.

But were you in that field?

You keep your back turned to me and do not reply.

Were you, Hermine?

Still nothing. The skin pulls tight round my temple. You emit a deep sigh.

Hermine, I whisper. I'm not a complete idiot. I know that some of the things I've heard must be true. You were there in the camp, so you must have taken part in some of those things. I don't blame you for it. I understand how difficult it was for you then. I'm not going to leave you, but I need you to stop pretending that you saw and did nothing. It's simply not possible. It cannot be true. After everything I've done for you, you owe me the truth.

Can't you see what they're doing? you whimper. They're trying to blame me for everything. For all of it, as if everything that happened was my fault. As if women and children aren't being killed now in Vietnam at the hands of Americans.

I'm fully aware of the hypocrisy of that, I say. I'm one of the few people who seem to understand the complexity of what happens in wartime. But we're not talking about Vietnam right now. We're talking about what happened in Germany. For God's sake! Today, I heard about children being loaded onto a truck to be taken to a gas chamber. It was horrific. That image is going to stay with me forever. I need you to acknowledge that what you were part of was wrong. I need to know that you understand that what happened in those places should never have happened. That's the only way I can make this work.

Tears roll down your cheeks.

I wish it had never happened, Russ, you sob. I know it was wrong, but it was a completely different time. I don't think you can ever really understand it unless you were there. What do you think I could do about it? I couldn't just leave. There were so many of them and we had to control them. If we didn't, they would have overpowered us. It's hard to describe what it's like to look back at it now; it feels like the person I was then was not even me.

I understand that it was difficult, I say. But I need you to be honest with me. Were you there when the children were loaded onto the trucks?

You cast your eyes downwards and whisper quietly, Yes.

The thought of you watching children being taken to their deaths fills me with the greatest sorrow I've ever known. My soul will forever bear its weight. However, in a strange sort of way, your confession comes as a relief. My shoulders let go of some tension. I breathe out slowly. I've known for quite some time that you must be guilty of some of the things you've been accused of. Hearing it spoken means we can stop the farce of pretence. I can face who you really are, what you've really done, and try to understand it. At least now we stand on the solid ground of truth.

OK, I say. I'm glad you're being honest with me.

There wasn't an option for children at the camp, you say mournfully. It was a work camp and they couldn't work. That was the policy. We were in an impossible situation. There wasn't enough food for them. We were told we had to do it. I can't really explain it to you except to say that it felt different back then. It felt like we had no choice.

But you must have had a choice.

That's the thing, Russell. We felt like we didn't. We didn't know what would happen to us if we refused to take part.

I pause for a second.

So, you didn't want to do it? You know it was wrong?

Of course I didn't want to do it. It was horrible. It made me feel sick. Please forgive me, Russell. I've been kind to children ever since. I wish none of it had happened. I wish I'd not been there. I wish I'd never taken that job. By the time I got to Majdanek, it was too late. I was in the middle of Poland. There was nowhere to go. Please, please try to understand me. I'm begging you to *really* try to understand.

Just as you owe me the truth, I owe it to you to try to understand. I cannot bear that you were made to work in such a horrible place. I believe that you were stuck there, that you could not leave.

I just needed the truth, I say. I know that you didn't want to take part. We won't talk about the children again. It's too awful.

Your eyes fill with despair.

I wish I could erase those years, you say. I wish that there'd never been a war.

You turn back onto your side and we lie in silence until your breathing slows down to a regular huff. I lie next to you, wide awake, unable to sleep. I go over the scenes I heard this afternoon in the courtroom and imagine you standing next to the truck. I need to stop doing this. I have to pull myself away from individual incidents and focus on the fact you didn't want to be there, that you were coerced. The people above you were to blame, not you. You were just a pawn in their game. At long last, I start to nod off. My body starts to float. I feel like I'm being pulled along in a river that's swollen with rain. The current turns me and spins me around; nothing can stop me from being swept along.

Hermine.
July 1943. Majdanek.

Ehrich is furious. Florstedt requested fifteen guards from Ravensbrück but only four have arrived. She shouts at Florstedt to contact Ravensbrück and demands for more to be sent immediately. She's right to be angry; we are completely understaffed. How the SS expect us to do this work is a mystery. There are incoming transports almost every day now. The workload is far too much for twenty-three guards, especially as several are always off sick. The number of prisoners we now have to guard is farcical.

The new guards that we do have seem decent enough, apart from Orlowski, who, at thirty, is quite a bit older than the rest of us. She's surly and has a cleft in her chin. Orlowski has already irritated the rest of the *Aufseherinnen* by going around saying she's a cut above the rest of us. She tells anyone who'll listen that she studied medicine at university; no one else here has set foot in a university, a point that Orlowski is all too happy to rub in. Despite this, Ehrich has taken to her on the basis that she is a good horsewoman. She asked her to join her and Lächert on a ride, a pairing that is suited, as both Lächert and Orlowski have an equally high opinion of themselves and are overly fond of using their whips.

I'm all in favour of whipping when necessary, but Orlowski does it merely for sport. On her very first day here, she started to brag immediately about her impeccable aim. She asked how many of us could crack a whip across both eyes of a prisoner at the same time, causing blindness. Of course, this kind of behaviour is against regulations. It's the kind of unnecessary bravado that the male SS guards engage in all the time.

I speak to Ehrich about it, but she says not to worry.

Orlowski's just joking, she says. All will be fine.

I'm certain that her response would be different if Orlowski could not ride a horse.

Russell.
March 1973. Maspeth.

It all happened so fast. Two days ago, the Federal Republic of Germany requested your extradition on charges of murder, and then yesterday Poland put in the same request. Police came to our door, arrested you and took you to Riker's Island prison. I've been up all night worrying and am in a state of delirium when the telephone rings. It must be the jail. Nobody else calls here anymore. I stumble to get it. When I pick up, your voice comes down the line, fast and breathless.

Russ! They've put me in a cell with prostitutes. They're completely disgusting. One of them even spat on the floor. Can you get me out of here?

Hang on, Hermine, I reply. I didn't sleep a wink last night. I'm very tired. Give me a moment to think.

I sit down on the floor and hold the telephone receiver to my ear. How can this be happening? I'm furious with Barry. I believed him and trusted him. He convinced us that we were going to win. He should never have advised us to give up your citizenship. As soon as that happened, it opened the gateway for extradition requests. On top of that, he failed to spot the word 'partial' in the small print of the amnesty papers. He'd argued that your amnesty meant that you didn't need to declare any previous convictions on your citizenship application, but without a full amnesty, that line of defence tumbled fast. The prosecution said you'd lied on your application papers, which is a crime. They ignored the fact that you did not lie. Quite rightly, you thought that the amnesty pardoned you, which meant you had nothing to declare. Now, your extradition looks more and more likely. I'm snapped back to the present by your voice down the line.

Russell, you say, sounding distressed. Are you listening? I shouldn't be inside a prison. I've already served my time for this. And why have they put me in with prostitutes? Is this some sort of additional punishment? I hate it here. Can you speak to Mr Barry and get me transferred out of this cell?

Try to keep calm, honey, I say. I promise you that it's going to be OK. I'll speak to Barry as soon as I can, but right now it's only 7am. I need to wait until his office opens. As soon as it does, I'll give him a call. If there's one last thing he can do for us, it's to get you moved to somewhere more humane.

After the phone call, I go into the kitchen to make myself coffee. Mitzi looks up from her basket and then closes her eyes. She's an old dog now; she doesn't move far. I didn't tell you the last thing that Barry said to me yesterday: that we're lucky that West Germany filed for extradition first because Poland still carries the death penalty. The highest penalty in West Germany is prison for life.

Hermine.

August 1943. Majdanek.

A transport arrives from Bialystock containing men, women and children. The men and women aren't a problem, but it's the first time we've had so many children at Majdanek, so there is no protocol. There are a lot of them, more than one hundred, in various states of health, some with parents, some without. It causes chaos.

Ehrich requests a meeting with *Kommandant* Florstedt to tell him that we can't keep them here. There isn't appropriate accommodation for them and they're too young to work. Florstedt is too busy to make a quick decision, so Ehrich starts a preliminary selection, separating off the sick, elderly and pregnant women for the gas chambers. The rest of the children are herded into a barrack next to Field V as a temporary measure. This causes a stir among the prisoners and even some staff. The constant calls for food and pitiful crying for Mama are hard to listen to, indeed they are too much for some of the guards. Bieneck won't stop pleading that the children should be given food and water.

How can we leave them there starving? she wails. Don't any of you have a heart?

I don't know what she thinks we can do about it. Of course, it's unpleasant, but doesn't she know there isn't enough food now to go around the prisoners who are needed for work? Several days pass while Florstedt decides what to do. All the while, we patrol the perimeter of the barrack to stop prisoners throwing bread to the children, whose arms stretch out through the barbed wire like twigs. Eventually, the order comes to liquidate the children's barrack. Of course, we know this is not going to be easy. Nobody wants to do this job, but it needs to be done. We need to get the children to come out into Field V, so we tempt them out with candy and apples and promises of Mama. We tell them that a truck is coming with more food and instruct them to wait quietly in line. From the outset, it's clear to me what a mistake it is to have the children in the women's field. As soon as the women see the children, they break ranks and run to embrace them. We shout that if they don't get back, no further food will be distributed to the children. The women retreat, but by now they are highly agitated.

As soon as Enders arrives with the truck, the children run forward, desperate for food. Our job is to grab them as soon as they're near enough to the truck to throw them in. We do this as quickly as possible, but once it becomes clear what's happening, all hell breaks loose. The women run at the truck, hysterical, and the children scatter like frightened rabbits all over the field. The women run after the children, trying to protect them, putting themselves between them and the truck. We are left with an impossible task. Some of us wrench the children out of the women's hands, while others try to beat them back. Lächert chases the runaways around the field like a hound amid hares. All the running churns the mud into thick ridges, which makes it almost impossible to move. Finally, Lächert fires several shots into the air, which stops all the running. The prisoners and children all stand stock still, as if suspended in a photograph.

I will shoot! I will shoot! Lächert screams, pointing the gun at the head of a whimpering boy, who clings to his mother.

The woman immediately relinquishes the child and shouts at him to get in the truck. Slowly, the field begins to move again. Lächert moves on to another prisoner, who is trying to grab a child out of Orlowski's arms. She pushes her face within an inch of the woman and screams at her, spraying her with spittle.

If you don't let go right now, I will shoot your child!

The woman lets go, whereupon Ehrich gives her a sharp kick. I grab a child from one prisoner and hoist it onto the truck. The prisoner throws herself at my feet and holds onto my leg so hard it feels like a tourniquet.

Let me go with my child! she begs. Let me go with my child!

This is obviously out of the question. I try to shake her off, but she's clamped on as tight as a vice.

Get off! I shout. Can't you see? You are good for work!

She won't let go, so I kick her, which is no mean feat as she is wrapped around my other leg. My foot strikes her, but still she will not let go. She keeps screaming that she wants to go with her child. It takes three more kicks before she slumps off me into the mud. Then, somehow, even though her head is bleeding badly, she finds the strength to get up and run at the truck. I sprint after her, fumbling for my whip, and somehow manage to hit her head hard with its wooden handle, which puts a swift end to the affair. She falls to the ground and lies there in silence, eyes wide open, blood coursing from her head. I have no time to stop. I turn around to look for the next.

The whole operation lasts about half an hour. Though it is short, it is exhausting and utterly fraught. Once the truck is fully loaded, I slam its lower door upwards. At once, a child starts to scream that its hand is trapped in the door. My nerves are completely shattered. I want to get out of here as soon as I can. We need to get the truck moving before the chaos starts up again, so I pull the tarpaulin down over the back of the truck. The child keeps on screaming, but the combination of engine noise and women wailing drowns out the noise.

By now, Lächert's shouting has reached fever pitch, and Orlowski is running around cracking her whip at the prisoners to prevent them from approaching the vehicle. As the truck starts to move off, a few of the children pull up the tarpaulin to wave at their mothers. Some of the women run after it screaming, but Lächert subjugates them with the lash of her whip. At last, the truck is gone. The field is a mass of prisoners lying in the mud, some wailing, some mute. The sky fills with cawing. Already the crows are starting to circle.

When I get back to my barrack, I go straight to bed without dinner. I cannot eat. The afternoon has left me feeling quite nauseous. On days like today, it is hard not to falter. The work we must do here requires nerves of steel. Even though I understand that the camp cannot accommodate that many children, loading them into the trucks was a horrible job. The landscape of Majdanek makes everything worse. All there is here is mud, mud, and even more mud. I close my eyes and think about Ravensbrück, the swims and the picnics, the lake and the forest. Most of all, I miss Maria, but she would hate it here. I would give anything to have a break from all this, to go back there and see her again. But I am stuck here. What is there here? Nothing but the camp.

Russell.

August 1973. New York.

A line of reporters stands between me and the boarding gate, jostling each other like hungry dogs. All I have with me is my ticket and passport. My luggage has already been put on the airplane. You are already on board, but I'm not allowed to sit next to you. When I protested this, the desk attendant said she was just following 'airport protocol for criminals' or some other words of equal affront.

The flight to Berlin takes off in forty-five minutes. After we land, we will be taken by the police to Düsseldorf, where you will go on trial. The past few days passed in a whirlwind. At the final hearing, Barry tried to argue that the German trial would constitute double jeopardy, but the judge ruled that this restriction only applies to crimes committed in the United States, not abroad. They couldn't wait to extradite you.

In the airport, one of the reporters shouts, Mr Ryan! Please look this way.

I look up and see four news cameras aimed at my face. A row of reporters stand next to them holding notepads and pens. The click and flash of photographers makes me blink. I need to get past them to enter the airplane. As soon as I move, they lunge at me, firing questions.

Mr Ryan, what do you have to say about your wife's deportation? Do you think she's innocent? Will you stick with her? Mr Ryan! Mr Ryan! Are you afraid of the German trial?

I look at these men in their cheap, shiny suits and take a moment to swallow the urge rising inside me to punch them in the face. I pull a piece of paper from my pocket, unfold it, and deliver the short speech I've prepared. I'm so agitated that I can hardly read my own writing. At first, I stumble, but then I manage to control my voice.

My wife worked for Germany during the war, just as I worked for America, I say. Now the country she worked for wants to prosecute her for crimes that the Germans committed back then. Germany is throwing her under the bus. The USA is no better. My country has deserted me too. The whole thing stinks!

One of the reporters steps forward. He stands so close that I can smell his stale breath. I try to step around him.

Mr Ryan, he says. How can you possibly think your wife is innocent after all that you've heard?

I push my face towards him, unable to control my anger.

How do you know that what *you've* heard is true? You guys have ruined our lives. She only did what everyone else did in her position, which was not a position of choice. This is a witch hunt. You should be ashamed of yourselves!

I push past him. The cameras continue to click and whir. Since I accepted your involvement, I've been able to turn my focus away from the things you might have done. The crimes were not yours, but those of a nation. If the Nazis had not been in power, your life would have been much more like mine. You're not to blame for what you were made to do. That's how I see it. Out on the tarmac, there is a slight breeze. I climb up the airplane stairs and get into the aircraft without looking back.

Hermine.
August 1943. Majdanek.

I wake up feeling much better after a good night's sleep and put yesterday behind me. However, I've barely finished breakfast when I am called to the next emergency, this time in the laundry. The laundry command is one of the easiest since the work there is light. But today the prisoners are running amok, searching through the garments in a total frenzy. Zimmermann has lost control of the situation. She coped well at Ravensbrück, but here she is totally out of her depth. Some of the prisoners have recognised the children's clothing from yesterday. One of them is grabbing piles of small shirts, vests and underpants and throwing them everywhere, shouting something about God's babies and screaming, *He will punish you all! He will punish you all!*

It takes both of us several minutes to restrain the prisoner. When we finally pin her down, she lies mewling on the floor, her hand clasped around a small jumper knitted in white wool. She vomits rancid smelling bile all over herself, and her chest heaves up and down. Zimmermann tries to soothe her, stroking the tufts of the hair on her head. This sight disgusts me so completely that I let go of the prisoner and take a step back. Does Zimmermann know nothing about typhus?

Don't touch the prisoner like that! I scream at her. Don't you know they carry disease just like the rats?

Zimmerman talks softly to the prisoner, telling her that the children are in heaven now. Far from consoling her, this makes the prisoner convulse and scream even more. She thrashes her legs about like a mule. I take another step back. The situation needs containing. I'm losing my patience. I go to kick the prisoner, but Zimmermann gets in the way.

That's enough! I shout at full pitch. Control yourself and get back to work!

This message is as much for Zimmermann as it is for the prisoner. Majdanek is a hard enough place to work without having to mop up after someone else's incompetence. There aren't enough of us here to have such a weak link in the chain.

Russell.
November 1975. Düsseldorf.

This trial is the third of its kind relating to Majdanek; the first two took place straight after the war. There are sixteen people on trial, nine men and seven women, including you. We've been allocated a defence lawyer called Hans Mundorf, a thoughtful and professional man, who puts both of us immediately at ease. In our pre-trial meetings, he tells us that under West German law, it's very hard to prosecute for crimes in the camps because each act must be proven to have been committed by a specific person at a specific time, date and place.

So many years have passed since the event that issues of memory prevent this from happening, he says. Prisoners from the camps struggle with exact details and are easy to catch out. Our legal system works in your favour.

Mundorf's English is good, which helps me enormously in the months waiting for the start of the trial. He places a list of the names of the defendants on the desk and asks if you remember any of the other guards from that time. I try to envisage you working alongside these people as you point out the names of the guards that you knew, but each time I try to conjure up an image of you among them, young, strong and in uniform, it morphs into the memory of you in your red swimsuit sunning yourself on the jetty at Wörthersee. I look down at my arms and imagine myself sitting next to you in the sunshine. You were so beautiful then.

Mrs Ryan, Mundorf says, bringing me sharply back to the present. I suggest that you don't communicate with the other defendants. Visible camaraderie will work against you. By far the best thing you can do is to remain silent.

That's easy, you reply. I was sick and in hospital for most of my time at Majdanek. I hardly remember it at all.

Good, he replies. That will be my line of defence, plus your youth; let's not forget that you were only twenty at the time. I will argue that you didn't know what you were doing. Say as little as possible. In fact, I advise you don't talk at all.

Hermine was conscripted, I add. She worked in the camps, but she never signed up to the Nazi party. She was never a Nazi. I hope you will make that clear.

Yes, Mr Ryan, he replies. I will.

On the first day of the trial, the journalists and television crews are out in full force. You file into the courtroom along with the other defendants, holding a newspaper up in front of your face. The press buzzes around you, shoving their cameras at you as Mundorf guides you to your seat.

The judges enter the courtroom and make their way to a block of desks. The wall behind them is panelled in wood with a large white cross affixed to it. The rest of the room is painted white and lined with rows of wooden seats for the witnesses, lawyers, onlookers and press, all facing the judges.

The chief justice is a round-faced man called Günter Bogen. When he talks, his dark eyebrows move up and down like caterpillars under his white hair. He tells the press to move backwards and, once they have retreated, the defendants sit. Bogen turns towards you with a look of irritation.

Mrs Ryan, he says. This is a courtroom. Remove your hat.

The hat you are wearing is homemade. Since our arrival in Germany, you've taken to knitting; it's helped you to relieve some of the stress. The trial starts. The first day is almost entirely administrative and, by the end of it, we are tired from sitting for so long. Outside the building, a television reporter asks me for a quick interview and I oblige. I stand in front of the thick-waisted pillars of Düsseldorf District Court in the cold November air.

This court and this country are prosecuting my wife for the crimes of a nation, I say into the camera. My wife worked for Germany like many, many people all over this country and now Germany attacks her. Shame on you all!

After the interview, we get into the car. I drive us towards the apartment we've rented in Bochum. The road takes us out of Düsseldorf to the north, towards Mülheim and Essen, through earthy brown farmland and woodland stripped bare. We reach the outskirts of Bochum and skirt round the south of the city and then head east to our road. The apartment is on the ground floor of a house. It has one bedroom, a kitchen, a sitting room and a small back yard. It's near to a lake and a park, so there's lots of greenery, which helps to keep us both sane. Despite all we've been through, I like where we're living, and the distance between here and the courthouse is helpful; each passing kilometre helps to alleviate the weight of the trial.

We've tried to establish some sense of normality over the past months. I've rented out our house in New York to give us an income, so we're not too badly off. You still do the cooking, but I do all the shopping so you don't have to meet anyone who might recognise you from the trial. Getting out and about has forced me to practise my German and I'm already more fluent now than when we first met. A small victory.

Inside the apartment, I turn on the light and unpack your bag while you prepare us a meal.

I hope we're not here too long, Russ, you say when I join you. I really miss Mitzi. I hope she's alright. She's so old now. I can't bear that we had to leave her.

Don't worry about Mitzi, honey, I say. She's in good hands.

George and Molly agreed to take her for as long as we're in Germany. I'm not sure they wanted to, but I asked and they couldn't easily refuse. The truth is that we have no idea how long we'll be here; Mundorf said this trial could go on for a very long time. The wind picks up outside the apartment. You hold out your hand and I take it in mine.

You are going to hear a lot of horrible things, Russ, you say meekly.

I squeeze your hand tightly to reassure you that I am here, solid and unflinching, for better, for worse.

Nothing that anyone says matters to me, Hermine. I'm here by your side.

Hermine.

November 1943. Majdanek.

When I finally come to, I have such a terrible headache that it hurts to open my eyes.

Fräulein Braunsteiner, you have typhus as well as jaundice and Wolhynia fever, the doctor says. I am extremely worried about your health. I'm going to keep you here in hospital until you promise me that you'll request a transfer out of Majdanek. I cannot state too plainly that if you stay longer at Majdanek, you risk losing your life.

Immediately, I know that I want to go back to Ravensbrück. I think of Maria, how much I want to see her. At this point, I don't even mind if Dieter is there. I tell the doctor that I will put in a request to leave. Ehrich will not be happy to lose her deputy. She's only just transferred Pfannstiel out of Majdanek because she is three months pregnant with Wallisch's child. Of course, a pregnant woman could not remain here. The conditions are too harsh, but Pfannstiel was a very good member of staff. And then there is Johann. In my haste, I have not thought about him at all. I plan to tell him, but when he visits me in hospital, there is so much on his mind that I do not mention it.

Things have gone crazy, he says. Last week, there was a mass execution. All the Jews in the Lublin district were exterminated to make the district *Judenfrei*. The order came from Himmler himself. There were so many to liquidate that it took us two days. Extra police units and guards had to be brought in to assist.

Did the *Aufseherinnen* help?

No, of course not. The camp was put on total lockdown and the *Aufseherinnen* had to stay in their barracks. It was far too brutal for women to watch. Loud waltz music was played to cover up the noise and prevent panic among the prisoners, but as soon as there was a roll call for all Jews, they suspected what was happening and became highly agitated. We rounded them up and led them to the back of the camp and then shot them and slung them into ditches. When the ditches were full, the bodies were burnt. The smell was atrocious. Many of the prisoners lost control of their bowels and that mixed with the stench.

That sounds simply awful, I say. How did you cope?

It was very hard work. Some of the men couldn't take it, but most of us managed to push on through. I will admit that after several hours, even I felt that I couldn't take it anymore, but I knew if I failed, someone else would have to do my work for me. I knew I had no other choice but to keep on.

You are very brave, Johann.

He smiles at me sweetly.

The *Kommandant* tried to make it easier for us, he says. He promised us two large bottles of vodka and 200 cigarettes each as a reward. The thought of that helped to keep us going. I can tell you, there were a lot of sore heads the next day.

He takes hold of my hand.

You should feel proud of your actions, Johann, I say. The camp has been getting so overcrowded. I'm glad that I missed it, but relieved to hear that the camp has been cleared.

Johann's second piece of news is even more shocking: *Kommandant* Florstedt has been removed from office under suspicion of embezzlement and charged with combing through the stores of property brought in by the prisoners to line his own pockets. He's in jail awaiting a military trial. Hearing this makes me think about Ehrich's fine pearls.

Who's replaced him as *Kommandant*? I ask.

A man called Weiss. He comes from Neuengamme Camp in Hamburg. I don't know much about him. We'll just have to wait to see what he is like. I miss you so much, Hermine. It's not the same there without you. I can't wait until you're back.

I don't have the heart to tell Johann that I'm applying to leave.

Russell.

April 1978. Düsseldorf.

Maryla Reich takes the stand, a Polish Jew from Lviv, small and mousy with short greying hair. Large glasses rest on her nose.

I survived Majdanek and Ravensbrück by using false identity documents that claimed that I was as an ethnic Pole, Reich says.

One of the prosecuting lawyers, a tall man with arched brows, walks before her.

Do you remember any of the defendants? he asks.

Yes, she says. I recognise three of them well.

Please identify them.

Reich points her finger at Charlotte Mayer and then Hildegard Lächert.

We called this one *Sloma* and this one *Krwawa Brygida*, she says.

Then she points her finger at you.

This one we called *Kobyla*.

Can you please explain to the courtroom what those words mean?

We didn't know the guards' names, so we made up nicknames for them in Polish. *Sloma* means straw – that one's hair looked like straw. *Krwawa* means bloody. We called her Bloody Brygida because she was the worst of them all, a real sadist; if she touched you, you were destined to bleed. *Kobyla* means mare, you know, a big, female horse. She wore boots with steel toe caps and she kicked like a horse. She wasn't as bad as Brygida, but she was still bad.

All eyes in the room turn to Hildegard Lächert and then to you. Lächert is a short, dumpy woman who looks like a grandmother, about as far from sadistic as one could imagine.

Your face reveals nothing. You sit there in silence, reading a newspaper under your desk.

Let's start with Frau Lächert, says the prosecutor. Can you describe her behaviour?

I remember her making us dig frozen ground, says Reich. It was so solid that our spades could not get through it. One day, she took the spade out of my hand and hit me straight across the face with the handle. I fell to the ground with my nose bleeding and then she kicked me in my stomach, but I was lucky because, for some reason, she decided to take out the rest of her anger on the woman next to me. She beat her across the head with my spade until she was dead.

The courtroom fills with murmurs. The judge tells the room to be quiet and indicates for Reich to go on.

Another time, there was this *Muselmann*, she says. That is the word we gave to the people so thin and weak that they walked on the crack between life and death. Brygida kicked him in the crotch and then, when he fell over, she kicked his head again and again until he too was dead. This is how she behaved all the time. She was pathological, completely inhuman. She sits here looking like an innocent old woman, but believe me, she terrorised us when she was young.

All eyes in the courtroom turn towards Lächert, who mops at her forehead with a handkerchief. It is warm in the courtroom and she is sweating. Reich continues her tale.

In the summer of 1943, I witnessed the hanging of a young woman, maybe nineteen or twenty years old. The girl had tried to escape. We were all rounded up and forced to gather around the gallows. I remember it clearly because when she was brought out, she was not wearing prisoner clothing. Instead, she was wearing a red sweater and a brown skirt. I can see her now quite clearly in my mind's eye; her head was shaved and she was barefoot. As she walked through us, she held her head high. She did not look afraid. I remember being in awe of her courage. When she got to the gallows, an SS man put her head in the noose. Just as she was about to be hanged, the young woman shouted out *Long live freedom!* across the assembled crowd. Brygida went completely berserk. She attacked two women in the front lines and beat them. By the time she had finished, they were not recognisably human.

Were such hangings common?

No. I just saw that one, but it will stay with me forever because that girl's cry gave us all hope and that's what we needed. It allowed us a glimpse of a future in which we were free. That hope was more precious than bread.

The trial goes on like this all day. Accusation after accusation as Reich tells tales about all of the guards, including you.

During the break, I go out to get some water. When I come back, I see Mundorf talking to you. He looks animated, so I move closer to hear what he's saying.

Mrs Ryan, he says. You must put it away. When you read a newspaper like that during the proceedings, it looks like you're not taking this process seriously.

You look at him in clear disbelief.

I'm not taking it seriously! you hiss. Is that what you think? Two and a half years I've sat here, being made to listen to lies. I've had everything taken from me, my citizenship, my freedom, even my dog. I'm not allowed to work. I have nothing else to do. And now what? I can't even read a newspaper?

Mundorf tries to appease you.

Mrs Ryan, he says. This is not about me; it's about the judges, the lawyers and the press.

Can you imagine what it's like to hear people call me those names? you say. How do you think I feel when they call me a mare? Do you know what it's like to hear myself compared to Hildegard Lächert? I could tell you a thing or two about her. She was the monster of Majdanek, not me! If you want to know how seriously I am taking this, then listen to me now. Sometimes I pray that I will join Alice Orlowski. And you want to know something? Orlowski was *even worse* than Lächert. I was a pussycat compared to those two.

I look at you, horrified. Alice Orlowski died two years ago during the trial. The strain was too much for her. She simply gave up.

Don't let me hear you talking like that ever again, Hermine! I say.

I turn to our lawyer.

Herr Mundorf, please, can you say something positive? Tell my wife that we're going to win this trial.

Mundorf shakes his head and sighs.

I do believe that there is a chance you will win this trial, Mr Ryan, but Mrs Ryan needs to help me to help her.

He turns back to you.

Mrs Ryan, people are watching you closely. It may seem unfair, but as a woman, you're going to be held up to a much higher standard than the men who are on trial. The press, the whole country, is watching you carefully. You cannot afford to put a foot out of place. Please, put the newspaper away.

When we get home, I make you some tea and you sit in the armchair, drinking it in tiny sips. I kneel before you and look into your eyes. The floorboards push hard onto my knees.

How could you say that you want to die, Hermine? Don't I count for anything? Has it not occurred to you that I need you too?

I'm sorry, Russ. I didn't mean it. I just can't bear to have the war hung round my neck anymore. If I hadn't been there, the same number of people would have died. Someone else would have been in my place. The fact it was me is immaterial, yet they blame me for everything. It's so unfair.

I know, honey. I wish it was me in the dock, not you. But I need you to be strong, not just for you, for me too.

There was no President Carter for me back in Germany, pardoning those who avoided duty, you say. And now Germany has decided to go after the people it made do its dirty work. You're lucky to be born an American. It's only Germany that rakes over the past like this.

You sit in front of me, shoulders stooping, full of self-pity, looking forlorn. Though lines cross your forehead and crease downwards between your eyes, I still see your beauty. I still see the woman that I first met.

Where are the trials for the people who bombed Dresden and Berlin? you ask. Why aren't Americans being tried for what's happening in Vietnam?

I stroke your hand. I don't know what to say to you.

I hate this country, you say. I don't want to be here anymore.

Come on, honey. Let's go out for a walk by the lake. It'll be good for both of us to get some fresh air.

I don't want to go out, Russ. It's dark and I'm feeling tired. You go. I'm going to bed.

I cannot persuade you. All you want to do now is knit or sleep. Outside, the cool air strokes my face. A lone cyclist whirs past me, ringing his bell. He calls out *Guten Abend!* and I call it back to him. When I get to the lake, it's completely dark. I stop by the shoreline and look out across the water; it's still and black as ink. I step forwards towards the water's edge and my shoes sink into mud. I retreat to the grass, wipe the mud from my shoes and close my eyes to pray.

Dear God, help me to withstand the horrendous things that I'm going to hear. Even though the events are unforgivable, help me to find it in my heart to remember that my wife had no choice. Help me to believe her when she tells me her side of the story. Help me to be strong for her and for myself too.

Hermine.

January 1944. Majdanek.

Sick and dying prisoners from all the other nearby camps are being brought to Majdanek now for gassing, which has pushed up our numbers to near breaking point. A new crematorium has been built, but there are still too many people to process; we are only nineteen *Aufseherinnen* guarding 380 women each. The level of disease is so high none of us wants to go near the prisoners for fear of catching typhus. I'm particularly concerned because my immunity is so low; if I catch typhus again, it is likely to kill me. I put in my transfer request more than a month ago as soon as I got out of the Military Hospital. Ehrich was disappointed, but when she read the doctor's note, she understood the urgency and promised to do her best to get me transferred back to Ravensbrück as soon as she could. While I wait, I'm exposed to the prisoners each day.

To make matters worse, Ehrich confided this morning that *Kommandant* Weiss is concerned about the advance of the Russian army. He's put the camp on standby to evacuate. If that happens, everyone in the camp, both prisoners and guards, will have to march west towards Germany. I thought it was impossible to be more frightened of dying than I already am, but the thought of the Russians brings new waves of dread. The Russians are brutal. If they get to us, they'll torture us and then they'll skin us alive. I pray fervently that my transfer request comes through before they arrive.

Russell.

May 1978. Düsseldorf.

Rachel Nurman tells the court she's originally from Warsaw. She emigrated to the United States after the war with her husband, who she met in a displaced persons camp. She's flown in from Brooklyn. She stands before the court, short and stocky, with white hair that clings to her forehead in wisps.

I was taken to Majdanek after the uprising in the Warsaw ghetto, she says. I spent six weeks in Majdanek before being moved to Auschwitz. It was the height of summer when I was there, unbearably hot, the type of heat that makes the air feel like treacle. There was not enough water and people dropped all around me like flies. Though the winter killed tens of thousands of us, the summer did a good job of killing us too.

The prosecutor indicates Hildegard Lächert.

Do you remember this woman?

Bloody Brygida? She's unforgettable. She picked on the weakest, not just the women and children but the men too.

Nurman pauses and runs her hand over her hair, smoothing it down, before she continues.

I remember there was this *Muselmann*. He stumbled to a water trough and dipped his food bowl in it to fill it up. Brygida ran up to him, grabbed him from behind and pushed his head down into the water and held him under. We never knew why she picked on the people she did. The *Muselmann* had no chance. He was a walking skeleton, whereas Brygida was big and strong and very well fed. We all watched, unable to help, as the man's body twitched and writhed. When he finally stopped,

Brygida let go. The woman standing next to me started to wail. Perhaps she knew the *Muselmann*, perhaps she'd witnessed one death too many, I do not know. Either way, we all knew it was stupid to make any noise. Brygida strode over and said she would be next. We expected her to kill that woman right there in front of us, but then she just walked away. Brygida was like that. You never knew when she'd go crazy, who she would choose, when it would be your turn to die.

Do you have any other examples of Frau Lächert's behaviour?

Yes. There was one particularly terrible day when all the children in the camp were brought out and loaded into trucks. Their mothers were in the field with them, screaming and crying, begging the guards not to take their children away. Brygida was grabbing children and throwing them onto the truck. I mean literally throwing them onto the truck like sacks of potatoes. We all knew the trucks were going to the gas chambers. I have never been able to understand how a woman could send a child to its death. I have children now. I cannot imagine what it was like, not just for the children, but also for their mothers. At Majdanek, the women were much worse than the men. How could women do that? You wouldn't believe a woman would be capable of such a thing unless you had seen it, like I did.

Nurman takes out a handkerchief and dabs at her eyes. The court waits for a few minutes while she composes herself. Then Nurman turns her attention to you.

Kobyla was there too, she says. She also threw the children onto the trucks. I remember that one of the mothers ran after the truck. *Kobyla* grabbed her and beat her to death.

I won't let myself believe this was you. You may have been there, but you did not do this. Nurman must be talking about someone else, another guard.

You saw Frau Ryan kill one of the prisoners? the prosecutor asks.

I saw her kill more than one person, Nurman replies. There was another time when I witnessed her kill a child. A man came into the camp in a transport. He was wearing a rucksack. *Kobyla* whipped the man from behind and a scream came out of the rucksack. She opened it and dragged out a small boy, maybe four or five years old, who'd been concealed inside. I will never forget it. She took out a gun and pointed it at him. The thing I remember most was the fear on his face as he whimpered to his papa to save him. *Kobyla* shot that boy in the face, in front of his father. The man collapsed on top of his child and she just left him there. The SS men came and took the man to the gas.

My chest tightens. This woman is lying. It cannot be true. You told me that you never had a gun. I want to shout out that this allegation is false, but I know I cannot. I sit silently, biting my lip.

Are you sure that was Hermine Braunsteiner? he says.

Yes, it was her, and do you know what disgusts me? That she lived free in America for so many years. How was that possible after all that she'd done?

Nurman dabs at her eyes again. She starts to cry and this time she cannot compose herself, so the court is adjourned. During the break, we walk out into the corridor. Nurman sits alone on a bench at the far side of the hall. Before I can stop you, you are striding towards her.

Liar! you scream. Why aren't you telling the truth?

Nurman looks up at you, startled. Her face fills with fear.

You stupid Jewish woman! you shout at her. Tell the truth in the courtroom!

I run towards you and hold onto your arm, trying to pull you away from her, but you stand firm. Your face is blotched red with fury.

Stop it, Hermine, I say. You need to calm down.

How can I calm down when she's lying in court? you say, your voice trembling. I didn't shoot a boy. It's a lie. We're in a court. She's meant to tell the truth.

You turn to me, pleading.

What will they do to me if they think that I was shooting children, Russ? Why did she say that? Why can't she tell the truth?

Two policemen approach us briskly from the other end of the corridor. Nurman puts her hand up to stop them.

I'm alright, she says.

She addresses you calmly, with much more composure than she had in the courtroom.

After the war, I said I'd never set foot in Germany, but I had to come here because of this trial. I came back here for the memory of my family and for all of the other innocent people who died in the Shoah.

Your body stiffens. You wipe your palms on your skirt.

We were nothing to you, Nurman continues. Faceless, nameless nothings, numbers, not people. But each life that was taken, each child on those trucks, each man drowned in a water trough, each small boy shot in front of his father, each one of those people had a name.

She pauses to take a breath. You stare at her coldly and she stares back in defiance.

I came here to speak for the voiceless, she says. I came here for my mother, my father, my brothers, for everyone that you killed. I speak for that boy in the rucksack. I speak for his father. I don't know how you can live with yourself. I don't know how you can sleep at night.

You shake your head and look at me beseechingly. I step forwards to defend you, putting myself between Nurman and you.

Mrs Nurman, I say sharply. My wife did not have a gun. She didn't throw children onto a truck. You are confusing her with somebody else. She's not responsible for the death of that boy. You cannot hold her responsible for the deaths of your family. It's not fair to pin your revenge onto her.

Nurman's eyes fill with steel.

This is not about revenge, Mr Ryan, she says, glaring at me. It's about justice. Each person involved was responsible for what they did. They all played their part. It was murder, Mr Ryan. How do you think so many of us were killed? All the people on trial here, including your wife, chose to become a murderer. Murderers should not walk free. They should face the consequences of what they did.

The policemen move in.

Frau Ryan, says one of them. We are arresting you for witness intimidation.

Russell, you whimper. I didn't shoot a boy. That woman is lying!

The policemen take hold of you and lead you away. Panic rises in my throat. My voice quivers as I run after the policemen.

Please, let my wife stay with me, I beg. She didn't mean to do anything wrong. This trial has been so hard for her. I promise she will never do it again.

Herr Ryan, there are laws that govern this courthouse. Your wife has broken the law.

Where are you taking her? Can I come with you?

Mülheim Women's Prison. You can visit her there.

The policemen walk you away. I walk back to the bench and slump onto it next to Nurman. She shuffles away from me, gets up and starts to walk back to the courtroom. After a few steps, she turns back towards me.

Mr Ryan, she says. I understand how hard it is for you to come to terms with what your wife did. I know that it's easier for you to think that I'm lying. But I am not lying. I was there. I will never forget it. I saw what she did.

I try to speak, but my throat swallows the words. However hard I try to believe that the stories are not about you, I cannot escape it: the image of the man, the rucksack and the petrified child.

Hermine.

February 1944. Ravensbrück.

I'd almost forgotten how beautiful Ravensbrück is. On my first morning back, I stand by the lake, feet sunk into a thick layer of snow. The water shines silver in the winter sun. A heron stalks the shallows, looking for fish. The tranquillity and beauty here is such a change after Poland's harshness, but the best thing about being back is not even the scenery. It's the fact that Maria's still here. I find her walking along the camp road with Herbert. He runs at me and covers me in great sloppy licks.

Hermine! she shouts. Is that really you? What are you doing here? Have you come back?

We embrace each other fiercely, and then I hold her out before me.

I'm so pleased to see you! I say. I'm so happy to be back.

Maria looks tired. Her face has a greyness and she has lost a lot of weight. We walk past the *Kommandant*'s house towards the *Aufseherinnen* quarters. I tell her all about Majdanek, how awful it was there, and how sick I kept getting. She fills me in on the gossip. The latest *Oberaufseherin*, Anna Klein, is alright, but Binz is her deputy, and she reigns with terror over the *Aufseherinnen* and prisoners alike. Binz has a boyfriend now, the *Kommandant*'s deputy, Edmund Bräuning. This link to the top means she gets away with murder. This doesn't surprise me. Binz was always hungry for power. Maria tells me how overcrowded the camp is, that there's been a huge influx of women and children from Warsaw, more than Ravensbrück can cope with.

A tent's been put up between blocks twenty-four and twenty-six, she says. It holds about a thousand prisoners, but there is not enough food to feed them all, so they're dying in droves. Their corpses lie frozen solid where they fall.

It sounds very much like Majdanek, I say. There are too many prisoners everywhere. It's placing terrible pressure on us all.

We enter the *Aufseherinnen* block and climb the stairs to Maria's room. It's so familiar. Even the staircase feels like being home. When she opens the door, I'm hit by a strong smell of dog, and I smile. Pure Maria! Two beds are crammed into the space where there used to be one and the desk has been removed.

To cope with all the additional *Aufseherinnen*, we share rooms now, she says. But I am lucky; I still have my own room.

The unmade bed is covered with dog hairs. Herbert jumps up onto it. Maria is completely oblivious to his mess.

Nobody wants to share with me because of Herbert, she says. I'm grateful because the new guards are rough. They get next to no training and the discipline of the camp's early years has been totally lost. Hermi, why don't you share with me?

Yes, of course, Maria, I say. But please can Herbert sleep on the floor? I draw the line at sharing my bed with a dog!

The dog looks at me forlornly and we both laugh. Maria sits on her bed and tells me about a recent visit by Himmler.

Do you remember his first visit? she asks.

Yes, of course. We all watched that movie, *Jud Süß*.

I feel a sharp pang. I remember sitting next to Dieter watching that movie. I was so happy back then. Life felt simpler; I'd seen so much less. Maria interrupts my thoughts.

Well, this time, Himmler came looking for women to work in his office because he'd lost most of his staff in recent bombings, she says. The prisoners were all lined up so he could take his pick. He chose four tall blonde women who could speak good German. His visit had quite a negative effect here.

Why?

It made everyone worried about the bombing raids. We're

not far from Berlin here. If Himmler's offices are being hit, we could be too. Plus, he warned *Oberaufseherin* Klein to be on guard against an uprising in the camp, which stirred up a panic. Everyone knows about the revolts at Treblinka and Sobibor.

I wouldn't worry about that here, I say. Those revolts were organised by male prisoners. The women are far too weak.

Klein is taking it very seriously, Maria says. The ratio of guards to prisoners is different from when you were here, Hermi. I think it is possible. She told us to use the dogs on the prisoners as much as we like.

Maria strokes Herbert, which makes even more of his hair shed onto the bed.

Of course, I won't use Herbert unless it's completely necessary.

Maria's as stubborn as always. I ask after Dieter.

He left about six months ago, she says. I don't know where he went. I stopped talking to him after you left.

I glow at this comment. Maria's loyalty is like a warm blanket. I'm so lucky to have such a good friend.

Later that night, I lie in bed wide awake while Maria sleeps. Even though the bed is much softer than the beds at Majdanek, I'm not sure I'll be able to share with Maria for long. The room stinks of dog. As I toss and I turn, I run through memories of my time here. My thoughts keep turning to Dieter. Despite everything, I find myself wishing I could see him again.

Russell.

October 1978. Bochum.

I'm helping an old man who lives a few doors down from us to rewire his kitchen as a neighbourly favour. The room is dim and it smells of stale air. Karl Hösler came to our door a few days ago and asked me for help because he'd heard on the grapevine that I'm an electrician. He's the first person who's wanted anything to do with me in a long time.

I'm an electrical engineer, I told him. But sure, I'll see if I can help.

Hösler sits at his kitchen table while I look at his wires. His hands curl with arthritis, his skin is mottled with age.

I've been following the trial, he says.

I brace myself, expecting him to launch into a tirade, but when Hösler speaks, he surprises me.

The hysteria surrounding this trial is quite shocking, he says. It must be hard for you and your wife. The young people don't understand it. They can't put themselves into our shoes. They turn on us. I have four sons, all of them good men, but I don't discuss the war with any of them. If I do, we just end up fighting, so what's the point? My wife passed away a few years ago and my sons are all I have left now. It's easier to keep quiet and keep the peace. You are a good man, Herr Ryan, for supporting your wife. You are so far from your home. You must miss your old life. Please, won't you sit down?

I join him at the table. He leans in towards me. His breath smells of alcohol. Let me tell you something, Hösler says. I worked on the railways in Düsseldorf as a train guard. A lot of the Jews were transferred through the station. I knew what was happening, but what could I do? It seems unforgivable now, but it felt very different back then. Düsseldorf was being bombed and people were dying all over the city. I was sick with worry about my own family. The Jews were not my priority.

I appreciate your honesty, Herr Hösler, I say. Very few people have the courage to say that. It's far too easy for us to judge now. None of us have any idea what life was like for you back then.

Hösler gets up from the table, opens a cupboard and takes out a bottle and two glasses.

Have a drink with me, he says.

I nod and he pours me a glass.

I'm pleased to meet you, Herr Ryan. You're a good man for helping me with the electrics. You're a good man for supporting your wife. Prost!

He chinks his glass against mine. The top of my glass is chipped. I turn it round to a smooth section, place my lips against it and take a drink. The liquid is sharp and strong; it's clearly homemade.

A lot of people of my generation are simply relieved that it's not us on trial, he says. We all bear the guilt.

Thank you, Herr Hösler, I say. It helps me to hear that spoken aloud.

He stares at his glass and says, We find ways to forget.

Hermine.
March 1944. Ravensbrück.

Within a week of arriving back at Ravensbrück, *Kommandant* Suhren calls me into his office. He's sitting behind an enormous desk, looking through papers. Suhren's an imposing man, tall, with white-blonde hair and a rectangular face. I stand in front of him, nervous, not knowing why he wants to see me.

You were second in command at Majdanek, Braunsteiner, he says without looking up. You have the War Merit Cross, extremely impressive, and you have good references from your time here at Ravensbrück. I am looking for someone with enough experience to run a women's subcamp.

He puts down his papers and looks up at me, eyes icy blue.

The camp is at Genthin, he continues. It's a work camp in Saxony. The prisoners make ammunition there. I'm sure you are aware that we are at a crucial stage of the war now; the need for ammunition is increasing and we must protect the Reich at all cost. I've had a request for 700 prisoners to move to Genthin from Ravensbrück. I would like you to go with them to run the women's camp. It's small, so you should find it quite easy.

Suhren looks at me, waiting for a reply.

Yes, *Kommandant*, I say, utterly delighted. I can do that.

He shuffles some papers on his desk and passes me one. I read through it briefly, sign my name and the date.

Thank you, Braunsteiner. Congratulations. You are now the *Oberaufseherin* of Genthin. You will transfer tomorrow. That is all. Heil Hitler!

And that is that, a promotion within a matter of minutes! I go straight back to my room to pack, folding my clothes amid all the dog hairs. Maria is going to be upset that I'm leaving so soon, but I hope she will recognise what an opportunity this is for me.

Once my suitcase is ready, I sit on the bed and look out of the window. Prisoners work the flower beds outside Suhren's house in the snow. This scene could be from five years ago, yet so much has changed. Back then, Maria and I were still working in the factory at Grüneberg. Here I am now, in charge of a subcamp of Ravensbrück!

When Maria returns, she is sad, but also genuinely happy for me.

Of course, I will miss you, she says. But it's so exciting for you and so well deserved.

Russell.
July 1979. Düsseldorf.

West Germany's dropped the Statute of Limitations for murder, a severe blow to our case. It raises the stakes sky high. I worry that you will go to jail. Outside the courtroom, you lean your body against me. You're convinced that you will be charged with murder.

That's not going to happen, I insist. The trial isn't over. Don't lose hope.

I try to guide you gently into the courtroom, but you resist. You breathe in short, sharp, quick breaths, hyperventilating.

I can't take it anymore, Russ, you say, pulling away from me.

Mundorf approaches us and I tell him you're not feeling well.

This is not a good day to be ill, he says. The press is watching.

Suddenly, you are hysterical.

Help me! Help me! you shout. I can't take it anymore!

You lean your full weight against me. I'm afraid you might faint. Judge Bogen appears in the doorway. Dark circles pull at his eyes.

What's wrong? the judge asks.

My wife is unwell, sir. She cannot go in.

Judge Bogen looks at you propped up against me. I stand firm, holding the weight of your body leaning against mine.

Very well, he says. You may take Frau Ryan home, but allow me to say something to her first.

Bogen walks towards you and looks you up and down with barely disguised contempt.

Frau Ryan, he says. After four years of silence, perhaps it is time for you to talk.

With that, he turns back into the courtroom and closes the door.

That evening, when we get back to the apartment, I make you some soup. You spoon it slowly into your mouth but only manage to finish half a bowl. I'm frantic with worry about your health. You're not eating enough and have become far too thin. You put the spoon down, mumble something inaudible and walk out into the garden. I follow and we both sit down on the grass of our small back yard. Birds dart across the sky.

Those birds are *Mauersegler*, you say. People often mistake swifts for swallows, but you can tell by their tails that they're swifts. The location is also a clue. The swift is a city bird, whereas the swallow prefers the countryside; we're at the edge of a city here, so those are swifts.

When you talk about the birds, your voice becomes liquid. As I feel you relax, the muscles at the base of my spine loosen too, releasing some of the tension I've been holding. This is what our life should be like: the two of us, sitting in the garden, looking at the birds. Of all the people to come after, why did it have to be you? We sit in peaceful silence as the light of the day starts to fade. A small white butterfly lands on the grass in front of us, then takes off again, in whimsical flight. You put your hand on my knee.

I'm sorry, Russ, you say quietly. I just couldn't take it anymore. Everybody talks about how difficult it is for the witnesses, but what about me? Nobody asks what it's like for me. Nobody understands what it was like to be a guard in those places. I wish Maria was here. She'd understand. Poor Maria. Oh how I miss her. She'd tell them what it was really like. That judge wants me to talk, but what's the point? No one will believe anything I say. They've already judged me. And I can't even remember it all properly anymore. It all feels so distant. When I look back, it feels like a series of photographs that are all blurred. It's like I'm looking at someone else.

Hermine.

March 1944. Genthin.

I'm riding to Genthin in a convoy of trucks. They move slowly, like caterpillars, back-to-back. Anni Schönwetter is in the seat next to me. Four other guards are spread through the rest of the trucks. I'm pleased with the staffing allocation; the *Aufseherinnen* assigned are all hard working and good at their jobs. We travel through the Ruppiner forests. The trees are full of spring and coming to bud. In Rathenow, we drive through streets lined with orange-roofed houses, each with a small front garden, dotted with yellow aconites and purple tulips. Germany is so beautiful in springtime.

After three hours of driving, we reach Genthin, a small town 100 kilometres to the west of Berlin. The camp lies in woodland just outside the town, surrounded by a high wooden fence with an internal layer of electrified barbed wire. Watchtowers manned with guns are spaced evenly along the fence. I'm relieved that we're far enough from Berlin to be safe from air strikes. We take the prisoners straight to their barracks. There is no camp uniform here; it's completely run out, so the women line up for large white crosses to be painted on the back of their civilian clothing. The clogs have also run out, so the prisoners must wear their own shoes. They go barefoot if they don't have shoes, which is not ideal, but what can we do? I allow them to rest in their barracks for what's left of the day. Tomorrow, they will start work at the Silva Metallwerk, the ammunitions factory run by Polte-Werke near to the camp.

Once I have settled, I report to the camp commander,

Lagerführer Otto Wahl. Wahl is in his late thirties, tall, well-built and very attractive. We get on immediately. He confides that he was recently promoted to run Genthin, and I tell him that this is also my first time being completely in charge. We congratulate each other on our new positions and promise we'll do a good job. Once the pleasantries are over, Wahl sets me some tasks. The first is to sort out the rationing in the kitchens.

The previous *Lagerführer*, Franz Ziegenfuss, was caught stealing food from the prisoners, Wahl says. He ran away from the camp a few weeks ago with one of the *Aufseherinnen*. The kitchen's a mess.

This surprises me on so many levels, not least that he would want to steal the prisoners' food, which is disgusting.

There's been a new edict from Himmler to change the prisoners' diet, Wahl continues. He wants us to stop allowing the vegetables to cook in the soup. He believes that adding them in raw at the end of the process will increase the vitamin content, which will improve the prisoners' working capacity.

I don't think that will work, I say. I think raw vegetables will be bad for their stomachs and that will in fact reduce capacity.

It's the latest in a series of Himmler's whims about diet, Wahl replies. We are under orders, so we obey.

I sort through the kitchens and try to get everything back into order. As it turns out, when it comes to the vegetables, I am proven correct. Within a week of putting raw turnips and carrots into the soup, dysentery is rife. With Wahl's blessing, I quietly reverse the orders and allow the vegetables to be cooked.

Russell.

November 1980. Düsseldorf.

This week is filled with accounts of the mass shooting of Jews that took place at Majdanek in November 1943. *Aktion Erntefest*, they call it: Operation Harvest Festival. All the women, both prisoners and guards, state that none of the *Aufseherinnen* were involved in this massacre. They were instructed to stay inside for the duration of the event, but the prosecutor is desperate to implicate the *Aufseherinnen*. He calls upon you.

You must have known, he says. The smell of burning bodies would have been strong.

Mundorf objects and I feel some relief. No doubt he'll repeat that you were not there.

Instead, he says, How could my client have known it was human flesh burning? How could she have known it was not the smell of animals being burnt?

There is a communal intake of breath. Mundorf pushes on, addressing Judge Bogen directly.

Your honour, it cannot be correct to say the prisoners knew that the smell was human flesh. Isn't it possible that it could have been the smell of work horses or other animals being burnt? We need to call in an expert witness on the subject of smell.

The courtroom erupts. Objection follows objection until the judge calls for silence. My hands clench into fists under the table. I pound on my legs. What on earth does Mundorf think he is doing? Why isn't he sticking to the very simple fact that you were not even at Majdanek at that time? This line of questioning is harming us.

During the break, you approach Mundorf in the corridor. Your voice bristles with anger.

What are you doing? I was in hospital with typhus when all that happened. Why are you talking about the smell of burning animals? How on earth is that going to help?

I lay into him too.

Herr Mundorf, this trial is already impossible for Hermine. You only need to look at the press to see how biased the whole thing is. Every move she makes gets her derogatory remarks. They analyse her hairstyle and clothing; they comment if she dares to smile. The men don't receive a fraction of the scrutiny and for once, we have an event where the female guards were *not even there*. You must have known the response your question would get!

Mundorf looks sheepish.

I was trying to prove that the women could not have known about it even if they had been there, he says.

You lean in towards him.

Of course, we knew about it, Herr Mundorf, you say. How would it be possible to hide such a thing? The point is that I was *not there*.

Hermine.

May 1944. Genthin.

Today, I inspect the factory. The prisoners feed metal into the machines at high speed. The room is filled with whooshing and screeching. Wahl is pleased that our output is up ten percent in less than two weeks. We know how to work the women hard. Their shift lasts twelve hours with only the briefest break at lunchtime for soup. We punish them each time that they miss their target. It's essential that we keep production to an absolute maximum. Wahl says there is talk of an Allied invasion of France, so we need to produce as many munitions as possible.

Schönwetter really knows how to keep the prisoners under control; they stand at their stations when I enter the factory. During the inspection, one of the prisoners releases her bladder. Urine runs down her leg and collects in a pool at her feet. It is disgusting. I shout at her, asking her what she thinks she is doing. The woman stammers that she could not hold it in any longer. She asked to go earlier but was refused.

That is correct, says Schönwetter. But it's just an excuse, *Oberaufseherin*. The women have use of the toilet first thing in the morning and then again after their shift. There is no need for them to go in between. She did it on purpose to get off her work.

Hearing this angers me. How dare she interrupt the line of work? I remember seeing a short metal stick on a bench near the factory doorway when I entered. I walk back to it, pick it up and return to the woman. She is trembling and muttering something over and over in a foreign language, presumably a prayer. I give her a thrashing over the head. After two or three blows, she falls to the floor. I tell Schönwetter to leave her lying there for the time being and to bring her to my office at the end of the day. Then I shout at the room full of women.

You use the toilet when we tell you, filthy cows! You are humans, not cattle. Stop behaving like animals!

When Schönwetter brings the prisoner to me later, her face is ashen and covered in dried blood. I can see her bones quaking under her skin. The woman's punishment for pissing on the floor like a dog is to stand outside her barrack for twelve hours with no food and no water.

If you wet yourself again, you will receive another beating, I say. Not just from me, but from all the guards.

Russell.
June 1981. Düsseldorf.

Each defendant is given the opportunity to make a final plea before the verdict is reached. It is your turn. You stand before Judge Bogen, shoulders stooped. This trial has aged you immensely. Your hair is snow white; it contrasts with the purple dress you are wearing, which hangs off you loosely. You pull yourself as upright as you can to address him directly.

Your honour, you say. The situation in the camps was extremely difficult. As a woman, it weighed heavily on my soul.

Bogen interrupts you immediately.

Frau Ryan, he says. If that is the case, then why did you select women to be killed and indeed kill women, as we've heard in this trial?

Undeterred, you continue to speak.

I may have been at the selections, you say. But we were instructed to be there. It was not possible for me not to take part. We were told that the prisoners were criminals, that they needed re-educating. I did not have access to the prisoner files. How could I know if they were imprisoned unjustly? I did not choose who was put in the camps. I was just a small link in the chain. I had no way of stopping what went on.

It's warm in the courtroom. Bogen's face has gone red. He tugs at his cheek and looks at you again.

People died because of your choices, Frau Ryan. Thousands of people died. Can you not see that what we are doing here is justice?

Your eyes scan the rest of the judges, searching their faces for even a hair's breadth of sympathy. This is your last chance to appeal to them, your last hope.

I was only twenty, sir. I had no life experience back then. It was a different time and a different place. People thought differently. We were at war. We were told the prisoners were the enemy. Everything we did, we did for our country. It's hard to explain how difficult it was. We were under extraordinary pressure. I may have hit the prisoners sometimes, but everyone did. I was not the most violent guard, far from it; I even helped the prisoners when I could. I've explained how I tried to improve the meals for them at Genthin. I may be to blame, sir, but I'm not a murderer. Please don't charge me with murder, so help me God.

You turn around and face out into the courtroom, directing the rest of your speech at the lines of press and onlookers. The whole courtroom looks at you. You look small and old. Your voice cracks and strains as you speak.

What do any of you know about what I went through back then? How awful it was. How often I was afraid for my life. What can you know of the daily struggles I've felt over the past five and a half years? What does anyone know of my suffering? What it's been like to hear unfair accusations, how I've fallen apart? What do any of you know about me? I'm just the person you read about in the papers, but for me this is real. None of you can possibly know what my life has been like.

You glance towards me and I nod at you, willing you to continue. You turn back to the judges with your final plea.

Your honours, when you are reaching your verdict, please think about me as the person I am, not a criminal, not a monster, but an ordinary woman, a young woman who had to do a horrible job at a difficult time. Yes, I bear some guilt. Like everybody else, I may have sometimes been rough, but I'm not a murderer. You expect me to pay for something that I neither planned nor thought up. It was my bad luck to work in the camps. I am not responsible for this piece of German history.

Bogen nods and you sit back down, looking exhausted. You cross your hands on your lap. It's impossible to know whether you have convinced the judges. All we can do now is wait.

Hermine.

June 1944. Genthin.

Production levels at the factory are twenty percent higher than when we arrived one month ago. I feel immense pride. It's the end of the week and Wahl's invited me into his office to celebrate with a bottle of red wine.

Music plays on the radio. I'm sitting in a comfortable armchair, pointing and releasing my toe in time with the music. Wahl's still in uniform. I'm wearing my favourite blue dress; it drapes over my knee when I cross my legs.

You look good in a dress, Braunsteiner, he says. You should wear one more often. I've put Schönwetter and Blum on duty for the evening. I told them not to disturb us.

He comes to stand behind me and I can smell a hint of fresh sweat.

You look tired, Hermine, he says, using my first name for the first time. My skin tingles and my heart picks up a pace. It's been a long week of work. Here, I'll help you to relax.

Wahl puts his hands on my shoulders and kneads at them softly. As the radio plays, his fingers inch forward and the blood warms in my neck.

Wagner, he says. Parsifal. It's beautiful. You know, the *Führer* is a very big fan.

His fingers trace the seam on my shoulders, then skim round my collar and descend to the top button of my dress. He prises it open and I lean my head backwards, closing my eyes.

Wahl whispers in my ear, This dress is very pretty, but you'd look better without it.

Outside the door, there's a cough, then a knock.

A voice says, *Oberaufseherin*?

Wahl removes his hand quickly, stands upright and moves back to his desk.

Wait a minute, I call out as I straighten my dress. Then, You may come in.

It's Blum. She looks from Wahl to me and then down to the floor, saying nothing.

Well, what is it? I ask, irritated.

I'm sorry to disturb you, *Oberaufseherin*. Good evening, *Lagerführer*.

Blum's caught two prisoners using the soap meant for cleaning munition shells to wash their underwear. She's not sure how to punish them. Wahl laughs.

Underwear, hey? Is it pretty?

We both giggle and Blum blushes. I think Wahl's a bit drunk.

What do you want me to do, *Oberaufseherin*? she asks.

Wahl is behind her now, smiling and pouring himself another glass of wine.

That is certainly bad, *Aufseherin* Blum, I say. But it's not urgent and right now I'm busy with the *Lagerführer*.

I can see Wahl behind her. He is licking his lips in a gesture that is half provocative, half grotesque. Blum looks at me, waiting for an instruction.

Tell the prisoners they are to report to me at 9am tomorrow, I say. There's no need to disturb me again. You can go.

Yes, *Oberaufseherin*, Blum says and then scuttles from the room.

When Blum is gone, I smile at Wahl. He is walking towards me with his shirt already half off.

Russell.

June 1981. Düsseldorf.

People have come from all over the country to hear the verdict. The courtroom is packed full. It takes ten and a half hours to deliver and Judge Bogen almost loses his voice. He pauses to take a long drink of water before delivering your sentence. This trial has aged him immensely; huge black rings circle his eyes. Nearly six years long, it's the longest trial Germany has ever seen and has cost the country more than twenty million marks. For what? To blame the cogs in the machine.

Judge Bogen coughs and calls you to stand.

Defendant Ryan, he says. Life in prison for the selection and murder of eighty people, aiding in the murder of 102 people, and selection and aiding in the murder of 1,000 people.

I look at Bogen in disbelief as you collapse against Mundorf. He holds onto you firmly and helps you to sit down. My heart is pounding. How can they take you away from me like this? You can't go to prison for the rest of your life. How will I manage without you? You are everything to me; all I have is you. Without thinking, I find myself standing and shouting.

This is victor's justice, not real justice! You're convicting my wife for the crimes of the Nazis! Shame on you all!

Sit down, Herr Ryan, Bogen says firmly. Justice has been served. You should count yourself lucky we're confined by our legal system. If the law allowed it, your wife's sentence would be much worse.

A policeman looms over me. I compose myself and sit back down. How can this have happened? Your sentence is the longest of anyone's, longer than Hildegard Lächert, longer than Hermann Hackmann, longer than all the rest of the women, longer even than all the men. This is not the outcome Mundorf prepared us for. We knew you were likely to go to jail, but not for life. At the end of the sentencing, three policemen approach you to take you away. You're slumped against Mundorf, unable to move.

Stop! I shout.

I push past them, unable to contain my distress.

Leave her alone! Can't you see she's not well? Where's your humanity? Give her some air!

Your eyes glisten with fear. Your voice is a rasp.

Russ, you say. I'm going to die in a prison.

I take hold of your face and pull it so close I feel the warmth of your breath.

No, you are not, I say. I will fight for you. I will get you out.

Outside the courthouse, people are waiting to see the defendants.

They're shouting, *Schande! Schande! Schande! Schande!*

Disgrace! Disgrace! Disgrace! Disgrace!

The shouting gets louder and louder. I whisper so only you can hear.

Hermine, I will stay here for you. I will visit you every week. I will wait for you and do whatever it takes to get you out.

You smile at me weakly. I'm powerless as the policemen lead you away. Out in the corridor, the chorus of shouting has reached a crescendo.

Schande! Schande! Schande! Schande!

It is a disgrace. Shame on this country for rewriting its history. Shame on it for pinning all this onto you.

Hermine.
April 1945. Genthin.

We're on high alert. A report arrives first thing this morning from above:

The Russians are moving closer. Destroy everything. Take your prisoners east to the crematorium in Brandenburg immediately to be liquidated.

We load all the women into six trucks. The prisoners are highly agitated. They keep asking what's happening. I lean into each truck as it departs and tell them they are going back to Ravensbrück, which appeases some, but many more start to cry.

The rest of the *Aufseherinnen* accompany the trucks, riding up front with the drivers. I stay behind at Genthin to await further orders, keeping one of the prisoners with me, a Polish woman called Mrozek. Mrozek can speak German and she knows how to type. I want her to remain in case I need to send messages. Mrozek sits in the corner and shakes uncontrollably, which worsens my mood. After a while, I tell her to go and sit in her barrack just to get rid of her. A short time later, Wahl bursts into my office, looking alarmed.

Braunsteiner, why haven't you started to burn all the papers? God knows what the Russians will do if they find the camp. Every last scrap of paperwork must be destroyed. If they can track us down, there will be retribution. We must leave no trace at all, absolutely no names.

Wahl rushes back into the stairwell and I follow. He sets up two large drums in the hallway at the bottom of the stairs. I help him fill them with paper and he sets them alight.

Destroy it all, no matter how small, he says.

I call the miserable Mrozek back from her barrack and set her to work. The three of us run back and forth from the offices, loading papers into the burning drums. The drums give off significant heat. Smoke billows out of them, making us cough. When at last we have finished, Wahl stands next to the drums as the fires die down. The firelight reflects in his eyes like tiny candles. In a strange sort of way, the scene is quite magical. Looking at him, I am filled with desire, but the fear in his voice snaps me back to reality.

It's not just the Russians, he says. The Americans and the British are approaching from the west.

Mrozek stands listlessly next to the drums, looking desperate.

Cheer up, I say. At least you're alive.

Barely two hours pass when we hear the noise of engines approaching. Something is wrong. The trucks are returning far too soon. Wahl runs out into the camp courtyard to meet them. I follow, trying to keep up. The lead driver, a fellow called Schulz, descends from the first truck. He mops sweat off his face with the sleeve of his jacket. Panic rises in Wahl's voice.

What the hell is going on?

We didn't make it, Schulz says. An army runner turned us around at Bensdorf. The Russians will take Brandenburg any minute.

Wahl raises his eyebrows and his mouth twitches. He sees that I'm looking at him and pulls himself together.

You need to take control of your prisoners, Braunsteiner, he snaps. Get them out of the trucks, call an *Appell* and then get them back to work. Mrozek, you come with me. I have my own work to do.

I do as he orders, heart beating as fast as a drum, all the while reasoning with myself that the Russians are more likely to push north of Berlin than in our direction. We must be ready to evacuate when the order comes.

Russell.

December 1984. Mülheim.

Mülheim Women's Prison is a five-minute walk from the train station towards the River Ruhr. I come here every week on a Tuesday after you've had breakfast and walked round the yard. At the entrance, I empty out the contents of my bag onto the desk: my wallet, the book that I'm reading, three books of crosswords, some packets of glue and two balls of wool. The guard looks at the pile and picks up the glue.

For my wife's craft work, I say.

The guard nods.

How is she? I ask.

Your wife is fine, Herr Ryan. Though she's been having trouble with nightmares again. We're giving her medication to help her to sleep.

She indicates that I may pass and calls one of her colleagues to show me into the prison. The second guard smiles. I know all of them now.

Good morning, Herr Ryan, the second guard says. Follow me.

She leads me through the building to the visiting area. Water condenses along the passageway on the stone walls. We enter the room, which is nearly bare, just three wooden tables, each flanked by two chairs. I sit at the nearest table and wait. A few minutes later, a third guard accompanies you into the room. You're wearing your prison uniform, a simple blue dress. I rise and walk towards you and hold onto you tightly, but the guard tells us we need to sit down. We obey and the guard stands by the door. We have just one hour.

How are you doing? Are you OK?

I'm fine, you say. I've been knitting a lot. I can still manage it despite my hands.

You lay them on the table for me to inspect. They're knotted and gnarled, twisted with arthritis.

Did you bring me the wool?

Yes, honey, I say as I fumble in my bag. I also brought crossword books and the glue.

I place the items onto the table and you pick up the glue.

I'm making a doll, you say. I'm allowed to sell them. It's something to do.

Clever you, I say. Industrious!

The hour passes quickly. You tell me about the sweater you're knitting and I tell you about some of the things that I've seen on TV. We discuss the weather, which has been bad. You've heard the high winds from your cell.

Are you warm enough in your room? I ask.

I ask the same things each week: Are you warm enough? Are you cool enough? Did you hear the rain?

Yes, Russ, I'm fine. I'm decorating my room for Christmas. I've been making paper chains. Next time you come, can you bring me some more coloured paper? I want to make you a Christmas card.

I can't bear to think of you alone in here for Christmas, I say.

I'm fine, Russ. Stop fussing. I'll be OK.

I've moved to Hattinger Straße in Bochum Linden. My upstairs neighbour, Leisl, has invited me to her apartment for *Heiligabend*. She lives with her ten-year-old son, a shy boy called Jens. I offered to teach him the trombone, but he's too introverted, which is a great shame. I so enjoyed teaching Joe back in Maspeth. When I think back to that time, I feel heavy with regret. Leisl is kind, but Christmas is never the same without you. The guard announces that we have five minutes left.

Hermine, I say gently. One of the guards told me you've been having bad dreams again. Are you sleeping OK?

You lean across the table and lower your voice.

I keep having the same dream, Russ. Not the one I told you about before. This one is different.

Can you remember it?

Yes. It's vivid. I'm in some sort of factory. I'm not sure where; it could be Ravensbrück, it could also be Genthin. I can't pinpoint the location.

Your face clouds over as you remember it.

What happens?

There are rows and rows of women working in lines. In the dream, I'm walking between the rows when one of the women does something that makes me really mad. I lift my arm to hit her, but my hand gets stuck above my head. It won't come down. When I look up, I can't see my hand, but I know I'm about to do something terrible and then I wake up covered in sweat.

It's not the first time you've had this kind of dream. Scenes from the camps fly through your head as you sleep like bats in the darkness, all jumbled and blurred. A few months ago, you told me you dreamt about shooting a boy. It upset you even though I told you it was impossible because you never had a gun.

Do you think these dreams are things that I did coming back to haunt me in my sleep? you ask.

No honey, I say firmly. Your brain is muddling up all the things we heard during the trial, confusing you, making you think that they're memories. The trial put thoughts into your head.

I take hold of your hands and look down at your fingers. We're both old now; our hands are wrinkled and spotted with brown.

You've got to clear your head of these thoughts, I say. What does any of it matter now, anyway?

On the way out, I ask the guard if she can give you more of the medication to help you to sleep.

Of course, Herr Ryan, she says. We all like your wife and we want her to sleep well. She's one of the easiest prisoners. She's polite and she keeps herself to herself.

As I walk to the station, the sky above darkens and it starts to rain. I pull the hood of my jacket over my head. While I wait for the train, I think about this latest nightmare you're having. Did you once beat a woman in a factory? Was that you? I'll never know for certain and it's better that way. I know that you took part in monstrous events, but I understand how you got there. You couldn't see wrong from right at the time; the warped logic of Nazism held you in its thrall, just as it held everyone. I see what this nation refuses to, that everyone was involved in one way or another, however big or small. You were one small part of a collective who were all doing wrong. If I think of each incident as performed by a series of guards, not you in particular, I can cope with what happened. This is how I've made peace with your past.

Hermine.
April 1945. Genthin.

Wahl unfolds a map and traces his finger across it, showing me the route.

We will cross the Elbe here, south of Tangermünde, he says. Then we'll head down towards Magdeburg. From there, we can go our own ways.

I look at the distance from here to Vienna. It takes me across nearly all of Germany. I'm so glad that I'm fully recovered. I feel physically strong enough to walk that far.

How long do you think we've got before the Russians arrive? I ask.

I don't know, Wahl replies, eyes wide with fear. One thing is certain, we've got to get out of here before they are near; they will rip off my balls.

And what about me?

Wahl says nothing. We both know that the Russians rape German women first before they kill them. It doesn't matter a jot that I'm Austrian. In the eyes of the Russians, it's all the same thing. I'm desperate to get going. All the *Aufseherinnen* are petrified by the Russian advance.

When do you expect the order to arrive for us to leave? I ask Wahl urgently. Surely, it's got to come soon.

I don't know, he says. It's messy out there. The chain of command seems to be lost. We cannot leave without a direct order, so we just have to wait.

Russell.
November 1989. Bochum Linden.

Everyone's watching the wall as it falls. I can hear the neighbours' TV sets through the surrounding walls as I stare at the screen in my own small apartment. Scores of people stand on top of the wall, singing and chanting.

Tor auf! Tor auf! Open the Gate!

The screen cuts to a young man holding a sledgehammer, whacking great chunks out of the wall. A huge section tumbles, creating a gap from the east to the west. People stream through it, jumping up and down ecstatically, hugging each other. One of them stops to speak to the camera, his face flushed with elation.

Communism's crumbling after all these years! he says. Today, the war is finally over!

The newsreel cuts to old news footage of President Kennedy speaking in West Berlin in 1963.

The Communist system is not just an offense against history but against all of humanity, he says. It's separating families, dividing husbands and wives, brothers and sisters, dividing people who want to be together.

I snort out loud. It's not only Communism that's done that! I switch off the television and go into the bedroom, open the wardrobe and pull out the top drawer. This is where I keep your jewellery boxes containing the silver necklace that I gave you and your favourite brooch.

I open the turquoise blue box, remove the necklace, place the pendant carefully in the palm of my hand, sit down on the bed and close my eyes. I remember the day I gave this to you, the day you became an American citizen. How proud I was of you; how happy I was that my country had taken you in. I place the box down heavily, thinking of the life that we should have shared, the life that we've lost. The walls of my apartment reverberate with the sound of celebration from the surrounding apartments. One wall is falling while another contains you. History is grinding its powerful teeth. History. It kisses some people but spits others out.

Hermine.
May 1945. Genthin.

When I report to Wahl's office before dawn, no one is there. He's gone. He must have fled Genthin last night. It turns out he is a coward. He left nothing, not even a note. I call the *Aufseherinnen* into my office and tell them that we're leaving in ten minutes. There is no order coming from above. They stare at me, petrified. Blum looks like she's going to cry.

Pull yourself together, I say. Now is not the time to get hysterical. We're going to walk out across Germany. All of you must dress like prisoners. Take off your uniforms but keep on your boots. Bring only what you need, food and water, some spare clothing, nothing else. Whatever you do, do not bring any papers; our position here puts all of us at grave risk.

Where should I go, *Oberaufseherin*? asks Wediner tearfully. I cannot go home. The Russians will be there by now. What should I do?

Wediner comes from Oranienburg, north of Berlin. It's certainly not safe there now. The *Aufseherinnen* look at me for guidance.

The Russians are coming from the east, I say. Wediner, you need to come west with the rest of us. If anyone stops us, we'll say that we're prisoners. If that causes suspicion, we'll need to split up. We'll walk towards the Allied powers; far better to be stopped by them than by the Russians.

It's only after the *Aufseherinnen* have left that I notice muffled wailing coming from the back of the room. It is Mrozek. She looks ragged.

What about the prisoners? Mrozek snivels. What should we do? What will the Russians do to us?

The truth is that I haven't given the prisoners a thought. Who knows what the Russians will do to them? Quite probably rape them too.

That's not my concern now, I say. Consider yourself free. You can do as you please.

The *Aufseherinnen* disperse to gather their things. I look round the room for the last time and then head downstairs into the hallway, past Wahl's two steel drums. Each contains a mountain of ash. All our work has been wiped out without trace.

Russell.

September 1993. Bochum Linden.

I sit next to the telephone, willing it to ring. A week ago, an ulcer appeared on your left foot. Two days later, the foot became gangrenous, so they took you to hospital. By yesterday, the infection had spread up your leg. The superintendent of Mülheim Women's Prison informed me that the doctors had decided to amputate your leg just below the knee. I try not to picture you lying on the operation table, scalpel slicing away at your skin. I feel like something unbearably heavy is pressing upon me, pushing against me from every side. At last, the phone rings. It's the superintendent. Her tone is civil and calm, which brings some relief.

The operation has finished, Herr Ryan, she says. Frau Ryan is conscious and stable. She's been put into recovery. She needs to stay in hospital for the next two weeks to allow her to heal. I can arrange for you to talk to her on the hospital phone once she's feeling a bit better. As soon as she's back at Mülheim, you can come and visit her in person.

Outside, a wagtail lands on the balcony and pumps its tail up and down, up and down. I watch it, thinking how much you'd like to see it, how you'd comment on it and tell me about its call and behaviour.

A week later, I speak to you on the hospital phone. You sound tired and breathless.

Hello, Russ. Is that you?

You sound tired, honey. Are you OK? How's the leg? Are you in pain?

It hurts less than I was expecting, but I can't bring myself to look at it.

I wish I could be there with you.

I'm glad you're not, Russ. I'm just a crippled old woman now. I'm no good to you.

Don't say that, Hermine. You're my wife.

You sigh down the phone line.

Do you remember how fit I was when we first met? I would give anything to go back to those days. How we swam and we hiked!

Of course I remember, honey. I remember how you practically ran up Hochobir.

I think about you hiking up that mountain all those years ago, striding ahead of me. I could hardly keep up with you. I think about our first night in the chalet in Eisenkappel-Vellach, the first time we made love, our bodies so young and so hopeful. The joy of the memory quickly shifts into melancholy, a deep longing to be those people we once were. How tangled and twisted our lives have been since then.

I used to be so strong, you say. Did I tell you that I walked all the way across Germany at the end of the war? More than 800 kilometres from Genthin to Vienna. Look at me now; you would not believe I was capable of such a thing. I remember Mutti's face when she opened the door, the first time she'd seen me in how many years, how she cried and cried. I hugged her and wouldn't let go.

You've told me this story many times. I still find it hard to believe that was you. I cannot fathom your life before I met you. What matters is the life that we've shared. You exhale loudly. A lifetime of memories expels through your mouth.

Once, my body could run up a mountain, you sigh. Now, I can't even take myself to the bathroom.

Are you getting enough help? I ask. I hope they're not neglecting you because you're a prisoner.

Oh no, Russ. The nurses are good. They help me wash and

they've been teaching me how to get myself in and out of the wheelchair.

That's good, I say.

I should have been a nurse, you say wistfully. It's a good job, helping people. I wish I had done that instead. I would have been good at it, and I would not have ended up here. If only things had been different.

I think about it often. How different our lives would be if the war hadn't happened. You would have stayed in Austria, married, lived happily with a family, of that I am sure. But what about me? Would I have met someone else? Or would I have ended up single, alone? What would my life have been like without you? There's no point thinking about it. I cannot change the course of my life now. There's no point feeling any regret.

Focus on your rehabilitation, Hermine, I say. I'm going to speak to the guards at Mülheim to make sure they monitor you better once you're back there. I don't want this happening to your other leg.

Hermine.
May 1945. Nuremberg.

My body chafes against the prisoner clothing as my feet pound the asphalt, backpack bouncing up and down on my back. It's stuffed with a map and compass, a cup, plate and spoon, spare clothing, some water and biscuits and, right at the bottom, my medal and brooch hidden away, stitched into a panel. Blum, Schönwetter, Schuster, Wagner and Wediner sprint behind me. The road is filled with people running and shouting.

The Russians are coming! The Russians are coming!

We keep up the pace from dawn until dusk. Fear drives us on. By the time we make Magdeburg, it's already dark. We pick our way through the city. It's been bombed to oblivion, streets mounded high with rubble. Eventually, we find shelter in the husk of a church and hunker down together in the burned out remnants of one of its wings.

I sleep with my head propped up against a pew. When I wake, my neck is sore, so I stretch and get up. It's before first light and no one else is awake yet. When dawn breaks, I look out of a window and see the city shaded softly with colour. Tumbledown buildings emerge from the rubble, orange and brown, still and so quiet, with no sign of life. From this vantage point, I can see the Elbe flowing gently below us, reflecting the first rays of sun in flashes of gold. A heron flies low over the river, wings stretched out wide, looking for fish, its shadow stroking the water. I lose myself to the sound of the river, but distant gunfire snaps me wide awake. We need to get going as fast as we can. Blum, Schuster, Schönwetter and Wagner are up and ready, but Wediner's still not fully dressed. She's crying and Blum is consoling her.

Oberaufseherin, she says. I don't think Hildegard's in a fit state to walk.

You better stay here with her and follow on later, I say. Schuster, Schönwetter, Wagner, you come with me. From now on, no one is to call me *Oberaufseherin*. My name is Hermine. I am twenty-five years old, a prisoner from Genthin, displaced by the war. You need to make yourselves invisible. Leave the past behind you, forget it, bury it deep down inside. Practise your stories and make them your own. Repeat them until you believe they are true.

I clamber out through the church onto the street. The sun is rising, dipping its fingers into the river and stirring the air. I need to head south towards Leipzig and Nuremberg, then southeast to Passau and across the border into Austria. I'm determined to make it. It's up to the others to peel off along the route whenever they want to make their own way home.

All of Germany is moving, prisoners, labourers, soldiers returning from war. Lines of people trudge the length of the road, carrying suitcases. A man cycles past and a few minutes later, three tanks roll by. A German soldier leans out of the top of one of them, shouting greetings and tossing great hunks of bread to the ground. They land in the dirt and cause a huge scramble; we're starving already and we've only been walking for two days. When we reach Leipzig, we're told that the Americans are coming, so we decide to stay only one night.

The stretch on to Nuremberg takes nearly two weeks. We walk all day and spend the nights sleeping in barns. Occasionally, we get a room in a house and bunk down together on the floor. I try to sleep, but I toss and turn, ears ringing, bones scraping the ground. A few days later, I start to feel sick. Our rations are low and I have a high temperature. Sweat drips steadily into my eyes. At one point, I see Schönwetter standing before me.

She's saying something, but I'm not sure quite what.

A few kilometres from Nuremberg, I need to sit down. I feel light-headed, like nothing is real. I slump down by the road and lie under a tree. My nose fills with the sweet smell of almonds, or is it vanilla? I look up into huge puffs of blossom under a canopy of moving white clouds. Schuster comes to sit next to me. Her voice is a mumble. I can't make out her words. She lifts my head and tips water into my mouth. It feels good. Petals drop down from above, like snowflakes in summer. I close my eyes.

When I wake up, a woman is standing next to me in a white uniform. It takes me a few moments to realise that she's speaking to me in English. I dredge my brain in search of the right words.

Where am I? I ask.

This is a field hospital in Nuremberg. Some soldiers found you, collapsed by the road. You're quite safe now. The Germans have gone.

I look around me. Blackboards line the far wall. This make-shift hospital must have once been a school. Rows of beds line the room, filled with injured soldiers and prisoners. I'm not sure who any of them are. I drift back to sleep and when I wake up again, the same nurse is there.

I wondered when you'd come round, she says, smiling. You've been shouting out things, but I don't speak any German, so I don't know what you were saying. You kept shouting out the name Maria. Your sister, perhaps, or a good friend?

Groaning interrupts us from the next bed where a body lies wrapped entirely in bandages. There is a yellow stain on the head where the eyes should be and a hole in place of a mouth. I look away, feeling queasy.

Where are the others?

What others?

The other prisoners. The people who were with me.

You were alone when we found you.

I close my eyes. What's happened to Schuster, Schönwetter

and Wagner? Where are they now? Did they abandon me by the road under the tree?

How long have I been here? I ask.

Just over a week, the nurse says. It was a bit touch and go. I wasn't sure you'd pull through.

I try to sit up in the bed, but the nurse stops me.

Not so soon. You are far too weak.

But I need to go home to Vienna, back to my family. Have you seen my bag?

It's here.

She points at the floor.

But you can't go now. You're not well enough to walk from here to Austria.

Russell.

April 1996. Bochum Linden.

I stand behind you, holding onto your wheelchair as your eyes scan the apartment. Your shoulders start to shake. I hurry round to face you and see that you're crying.

What's wrong, honey? Don't you like it? I spent all yesterday cleaning and making it nice.

The prison staff warned me that leaving jail can be a big adjustment; some people struggle to re-enter the world. Maybe it's too much for you.

Oh no, Russ! It's not that. I just can't believe that I'm back here with you. I thought that I would die in that prison.

Two days ago, Johannes Rau, the Minister President of North Rhine-Westphalia, pardoned you due to ill health. He was right to show mercy. You were the last of the Majdanek defendants still in jail; all the others have died or been let out. You wipe at your eyes with your sleeve.

I'm crying, but I'm happy, you say.

Wait here a second. I got you something to welcome you home.

In the kitchen, I pull a bunch of red and white roses out of the sink. I take them to you and help you uncurl your fingers and then wrap them back round the stems. You sniff at the flowers.

They're beautiful, Russ.

Just like you.

Don't be silly. I'm ugly and crippled.

I bend to reach your height. Though you are thick in the waist now and wheelchair bound, with only one leg, none of it matters.

To me, you will always be beautiful, I say. My beautiful wife. You smile at me wistfully.

I don't deserve your kindness.

Don't say that, honey. I'm your husband. I need to look after you.

All I ever wanted was to live with you in America, you say. For us to have had an ordinary life.

We are here now, I say. All I care about now is us being together, making the most of the years we have left.

Tears roll down your cheeks.

Thank you, Russ. Thank you for everything. Thank you for waiting for me all this time. Thank you for not going home.

Don't be silly, I say. I gave up on America a long time ago. This is home now, here with you.

I need to rest, you say. I get tired so easily now. Can you help me out of my chair onto the bed?

When you are settled, I leave you to nap and go into the kitchen to prepare us some food. By the time I walk back to the bedroom, you are fast asleep, lying on the bed, flat on your back. Your breath rakes at your throat as if at dry leaves. I've never seen you sleep on your back before. You always used to sleep on your side. I sit on the chair next to the bed and lean in close to your face. Your skin's deeply lined and it sags to the side. I look at my hands; the skin's just as wrinkled as yours. I have aged too, though inside I feel just the same. How well do I know you after all this time? Are you the same person you were when I met you? Were you ever the person I thought that you were? Am I the same man I was back in Austria? Or have I changed so slowly and in such tiny increments that I haven't noticed that I've turned into something quite new?

Hermine.

June 1945. Nußdorf.

Over the next few days, I regain my strength. The nurse brings me some clothing and food for my bag. I thank her profusely for her kindness.

Good luck! she says as I set off again. Safe journey home.

At Regensburg, I stop to look at the Danube over a wall. If I follow this river, I will get home. A soldier interrupts me and asks for my papers. My heart leaps directly into my mouth. I raise both of my arms up in surrender, trying to hide the panic that must be showing on my face. The soldier looks amused. He's chewing on gum.

I'm not gonna hurt you, Miss, he says. I just need to see your papers.

I don't have any, I stutter. The Germans destroyed them. I was a prisoner in one of the camps.

My arms are still up, pointing skywards. The soldier beams a great smile.

You can put your arms down, Miss. I'm sorry for what happened to you. You're free to go. Are you on your way home?

The relief is so great that I almost collapse.

I'm Austrian, I say. I'm going to Vienna. That's where I live.

The soldier shouts down the road to one of his colleagues.

Hey, Atkins, do you know if any trucks are going towards Passau? This young lady here wants to get to Vienna.

Wait there, the other soldier shouts back. I'll go ask.

As we wait, I repeat the story that I've prepared over the past weeks, that I'm a prisoner, who was held at Ravensbrück, then

Genthin, for political work. I keep the details as vague as I can, but the soldier's not interested; he's much more keen to tell me about himself. Sam Foster is from Ohio and used to be a schoolteacher before the war.

We both wanna go home, Sam Foster says cheerfully. We got that in common.

A truck pulls up and another American soldier leans out, smoking a cigarette. He indicates for me to jump in.

I hear you're going to Passau, he says. You'll be safe there. It surrendered last month, so it's in our hands.

More soldiers sit on benches on each side of the truck. One of them offers me some bread and some cheese. I take it gratefully and eat hungrily; I've become very thin. The journey takes a few hours. I look out the back of the truck across flat open farmland. Young wheat sways in the fields, creating carpets of green.

The road is littered with discarded equipment, piles of old helmets, used ammunition, broken guns. My thoughts wander to friends and family. What's happened to Maria? I imagine her walking this road with Herbert, the two of them together right up to the end. Dear Maria, I hope you escaped. What about Lächert, Ernst and Pfannstiel? Ehrich and Langefeld, Johann and Dieter? My mind turns to home. I can't wait to see Mutti. I hope above everything else that she is alive, as well as Luise and my other sisters and brothers. Please God, let all of them have survived.

When the truck reaches Passau, everyone gets out. There are soldiers milling around everywhere. I'll feel much safer once I'm on my own soil. I walk through the town to the bridge that crosses the river and look down. The river swirls below, muddied brown with silt. When I reach the other side, I look back across the bridge from the safety of Austria. What will happen to Germany now?

After four days, I make it to Linz. From there, I hitch a ride with a truck as far as Sankt Pölten. After nearly two months of constant moving, scavenging and sleeping rough, I can barely stand. Two more days and I will reach home.

The last few kilometres are the hardest; my feet scrape the ground through the holes in my boots. North of Vienna, I tramp across farmland and the remnants of unattended vineyards, whose owners must have been called to war. Vines tangle and sprawl over each other, unchecked and unkempt. At the top of the hill that overlooks Nußdorf, I stop and look down. A kestrel glides over me and swoops down the valley, searching for mice in the unploughed fields. The sight of it fills my heart with joy.

Once down the hill, I pass the cemetery, filled with new gravestones. How many lives have been claimed by the war? I turn away, not wanting to see if there are new stones next to Vati; I cannot face the thought of any more of my family dead. When I reach the stream, I take off my shoes and dip my feet into its coolness. The water makes my torn feet sting. A dragonfly lands on a rock, iridescent and blue, spreads out its wings and curls in its tail. I wash as much dirt as I can from my face, discard my boots and walk the final stretch barefoot, pushing past the pain in my feet.

The gardens of Nußdorf have all been neglected; summer flowers poke out through undergrowth, fighting with weeds. When I reach Kahlenberger Straße, I break into a run. My feet catch on the cobbles, making me trip. The door to our building has been left open. I stumble through it, climb up the stairs, and stop for a moment outside our apartment. I reach out to the wall and pull off a flake of old paint. It feels so familiar, just like an old friend. The sound of soft singing seeps through the doorway. It is Mutti, dear Mutti. She is here! She is here! My head is pounding. My heart is a drum. I look down at myself. My clothes are in tatters and I'm covered in dirt, but none of it matters because I've made it back home. I wipe away tears, put my hand to the door and knock.

Russell.

November 1998. Bochum.

The lake is flat and grey, its surface dull as lead. Bochum rises in the distance, cold and solid. The sky looks like ice.

It's wintry today, I say, pushing your wheelchair.

Air puffs from your mouth like a snort from a horse. You pull your hat down and straighten your rug. A bag of bread from the bakery rests on your lap. The ducks see us coming and paddle furiously toward us.

Do you want to feed them, honey?

Again, no response. I push the chair off the path towards the water; its wheels struggle to stay straight on the grass. I lean over your shoulder and take some bread from the bag, rip it and toss it out to the ducks. They tug at it in a frenzy of quacking while we both watch in silence. Perhaps you are right, there is nothing to say.

I clip the brake onto your wheelchair and walk a short distance away to a bench, leaving you there, throwing bread to the ducks. A child rushes past on a scooter, followed by his mother, who runs after him shouting for him to slow down. We wait a while longer and then I get up.

I guess we should go home now, I say, releasing the brake on your chair and turning you back towards the path.

Wait, you say. Can we stay a bit longer?

Yes, of course, as long as you want.

I turn you back round so you can see the lake. You close your eyes and sniff at the air.

I'm imagining we're in Austria, you say. Back where we started, the lake and the boat. Do you remember? We drank cider and you gave me those seeds. Did I tell you I planted them? They grew and they flourished.

My heart cleaves. I remember it as if it was yesterday. You looked so good in your red swimsuit.

I will never forget it, I say. You swam so well. I couldn't keep up

I sit down next to you on the grass, take hold of your hand, squeeze it gently and close my eyes too. We're back at Wörthersee together, rowing, diving, laughing, kissing, carefree and happy, shimmering, the best versions of ourselves.

If I could go back there, Russ, I would swim to the bottom and never come up.

Then I would swim down after you and pull you back to the surface.

You turn towards me and I look into your eyes. They're as blue as they were the first day we met. I see my whole life in them, all of it from beginning to end. You turn away to look out over the lake and let go of my hand. I can feel your mood shifting, like the wind on the water.

I'm sorry, Russ, you say. I know that I've ruined your life.

Tears well. I stifle them. My voice starts to crack.

Nothing has ever changed how much I love you, Hermine. I want you to know that.

Your face fills with gratitude. I think I see hope. What comes next is so quiet, it's almost a whisper.

Do you forgive me?

You've not asked this question in a very long time. I pause for a moment while I think what to say.

What is it that you want me to forgive, honey?

The things that I did.

It's not a question that I want to answer. I've spent more than thirty years living in the shadow of your past. I found my way through it to get to this point.

I clear my throat and say, I understand why you did what you did.

But do you forgive me?

I take a deep breath and choose my words carefully.

I understand why you did what you did.

That's all I can give you. Your eyes fill with sadness. It snuffs out the hope. You look at me and nod. The wind's picking up. It's sending out ripples across the lake's surface.

Come on, I say. The weather's getting worse. We need to get back to the car before it starts to rain. I want to get home and make us some stew.

I pull your chair back onto the track and start to push you towards the car park. The path below us is flecked with dark grey, like compacted ash. Your chair tracks across it, its wheels turning slowly. As I push you, I blink away tears. Have I loved you enough? Have I loved you too much? Have I tried hard enough to understand you? Have I tried too hard? I've believed you and doubted you, loved and resented you. I've swum in your tide. I stop for a second, put my hand on your shoulder and feel you relax. This journey we've travelled was not of our choosing, but we are still here.

The sky above darkens and the air starts to chill. In the distance, sheets of rain slice through the city. I push the chair harder, to pick up the pace. A plover flies low over the lake, balanced on wingtips. It skims the water, piping out mournfully. The wind is pushing it this way and that.

Historical Note

While both main characters in this novel were real people, this book is a work of fiction. I shaped Hermine Braunsteiner through what I learnt about her from court records, witness accounts, newspaper articles, Simon Wiesenthal's files in the Vienna Wiesenthal Institute, plus historical analysis of the *Aufseherinnen*. Nonetheless, she is fictionalised. The character of Russell Ryan is entirely fictional in this book. Other real people who appear in this book have also been fictionalised.

I found the following books particularly helpful during my research and would recommend them to anyone wanting to find out more about Hermine, the *Aufseherinnen*, the time and places that they existed in, and the psychology behind perpetration: *The Camp Women: the Female Auxiliaries who Assisted the SS in Running the Nazi Concentration Camp System* by Daniel Patrick Brown, *If This is a Woman. Inside Ravensbrück: Hitler's Concentration Camp for Women* by Sarah Helm, *Female SS Guards and Workaday Violence: The Majdanek Concentration Camp, 1942-1944* by Elissa Mailänder, *The Ravensbrück Women's Concentration Camp: History and Memory* edited by Alyn Beßmann and Insa Eschebach, *Im Gefolde der SS: Aufseherinnen des Frauen-KZ Ravensbrück* by Simone Erpel, *Die Frauen von Majdanek: Vom zerstörten Leben der Opfer und der Mörderinnen* by Ingrid Müller-Münch, *Ravensbrück* by Germaine Tillion, *Into that Darkness: An Examination of Conscience* by Gitta Sereny, *Account Rendered:*

A Dossier on my Former Self by Melita Maschmann, *Justice not Vengeance* by Simon Wiesenthal, *New Lives: Survivors of the Holocaust Living in America* by Dorothy Rabinowitz, *Omaha Blues: A Memory Loop* by Joseph Lelyveld, *The Ratline: Love, Lies and Justice on the Trail of a Nazi Fugitive* by Philippe Sands, *The Destruction of the European Jews* by Raul Hilberg, *Rethinking the Holocaust* by Yehuda Bauer, *Becoming Evil: How Ordinary People Commit Genocide and Mass Killing* by James Waller, *The Nazi Doctors: Medical Killing and the Psychology of Genocide* by Robert Jay Lifton, *Eichmann in Jerusalem: A Report on the Banality of Evil* by Hannah Arendt, *Eichmann Before Jerusalem: the Unexamined Life of a Mass Murderer* by Bettina Stangneth, and *Ordinary Men: Reserve Police Battalion 101 and the Final Solution in Poland* by Christopher Browning.

I would encourage anyone with further interest to visit the Ravensbrück Memorial and the State Museum at Majdanek.

Acknowledgements

My profound gratitude to Dr Isabelle Hesse and Dr Beth Yahp at the Department of English, University of Sydney, Dr Michael Abrahams-Sprod at the Department of Hebrew, Biblical and Jewish Studies, University of Sydney, Professor Sue Vice at the School of English, University of Sheffield, Professor Sara Knox at the School of Languages and Humanities, Western Sydney University, Professor Konrad Kwiet and Tinny Lenthen at the Sydney Jewish Museum, René Bienert at the Vienna Wiesenthal Institute, Angi Meyer at the Ravensbrück Memorial, Joanna Cieślik at the State Museum at Majdanek, and Dr Elisabeth Stöve at Düsseldorf District Court. Thank you all for your help, advice and input during the writing of this book.

My gratitude to Julius Dem, Dr Tim Corbett, Julia Dautermann, George Szenderowicz and Lauren Wagner, who translated documents for me from German, Polish and Yiddish.

Thank you to the following people who accompanied me on research trips: my dear friends Bec Clarke and Camilla Sherwin, and my parents Charles and Clodagh Law. I'm grateful to John Thompson for trekking around Queens taking photos for me, and to Ronan Donohoe for answering my many random questions about life in America in the 60s and 70s. Thank you to Marcus Evans for advice about contracts and Lizzie Waterfield for artwork related to this book.

I'm indebted to the following people who read and

commented on my manuscript at various points of completion: Godwin Busuttil, Caileen Cachia, Anna Gleadall, Sam Guy, Natalie Kestecher, Sarah Lazarus, Sofia Mavros, Lisa McNight, Philip O'Loughlin, Chris Pearson and Libby Santella. Extra special thanks to Sarah Lazarus for being the Queen of All Words, and to Chris Pearson for proofreading this book several times: you were instrumental in helping me to shape it.

The most enormous thank you to my literary agent Morwenna Loughman for your continued belief in *The Mare*, and to James Keane, Ted O'Connor, and Amy Leacy at Northodox Press for having the courage to publish such a difficult story.

By far the biggest thanks goes to my husband Alastair for your love and support, everything you do for me and our family and for your unwavering belief in both me and this book. I couldn't have done this without you.

References

Cover images, *photograph of Hermine Braunsteiner & Majdanek, Poland*, reproduced courtesy of Yad Vashem.

Page vii, *Ordinary Men* (2001), quote by Christopher R. Browning, reproduced courtesy of Christopher R. Browning.

Page vii, *The Maya Angelou Autobiographies* (1969), quote by Maya Angelou, reproduced courtesy of Hachette Libre.

Page vii, *Modernity and the Holocaust* (1991), quote by Zygmunt Bauman, reproduced courtesy of Polity Books.

Printed in Great Britain
by Amazon

49701979R00182